Southbound

■ ■ ■

An Escapist Novel

Jerry S. Drake

This is a book of fiction. Names, locations, and all the events that take
place and the characters portrayed are creations of the writer's imagination or are used fictitiously, and any resemblance to actual persons,
living or dead, is purely coincidental.

Library of Congress Case Number: 1-780977087
ISBN-13: 978-0-9856970-0-6
ISBN-10: 0985697008

Front cover photo by the author
Printed in the United States of America

Other Books by Jerry S. Drake

Western Novels:

Aftermath
*Treasure Mountain

The Tom Patterson Western Series:

Breaking Trail
The Gunfighter's Apprentice
Sierra Skullduggery

Action-Adventure Novel:

**Schooner

*   Anticipated publication – 2013
** Anticipated publication – 2013

Praise for Jerry S. Drake's Western Novels:

Breaking Trail

"The book is stylishly written and – like Thomas Harris' *Hannibal Rising* – fills in the background of a character whose past has always been something of a mystery. Fans of the Patterson novels will want to seek this one out"

-Booklist Reviews

The Gunfighter's Apprentice

". . . the author, in his first western, pulls it off with panache. Although thematically gentle, the book is written in the tough, gritty, violent style of the classic pulp western. Fans of the genre will have a good time."

-Booklist Reviews

Sierra Skullduggery

"A gripping plot, knuckle-biting adventure, and sharp delineation between good and evil distinguish this sequel to *The Gunfighter's Apprentice*. The plot adds up, and Drake puts Tom and Betty Patterson in fine form."

-Publishers Weekly Review

*Dedicated in loving memory of Virginia
and all the wonderful people she
brought into my life.*

1

"Mathias! Get your butt over here!"

Customers' heads swiveled as quickly as mine to the squat little manager in the foyer of the HappiTimes Restaurant. Just as quickly, customers searched for Mathias and his butt, finding and focusing on me - red-faced and embarrassed – the incident interrupting my friendly conversation with a group of four at a table. I'd been "working the room," circulating in shirt, tie, dark trousers, and polished shoes; the genial Assistant Manager glad-handing the guests. The little toad, Jack Turley, gave me a summoning gesture, almost stamping his foot in his pique.I was tempted to give him an obscene gesture in return. Instead, I excused myself from my customers and walked slowly toward him, trying to hang onto whatever dignity I might salvage. "What's wrong, Jack?"

The little man glared. "Did you tell Mary Ann to take off early?"

I nodded. "Yeah, her kid's sick and she asked."

"You ain't got the authority for that," he said, jabbing a finger at me.

I gestured around. It was a smallish crowd; a Monday evening in Denver isn't a really big night in the restaurant business. "We're not too busy. Everybody's handling it."

Again, he jabbed his finger, this time into my chest. "You ain't nothing but a goddamned trainee. I tell people whether they can stay or go." He jabbed me yet again for emphasis.

"Do that one more time and I'll deck you," I said, loud enough for people around to hear.

"What? What?" Turley screeched, flustered and turning red. "What did you say to me?"

"I'll not only kick your butt, but I'll toss you through the window for good measure!" I said, even louder.

"Are you threatening me?"

"Absolutely!"

"You're fired! Get out of here! Right now!"

I spun away from him and headed for the kitchen, taking long, angry strides, muttering oaths at the little prick, most likely heard by the people as I passed. I went out the back door and turned toward the area where employees are required to park their cars. Halfway across the lot, I realized I'd left my suit coat and some other belongings in the office.

Should I go back in? No, better wait 'til we both cool down, no sense in taking a swing at the little sonofabitch!

Once in my car, I made myself behave as I drove out of the parking lot. This *HappiTimes Restaurant*, one of seven of the chain in the city, was on a busy intersection, so I was careful as I eased into the stream of traffic. In my testy frame of mind, I didn't want to end up with a fender-bender, and take out my frustration on someone who happened to be in my way. I didn't have much of an idea of where I'd be going, so I just drove aimlessly for a while, trying to calm down. Going home was not an option. In the unlikely circumstance that Gloria would be there, she'd want to know why I was home so early and, when she found out what had happened, there'd be another confrontation.

I didn't need that.

Actually, I shouldn't have been so upset about losing my job. It was only that this would make the third one lost in less than five years. First, there'd been the downsizing at the big communications company, then the electronic sales slot that hadn't panned out. Finally, more or less out of desperation, I'd signed on as a trainee in the "exciting field of restaurant management." Maybe "exciting" for some people, but for me, it was pretty much the same thing over and over, until I thought I'd go bonkers. If I hadn't lost the other two jobs in such a short period of time, I think I'd have taken a walk from this one after the first two weeks. Not only was the work repetitive and boring, my boss, Turley, was officious and overbearing. From the day I started work, he'd been sarcastic and demeaning, telling me that the company was wrong in "hiring just anyone off the street." He'd brag that he was a second generation in the restaurant profession. However, one of the server girls told me that Turley's parents had once owned a small town slop shop for a couple of years, but never made a go of it.

Even after I'd finished the initial phase of training, he'd kept after me, always critical, finding fault even when there was no fault to find. He'd made references to wasted food, lost tableware, even money being lifted from the till.

"It's your job to watch these bimbos," he'd once blathered, referring to the servers. "They'll steal you blind, and I'm holding *you* accountable."

"At what you pay, I'm not sure I'd blame them," I'd told him.

"I ain't counting you out either, mister," he'd growled. "I'm keeping an eye on you, you betcha!"

I think he'd have fired me that day, except that the home office management of the chain had probably heard a lot of complaints about Turley before. Ours was a corporate-owned restaurant, not a franchise. Turley's management position had been assigned by someone up in the corporation hierarchy who had probably come to regret the choice. There was an extraordinary employee turnover in his restaurant and, recently, he was walking tender, trying not to bring the company down on him. The dining room staff loathed him and hoped he'd be replaced. In the kitchen, the cooks called him Mister Turkey. Only one of the staff got along with him, Wanda Dale, the evening greeter. She was thirty-four, pretty in a sharp, bony sort of way. She'd cozy up to him and do, Lord knows, whatever to keep him happy. He certainly kept her happy. He paid her at least twice what the others made, and it was rumored she earned bonuses for certain services rendered.

Not knowing what exactly to do, I drove around for quite a while, burning gas that I'd probably not be able to afford in a couple of weeks, watching the city turn from dusk to a darkness studded with the glittering lights. I thought about my prospects and, for a guy just about to turn thirty, they seemed pretty dismal. I thought about my wife, and that situation did nothing to lift my spirits. I also thought about my parents and wished to hell they lived in another city. For sure, I wouldn't want to face the two of them again after this latest dismissal. They thought my restaurant job reflected poorly on their social status, but my repeated inability to hold even such lowly jobs was even more of a shame to their upper-crust affectations.

I kept driving and driving, until I realized that it was about time that the restaurant would be closing. Stores in the *HappiTimes Restaurant* chain opened right at 5:00 AM and closed at 10:30 at night. I figured now was the time to go back for the things I'd left behind and, not to my credit I suppose, I harbored the thought that Turley might have cooled off enough to give me my job back. I realized I'd have to crawl to the despicable fart for that favor, and I wasn't sure that I could sink that low.

A little before eleven o'clock, I pulled into a spot behind the restaurant. The big sign on the main street had been turned off and no cars were parked up front. I got out of my car and walked to the back entrance. My thoughts were intent on what I might say to Turley; I even wondered if we might possibly shake hands and forget about it. Not likely, but there might have been a possibility.

The back door was open and I stepped in. To my left, the kitchen had been cleaned, the night cooks and swampers gone home. From what I could see through a hallway door, all the dining room ceiling lights were dark, leaving just the row of lights over the front counter and the cash register. Framed in the door, I could see Wanda - and there was something funny about the way she was standing. She was rock still, like a statue, not moving a muscle. I couldn't see Turley, and I thought he was probably back of the cash register counting up the money for the night. It entered my mind to slip back to the office to collect my things without a fuss, but I thought I'd probably piss Jack off if he found me there without his knowing, so I decided to walk right out and face him.

Except, something was not right.

Wanda was still standing stiff.

Scared stiff.

To tell you the truth, my immediate thought was to sneak back out, and not put myself at risk for whatever was happening. Instead, I crept up the hall to the doorway and peeked around.

Behind the cash register, Jack Turley was shoveling bills into a bank sack while a raggedy young man, on the other side of the counter, was confronting him in a threatening stance. He could have had some Asian blood in him, Hispanic, maybe Indian or maybe not; it was hard to tell since he was standing in the shadows.

Then, too, I saw the gun in his hand, and I expect that was what I was focused on instead of his features. I could see Jack, so scared and nervous, was on the verge of peeing his pants. He kept his head down, not looking at the young tough, as though to show he wouldn't make identification later.

For a moment, I thought it was going to be all right. The robber reached for the money sack, and I thought he'd take it and go. Instead, he placed the money sack back on the counter and, without the slightest bit of provocation, aimed the gun and fired into Jack Turley's chest. He leaned over the counter as Jack dropped to the floor and then fired again. Wanda screamed, and the hood turned toward her.

I didn't think about it, I just charged. Looking back on it, maybe I shouldn't have. I hit the gunman just as he fired, and the bullet aimed for her body entered her brain. Of course, I didn't know that at the time. I knew only that I was wrestling with a hard young body, and only my surprise attack helped to even the odds against his revolver. I struggled with him, getting both hands on his gun hand wrist, slamming it again and again on the floor, finally knocking the gun loose.

We both scrambled up and, as I dove for the gun, he ran for the front door. Not familiar with handguns, I took moments to look at the revolver and to make sure I knew how to use it. Far too late, I ran after him, too frenzied to think clearly, thinking only of not letting him get away. I went through the front door, spotted him, and gave chase. He had a good lead, but I was gaining on him as he left the parking lot to sprint down a side street.

"Stop!" I shouted.

The bastard veered suddenly, and then headed toward a dark alley. I skidded to a stop, planted my feet wide apart and, just as I've seen in movies and television shows, I held the gun in both hands and fired twice.

That's when the patrol car came around the corner.

As you might well guess, my second bullet hit the upper left corner of the patrol car's window, crazing the glass, making the cops believe I was firing at them.

If you can believe that a police car can look angry, that was one mad sonofabitch! The red and blue flasher came on, the siren wailed up to a scream, and the patrol car came at me like a banshee!

I threw the gun aside and held both hands up high.

The cop car skidded to within two feet of me and, in seconds, two uniformed men were swearing and slamming me down on the parking lot pavement, wrenching my hands behind my back, handcuffing me, searching me, shouting at me.

"What the hell do you think you're doing?"

"Shoot at us, will you? You damned asshole!"

One officer held me down, his knee in my back with enough pressure to nearly break my backbone, while his partner returned to the patrol car to radio for backup.

"Hey, take it easy! I'm not the guy!" I protested, struggling a bit, trying to relieve the pressure. "He's getting away!"

"Shut up!" The cop gave me a hard rap on the head as he stood up, and then retrieved the revolver I'd cast aside.

"What the hell's the sonofabitch up to?" the second cop asked as he returned, both of them now standing over me.

"We'll find out in a couple of minutes," the guy with the heavy knee responded. "Looks like he was coming out of the restaurant." He examined the revolver. "Five gone." He shifted his gaze to the building. "It don't look good, no, sir."

They continued to talk as if I was not there. Occasionally, one reached out a booted foot to bounce my chest and head on the asphalt, while they spoke about shift schedules and days-off plans. All the time, I kept trying to tell them about the killer that they wouldn't chase, about the man who had shot the people inside. They didn't listen at all. They kept me flat on the blacktop as a couple of other patrol cars came speeding out of the darkness. On my belly, twisting to see, the parking lot was becoming a scene of frantic activity. Policemen were rushing here and there, some coming over to look down at me, while others moved with caution into the restaurant. Next, I was roughly pulled to my feet and, with four policemen assisting, I was half-dragged and manhandled into the cage of the first patrol car, one of the officers making sure that I banged my head on the way in.

Probably the one I'd almost shot on the passenger's side.

Three officers stood outside the patrol car while still more police cars arrived, followed by an ambulance. All this time, I was trying to get someone to talk to me, to hear what had happened. The policemen must have heard my pleas, but they gave no sign. They merely stood their vigil, one at the front of the car, the other two on either side, watching the activities at the front of the restaurant.

I saw the medics coming out with someone on a gurney and, the way they rushed, I figured it had to be Wanda. I felt good, thinking that she was alive, and I hoped she hadn't been badly injured.

It never even occurred to me that I was really going down for the shootings. What was happening to me was a mistake, and something I could clear up if somebody would only give me a chance to explain. The shooter was long gone by now, but I could give a description. I hadn't seen him clearly, but I thought I'd be able to pick him out of a lineup or a criminal photobook. The cops would probably take me to jail, discover their mistake, and go about their duty to find the real criminal.

After a long time, a portly, gray-haired officer came out of the restaurant, walked to the car, and bent down to look at me through the open window, his face grim and angry.

"You do this?" he asked.

I shook my head. "No, sir! I just walked in on it. Young guy was robbing the store. He shot Jack and Wanda." I nodded to indicate the direction the killer had fled. "You're letting him get away!"

"My officers told me that you were shooting at them."

"No, sir! I was shooting at him. I hit them by mistake."

The man didn't appear to believe me. "You know those people inside?"

I nodded. "I'm the . . . I was the assistant manager here."

"Was?"

I knew then I had made a mistake in the way I said it, but there was no way out of it now. "I was working there today."

"What do you mean . . . was?"

"Well," I began lamely, "Jack and I had words today, and I guess he was going to fire me."

The officer's reaction told me nothing. He continued to stare at me, and then straightened up to walk over to another officer. It was clear he didn't believe my story, and he was the first of many. Perhaps it's even more so when a killer is caught red-handed.

I was advised of my rights and, at the police station, I was fingerprinted and told that I was entitled to have an attorney. I was informed that I could make a phone call, and so I did. I called my home only to encounter my voice mail instead of my wife. What she was doing out and away from home at this time of night was another of my problems, a pretty good indication of the rocky condition of our marriage. Nonetheless, I left a message. Since I was unable to make a contact, I was allowed a second call to my parents and left a pitiful plea there as well.

While I waited for someone to come to my aid, I spent what remained of the night and the next morning being interrogated by the police. The homicide people, two men and one woman, were brusque and impassive as they listened to my story. They went after it again and again, picking at small details until my narrative began to shatter. My fatigue and anxiety introduced confusion into my endless recountings. I said too many things, offered too many candid comments, told my story with various inconsistencies, vaguely agreeing to motives and angers they'd invented.

It was a wonder I didn't confess.

When they were exhausted themselves, they put me into a cell all by myself, certain of my murderous nature, no doubt concerned for the safety of other inmates in general holding cells. I stayed there for two full days without a word from family, friends or acquaintances.

Looking back, I wonder why I had any such expectations.

2

On the morning of the third day, my father came to the jail. He was waiting in the visitors' facility, as a guard escorted me into a cubicle on the prisoner's side of a screened partition. He sat across from me with obvious reluctance. "Kevin, what the hell have you done?"

"Nothing at all, sir. I'm completely innocent."

Of course, he didn't believe me.

He looked at me for a long time, his handsome, mature face with just a hint of a sad smile, an expression that some took for compassion, but those who knew him better recognized as mocking arrogance. He was a successful and skillful surgeon, feared and revered by his patients, well respected by his medical colleagues, and equally despised for his glacial personality.

"I've hired an attorney for you," he said finally. "I understand he is a capable man, and he'll do the best he can for you."

With that, he arose abruptly, the visit over as quickly as it had begun.

"However it turns out," he said with his body already half-turned to leave "This will be the last we will have to do with you. Your mother and I are in complete agreement on that.

You've brought shame to my name, and heaven knows what it will do to our lives."

"I haven't done anything wrong!" I shouted. "This is all a mistake! You've got to believe me!"

His lip actually curled. "You'll likely be spending the rest of your life in prison, or even be executed." He hesitated for a few seconds, and then added, "God forgive me, I'm sorry to say this about my own son, but you probably deserve the latter."

I looked at him in astonishment. "Did I actually hear you say that?"

He grimaced, uncomfortable at the confrontation, but neither ashamed nor repentant. He continued, "I always knew you were an inadequate fool, but murder?" He shook his head as though to shed himself of my presence. "We'll do whatever we must do to live through the disgrace but, whatever happens, you are never to contact us again."

He began to stride away.

"Sir!" I called, checking his departure for a few moments more. "What about Gloria? Have you heard from her?"

He turned once more to me and made a brushing motion that I'm sure was an involuntary dismissal of my irksome spouse. "We've not taken her calls, nor will we," he said brusquely. "I doubt if even she will contact you." He walked away, not looking back, walking out of my life forever.

You should understand warmth was never a part of my upbringing. As I've said, my father was a cold-hearted man with singular interests only in his work and his comforts. Avoiding marriage until well established in his medical practice, Dr. John Edward Mathias had carefully selected and taken himself a trophy wife. Mary Ellen Markham, my mother, was the beautiful and socially prominent daughter of a wealthy Maryland family. It had been a successful pairing; the mating of an ambitious, self-centered man with a near-mannequin wife whose self-interest neatly matched his own. She kept herself attractive as she aged, aloof in her supportive role, secure with the wealth of her own family, and well satisfied with the additional riches of the doctor's lucrative practice.

I had been a dreadful mistake, a child neither had wanted.

If Mother would have had her way, I would have been aborted. My father had enough medical associates to knife away my life if he would have asked. He could have done the job himself, in the bathroom or in the kitchen of our palatial home. No one would have probably been the wiser. The only thing I believed to have saved me was that my father operated in at least one Catholic hospital. An abortion, even suspected, would have jeopardized that portion of his income.

Needless to say, I'd been an only child.

An hour after he'd, left, my attorney came to the jail, and I was ushered into a vault of an interview room furnished with only a couple of straight chairs and a cheap table. He was standing behind the table, a slim, sober-faced, balding man wearing a dark blue suit, white shirt, and a navy-blue tie. He looked forty-something; early or late, I couldn't tell.

"Howard Warnell," he introduced himself. "Your father hired me to represent you." He sat down across the table from me, but did not offer his hand. "It's either Howard or Mr. Warnell. I won't be called Howie or anything like that, is that clear?"

I nodded.

"I don't know how much help I'm going to be to you," he said, folding his hands on the table. "I'll try to keep you from being executed."

"I didn't do it. This is a terrible mistake."

He passed right over that. "I got a call from your wife this morning," he said matter-of-factly. "She's planning to start divorce proceedings immediately. I don't know why she would've come to me about it, but I told her that she'd have to find another attorney."

Even with what I knew about Gloria, it was stunning news.

"That won't help our case," he continued, and then looked at me with the first sign of compassion. "I hope you have some friends somewhere, because your relations are shit."

"They are, indeed," I muttered. Again, I tried, "Mr. Warnell, somebody's got to believe me. I *am* innocent."

Warnell's slight sympathy faded into seriousness. "I've read the account you've given." He shook his head. "I haven't decided exactly how we'll go about defending you, but your ludicrous, unbelievable story is something we might have to stick to. Tell it well and perhaps a jury might believe it."

"But you don't."

"It doesn't matter whether I do or don't."

"It matters to me."

He shrugged. "I may plead temporary insanity. I really don't know at this moment. I'll think about it as we go along."

"Are you any good?" I asked, my anger seeking a target.

"Probably not good enough," he admitted. "I've won some, lost some. I'll consider this a win if we keep you out of the execution chamber." He glanced at his watch. "I'll be back."

"Can you get me out of jail?" I asked, hating the pleading tone that came into my voice.

"No one has offered to put up any bail money," he said with a slight shake of his head. "It's likely to be astronomical if bail is allowed at all." He paused, and then added, "Your parents might have the wherewithal, but they'll not offer it." He gestured to the walls. "Get used to it."

I never would.

■ ■ ■

I was transferred to the County Jail and held in a single cell to await trial. My chamber included a metal slab with a thin mattress on top for a bed, a stainless steel stool lavatory, a chair, and a table fixed to the wall. Overhead, a harsh flores-cent glare beamed down on me, relieved only at lights-out at ten o'clock at night. I was allowed out of the cell for meals, for showers, and occasional brief recreation. Considered a dangerous criminal, most of my days went by in lonely lockdown. My only regular visitor was my attorney, Howard Warnell.

One day, on one of his visits, he seemed more downcast than usual. "How are you doing?" he asked automatically.

"Okay, I guess. Something bothering you?"

"Bad news. The woman in the coma? The one at the res-taurant?"

"Wanda Dale?"

He nodded. "She died about an hour ago." He sat silently for at least a minute.

"Damned shame she couldn't have stayed alive 'til after the trial."

"Well, that's a hell of a thing to say!" I said, offended. "She was . . . kind of a friend." Even so, I recognized the newly added jeopardy to my life's expectancy.

"Of which you don't have too many."

"Anything good to tell me?"

He shook his head, and then offered what he considered a cheerful note. "Other than the woman's death, you're becoming pretty much yesterday's news. Not even in the back pages most of the time. Of course, her death will bring it up again, but by the time of the trial . . ." He shrugged as if that was an accomplishment.

"Tell me something positive," I pleaded. "Like you have found a witness, or the cops are tracing the gun."

Again, he shook his head. "They're not looking. They think they've got the right guy."

"I gave them a description!"

He nodded. "Asian, Indian, Caucasian . . . maybe Mexican. Young, not so young, not too tall, not too short, no identifying marks."

"Hell, it all happened so fast!"

"So you say."

"Find something, please," I begged.

He rose from his chair, cutting the visit short. "I'll do what I can."

■ ■ ■

One day, I had a different visitor.

Gloria.

"I'm sorry you're in here, Kevin," she said in the up-tight tone of voice she gets when she's doing something she doesn't want to do. "Goddamn it, Kevin!"

"Thanks for coming," I said, letting the bitterness show. "I'm surprised."

"Kevin," she said, fishing in her purse. "I brought divorce papers."

"Yes, I've heard."

"Can I give them to you?"

"Not to me, personally. You'll have to give them to the jail people."

"Will you sign them?" she asked anxiously. "And not make a fuss?"

I hesitated, wanting to make a fuss.

"You could fight it if you want, but what's the use?" she whined. "You know you're not going to be around to be a husband any more."

"Okay," I agreed. "Let's make a deal. I sign them, and you agree not to bad mouth me."

"What do you mean . . . 'bad mouth' you?" she sputtered.

"You've said some things to the press," I reminded her.

"Oh, that!" she exclaimed, waving the divorce papers. "You know how the media distorts things people say."

"If you're asked, don't say them at my trial."

"Don't be silly," she said in irritation. "I won't even be at the trial."

She threw me a kiss she didn't mean and walked out. Later that day, I signed the papers and made myself a free man.

So to speak.

When I'd first met Gloria Bennett, I thought she was something very special. In the fall of my senior year in college, a friend had introduced us in the campus cafe, not before telling me in a whispered confidence that she had found me "interesting."

"*Interesting*" in that she believed I was heir to scads and scads of money. And, as I later discovered, her purpose at an institute of higher learning was to snag a rich husband.

Her name was Gloria Louise Bennett, a second-year transfer from an eastern Colorado college. Attractive, smart in some ways, and not so much in others, she seemed to be very much a supportive person who was most interested in everything I said, felt, or did.

She was skilled in her pursuit of me and, to be sure, I admit that she could really arouse me. Lust was probably why, during the Christmas break of that college year, we got married. Both of legal age, we did it quickly, just a civil service, a few words muttered before a judge. This magistrate admonished that we should consider this wedding as binding as one in a church with pomp, incense and ceremony.

"Your parents didn't come," Gloria said pointedly as we left the city hall; my first inkling all was not right with this marriage.

"What do you mean?" she shrilled, after I told her how things stood with my parents. "They don't like you?"

I nodded.

Gloria hung on in the marriage. She stayed, not for the little money I could provide for her, but in the stubborn hope that my folks might change their uncaring ways. She even thought she could win them over with her practiced charms. As the few years passed without success, we both realized our discordant union was doomed.

When and with whom her extramarital affairs began, I found I didn't care. Eventually, I knew that the huntress would find what she was looking for and our wedlock would end. I'd married a shrew that had made my life as miserable as her own. Now, after eight years of a loveless marriage, I was well rid of her.

3

The jail days became weeks, and the weeks became months. By comparison, the trial was short and unmerciful. Attorney Warnell decided to plead me innocent, saying I looked too rational for temporary insanity. The courtroom was packed with newspaper and television reporters, sketch artists, and a whole lot of people I didn't know from Adam. There were neither friendly faces nor consoling relatives. Dr. and Mrs. Mathias had gone abroad six weeks before the trial, and stayed until it was well over. Away from the press, and out of the public eye, they assumed their abandonment of me would fade in time, bringing them only a minimum of criticism.

Warnell had me carefully groomed and conservatively dressed in a nice, yet not ostentatious, dark blue suit, a white shirt, and a muted blue striped tie. He'd coached me on the manner that I should use to create a favorable impression: I was to sit up straight, pay a lot of attention to what was being said, and not to smile too often, nor too little. Once in a while, I should glance at the jury with a pleasant expression, but not to overdo it lest they think I was trying to influence them. I was warned to neither show anger nor undue irritation at comments made by the prosecution. I was allowed to raise an eyebrow or give a small shake of the head should I hear something I considered untrue or preposterous. Always, I should present an image of a really nice guy who is being hurt by unfair accusations, bewildered by unproven circumstances.

"Play your part well," he whispered to me as we took our seats at the defense table. "It's your life and my reputation."

I wondered which he thought to be of greatest importance.

◼ ◼ ◼

Judge Purcell was a small, wizened man of considerable years, enough of it spent in courtrooms to have developed a permanent bad attitude toward any and all who appeared before him. He had an ill-concealed contempt for the attorneys and other courtroom personnel, and an apparent disdain for the jurors.

"Ladies and gentlemen," he said to the latter in his condescending manner. "You will do well to remember that I am completely in charge of this court, this trial. I am the one who will decide the laws that apply to each phase of the proceedings. It is my responsibility to judge the presentation of the facts, and it is your responsibility to determine what facts are applicable to the final outcome. I will do my job well, and I expect you to do the same. There are rules for every person involved in this trial, and each and every one will abide by those rules or suffer consequences that I can impose." He paused to point an accusing finger at me. "We're here to try him, and not my patience!" Judge Purcell didn't smile during the entire proceedings, and the jury was pretty grim, too.

The lead prosecutor, a smooth, experienced devil, delivered an opening statement that made me out as something between Charles Manson and John Wayne Gacy. I was pictured to the jury as an indolent ne'er-do-well, a problem as a child, and a failure at life and success. I was described as

21

ill-tempered, aloof and disdainful with fellow workers, condescending to one and all. It was said I considered myself too
good for the work I so ineptly performed.

Then came a string of witnesses, some people I scarcely
knew from my previous employment situations who, for whatever reasons I had no clue, seemed to have developed a surprisingly intense dislike for me. There were other witnesses,
customers of the restaurant who were there when Turley and
I had exchanged our heated words. Somehow, they seemed
the most sympathetic toward me.

One at a time, the prosecution brought on the two police
officers that had been in the first patrol car. The driver made a
brisk, no nonsense report, and was quickly excused with little
questioning either by the prosecuting attorney or my guy.

The second officer, Michael Kahn, was a different story. "A
few more inches," he said, turning to address the jury, "and my
wife would've been a widow."

"Officer Kahn!" the judge intoned warningly.

The policeman gave an apologetic shrug, and turned back
to face the prosecuting attorney. "Well, it was a close call."

"Did the defendant offer any resistance after that shot?"

Officer Kahn shook his head emphatically. "He gave up
when he knew he had no chance. We were on him like white
on rice."

"Officer!" the judge spoke again in a doomsday voice. "I
won't warn you again. State the facts as you know them without embellishment."

"Yes, your honor," the policeman responded with appropriate contrition.

"Did he seem remorseful when you confronted him?" the
prosecutor asked.

"Objection," murmured my attorney.

"Sustained."

"Can you describe his attitude when you arrested him?"

"He was highly agitated," the policeman answered, glancing at the judge, seeking approval for the short response.

"Do you recall what he said at that time regarding the incident?"

"A cock and bull story—"

"Objection!" Howard Warnell's voice was up a decibel or two although not really sharply.

"Sustained."

The policeman shrugged his apology once again. "He said there had been an attempted robbery, and that he was shooting at the robber."

"Did you discover a money sack on the counter," the attorney asked him.

The officer nodded. "Not me, personally. Other officers said the money was still there. To them, it didn't look like a robbery, just sacking up money to take to the bank . . . and we didn't see anybody at that restaurant other than Mr. Mathias."

"No more questions," the prosecutor said with a nod first to the judge, then another to the witness.

When it was our turn, Howard Warnell walked up close to Officer Kahn, and spoke to him in an affable manner. "You say that the bullet that hit the patrol car came close to you?"

"Yes, sir."

"The upper corner of the windshield on the passenger side?"

"Yes, sir."

"If you were trying to get away undiscovered, wouldn't shooting at a patrol car be a foolish act?"

"Objection! Calls for conjecture!"

"Sustained."

"Could that have been an accidental shot rather than a deliberate one?"

"Objection! Again, calls for conjecture—"

"Overruled," the judge cut in. "It doesn't sound unreasonable."

"I suppose so," the policeman said grudgingly.

"And you say Mr. Mathias laid down the weapon as soon as you approached him?"

"Yes, sir," the officer agreed reluctantly.

"And when he told you about the other person, the one he told you had done the shooting . . . did you institute any kind of a search for that person?"

"There wasn't any need," Kahn responded. "We knew we had the right guy."

"Your honor," Warnell said with mild exasperation.

"The jury will disregard that comment," Judge Purcell declared, and then nodded to the court reporter. "Strike from the record."

"You did not search the neighborhood?" Warnell asked, inserting a note of disbelief into his voice.

"No, sir, we did not," the officer reluctantly admitted. "If he was shooting at somebody, it seems likely we'd have seen him, too!

"Your honor," Warnell said tiredly.

"Jury will disregard," Judge Purcell instructed, and then glared at the policeman. "We believe in evidence here, Officer Kahn. Not offhand opinions."

Kahn wilted under the judge's blazing stare.

Howard Warnell seemed ready to ask another question, but turned abruptly and walked back to our table. "No further questions."

So far, I hadn't seen Gloria in the courtroom and, giving me a modicum of relief, there had been little in the papers concerning her. The divorce was proceeding smoothly, and I had little reason to believe that she wouldn't live up to her agreement.

Then, the unthinkable happened.

The prosecutor brought Gloria to the stand. She took the oath, and never once looked at me or even in my direction. She was as attractive as ever and, I thought, male members of the jury seemed to perk up a little at the sight of her. She, in turn, gave them one of her best smiles, one much like those given to me in the early days of our courtship.

"Did your husband ever abuse you?" the prosecutor asked after going through preliminaries.

What the hell!

She twisted uncomfortably. "I was afraid of him."

My mouth dropped open, and I almost rose from my chair until my attorney put a restraining hand on my arm and called, "Objection!"

"Overruled!"

"Did he ever strike you?" the prosecutor asked.

"Oh, yes," she replied. "Several times."

Despite Warnell's warning, I showed anger, worrying him as he shouted, "Objection!"

"Overruled!"

I slumped in my seat, too frustrated to sit up straight and look innocent. I'm sure the jury must've considered me capable of murder because, at that moment, I just might have been.

When it was Warnell's turn, he asked, "These times when you say he struck you . . . did you call the police?"

"No."

"Make out a police report?"

"No."

"Go to the hospital?"

"No."

"To your doctor?"

"No."

"Report these incidents to any friends or members of your family?"

"No, I guess not."

"Then . . . all we have is your word on this?"

"Objection, your Honor!"

"Overruled!" The judge showed he was impartial. "The defense has said nothing to merit an objection. Proceed, Mr. Warnell."

"No more questions, your Honor."

"You are excused, Mrs. Mathias," the judge said.

Gloria left the witness chair with her head stiffly turned so that she would not have to look at me. She walked up the central aisle and left the courtroom.

My lawyer sat down, looked at me and gave me a shrug.

Witnesses for my defense, a couple of boyhood friends and some former fellow employees, gave lukewarm testimonies to my general good nature and lack of previous criminality. Witnesses, who had had anything to say pertinent to the case, seemed to have been on the side of the prosecution.

As the trial neared the end, Warnell put me on the stand. I told my story, putting on my best appearance of sincerity, explaining how much I'd been a victim of circumstances. I thought I'd done well; several of the jurors seemed to be impressed, even sympathetic.

"How'd I do?" I whispered to Howard.

"Not bad," he conceded. "We'll see."

■　■　■

The jury declared me guilty and, at a later court session, the judge gave me a sentence of life imprisonment for each death, with no possible chance of parole.

"Hey, we did it!" Warnell crowed in our final moments as they led me away. "No lethal injection."

"Can we appeal?" I asked, unable to believe my dreadful fate.

"Not with me, kiddo" he said, giving me a disinterested wave as the guards pulled me along. "Try the born-again religion thing in a few years . . . and watch your ass! Literally!"

4

I was transferred the next day to the state's diagnostic center; a detention facility for processing, evaluation, and prison assignment. Sort of a halfway house for those on their way in, the center was a formidable prison in itself. Surrounded by double rows of high metal fences, each topped with concertina razor wire, the thick-walled contiguous buildings enclosed a large grass courtyard, bordered by concrete walkways. Along with four other convicted prisoners, I entered the 'take-in' building.

"There are rules that you will follow, and you will follow them exactly," a uniformed captor informed us at an orientation session. "You'll be here, ranging from six or seven days, up to three weeks at the most. You'll be given a complete physical examination. Any medical or dental problems will be taken care of by our medical staff while you are here. You'll be given written tests and aptitude tests. You'll be interviewed and evaluated. Your behavior during this short period of time will have a significant effect upon your imprisonment." He paused, and then continued in a more sympathetic manner. "We know from experience that this is a very difficult time for you. This is the place where you will have to face the reality of your sentences. Knowing this, we'll do whatever we can to make your adjustment easier, but don't mistake decent treatment as softness or weakness. We are used to handling tough guys and troublemakers." He paused once again for effect. "Learn to get along."

Placed in a holding cell, we were taken out individually to surrender our personal belongings. I was told to strip and shower. In the nude, I was examined for signs of needle use, self-mutilation, devil-worship tattoos, or any illegal substances that I might've stashed in or up an orifice. Once my jailers were satisfied, I was provided with new jailhouse clothing, fingerprinted, and photographed once again.

After my physical exam, two guards escorted me to one of the housing unit buildings. Inside, we entered a *pod*; an open lounge area with three tiers of solitary cells rising against the back wall, each level accessible by a central steel stairway. On the ground floor, in a secure wide-view glass chamber, guards kept a constant watch overall. Out in the lounge area, several men in regulation orange jump suits were watching a daytime soap opera on a TV set mounted high out of reach on a wall. One inmate glanced at me as we crossed to the central stairway, but the others were too engrossed in the program to look away.

"You'll be allowed out of your cell for testing and evaluation," one of the guards told me, as he led me to the second level. "There are forty-eight cells, and we take half of you at a time to meals three times a day. You're also allowed one hour down there," he continued, nodding his head down at the lounge area.

He opened one of the cells and gestured for me to enter. "You're in lockdown all the rest of the time," he said, closing the steel door behind me.

And closed in despair.

For the first time, I was without hope. I looked around this tiny chamber, and realized that this was not just my present - this was to be my future, the rest of my life. I knew that there would be no miracle to save me, no unfound evidence to prove my innocence. I would be a young convict, a middle-aged convict and, finally, an old convict, confined to an above ground crypt until the day I would gratefully die. I'd be able to wash and shave, piss and shit, and have to find some way to spend those endless years ahead without losing my sanity.

I sat down on the hard bed and began to cry.

■ ■ ■

On the second and third day, along with others, I was given a battery of intelligence and educational tests, oral and aptitude exams.

Three days later, my cell door opened. "Interview time," the guard announced.

In a private office, the name on the desk sign identified her as Ms. Beatrice Shelton. She was a young, dark-haired woman, not much older than me, attractive in a severe sort of a way. She was reading a file when I entered, looked up with a nice smile, nodded me into a chair, and resumed reading. The guard closed the windowed door behind us and stood outside where he could watch.

She looked up again, the nice smile replaced by a wry one. "You make interesting reading, Kevin."

"I expect everyone here does," I responded, intending no flippancy.

"Are you playing games with us?"

"How do you mean?"

She touched the file folder. "Your tests . . . especially the math," she began, a slight frown showing on her face. "You solve some of the hard problems yet you didn't bother with the others." She gave me a steady gaze. "Why is that?"

I shrugged.

She sat back in her chair and studied me. "You're intelligent. You're well educated." She touched the file folder again. "You've been to private schools, graduated from a college, and you come from a well-to-do family. You have no prior history of violence . . . unless the story given by your wife is true." She opened the file and leafed through several papers. "Is that true?"

"Not a word of it," I answered.

She didn't show belief or disbelief. After a few moments, she raised her eyes to mine once again. "Something about you doesn't fit, Kevin. With your background and opportunities, I'd think you'd have shown more achievements in your life. With your intelligence, I'd assume you'd have more to show." She tapped the papers with her finger. "It's as though you strive to be . . . average."

I let the silence hang between us for a long time. Finally, she gave a little shrug and returned her gaze to the papers in the folder. "Your wife started divorce proceedings almost as soon as you went to jail. How do you feel about that?"

"It wasn't much of a marriage," I confessed. "Even before the . . . incident."

"What was the problem?"

"She wanted more than I could provide."

"Money was a problem?"

"She wasn't content with just getting by."

Ms. Shelton gave me a slightly trenchant look. "Do you find fault with that?"

"I can't blame her," I replied. "She picked the wrong guy, I picked the wrong girl."

Ms. Shelton studied me for a little while. "Are you really that calm about it?"

I nodded. "I think we're both relieved that it's over."

She turned papers. "Your father made only one visit to you. Neither of your parents, mother or father, attended the trial."

Again, I nodded.

"Let's talk about them."

"Let's not," I said matter-of-factly.

She raised an eyebrow. "Not so calm about them, are you?"

"Let's not go where you're going," I said, a request, not a demand.

"Perhaps we should have you speak with our psychiatrist," she ventured.

"Fine, if you'd like."

"It might explain what happened at the restaurant," she said, probing.

"No, it wouldn't," I said tiredly. "It wasn't my crime."

"Only a few admit theirs," she countered.

"I'm unique," I responded. "I'm innocent."

Like all others, she had no doubts about my guilt.

We talked for a longer period of time, most of the conversation pragmatic in content, cordial and polite in manner. She made a number of notations and gave me some well-intentioned advice about the life I was about to enter.

At the end of the interview, she stood and nodded toward the door. The guard moved before I did, entering to be at my side as I rose from my chair.

"Good luck, Kevin," she said.

As I left, she was extracting another file folder from a stack on the credenza behind her.

"What's next?" I asked the guard on my way back.

"They'll let us know," he said, a standard and dissatisfying answer, his way of saying he wanted no further questions. In silence, we crossed the courtyard to the housing unit, and marched up the steps to my cell.

"Sleep tight," he said as he shut the door.

"And don't let the bedbugs bite," I said to myself.

I curled up on the bed, feeling the hard steel through the two-inch pad, and thought about the interview.

Striving to be average - that's what she had said.

Striving to be average - a way to get back at my parents.

I don't remember at what age I knew of their lack of caring. Pretty young, I guess. Hurt as only a child can be hurt, nevertheless, I somehow adapted. The very early years were the hardest: There was a succession of paid nannies to take the place of motherly love. When I was barely old enough, my parents shipped me to an out-of-state military school for boys during the winter, and then sent me off to camp during much of the summer. When I was briefly home to actually spend time with mom and dad, there were constant scoldings and reprimands. The only occasions they ever seemed to give a damn, was when I did something well. However, doing well was always something not so much attributed to me, but to my genealogical inheritance of their individual and combined superiorities. Achieving less than their expectations seemed to be my best bet to make them uncomfortable.

Some of my military school classmates, with similarly uncaring families, rebelled through bad behavior, by posting poor grades, by flunking out. Not me. Flunking out meant going home to that dreadful parental atmosphere. Being *just average* not only was a way of striking back at my parents, it also meant that I could stay where discipline was strict, but fair. It meant I could stay with teachers and dormitory monitors who showed, at least, a degree of compassion and under-standing. Of course, I wasn't the teachers' favorite. They expected more of me, and were disappointed when I cruised comfortably between excellence and failure.

For a time, while in the upper grades, I did excel in track. I was the top runner in the 100-yard, the 220, and I was the leadoff on the relay team. We won a few track meets against other schools of privilege and, somehow, word had gotten back to the good doctor and his wife that their son might have special athletic qualities. One spring day, with them sitting aloof and expectant in the stands at our most important meet, I purposely turned in my poorest day, win-ning no events, and my scores were scarcely noticeable in the standings.

They left early without bothering to see me.

By the time I hit college, being *just average* had become a way of life. To be sure, it wasn't a top-rated university or col-lege; it was an out-of-the way small campus that required little of their students and gave little in return. I passed my courses without working hard at them, spending more time in the pur-suit of attractive women than an education.

Now that I look back, by being *just average*, I'd hurt myself more than anyone else. If I hadn't been at that school, I wouldn't have met Gloria. If I hadn't been *just average*, I'd have had better career choices. Somehow, I'd chosen medi-ocrity as a fit reward for my parents, and it had turned into a way of life. I'd *just averaged* myself right into an attitude of apathy and unconcern.

On the Tuesday of my second week, I had my first encounter with prison jeopardy. Half of our pod had been taken to the cafeteria where we stood in line for our noon meal. A young black, one I hadn't seen before, was at the end of the line as we'd marched down from our cells. With considerable swagger, he brushed past the others and stepped in front of me, literally bumping me aside to show his contempt. He stared at me with insolent amusement, his eyes searching my face for my reaction. He was spoiling for a fight, waiting for me to step up to his challenge. If I didn't, I'd lose face and invite similar action from others. If I did, I'd brand myself as a troublemaker.

I had only seconds to make the choice.

From behind me, an older black man, stepped between us, turning his back on the troublemaker to make an obliging gesture to me. "Well, thank you, son," he said politely. "I appreciate your courtesy, inviting an old man like me to go first. Mighty kind of you." He gestured to one of the tables in the dining room. "When you get your food, I'd appreciate your company."

Whatever his reason, he had deftly defused the confrontation, interposing himself between my antagonist and myself. He turned around, took a tray, ignoring the mean stare of the younger man, and preceded me down the serving line. We walked together across the room to a table and sat down.

"Charlie Bryan," he introduced himself.

"Kevin Mathias."

He nodded. "Read about you."

I thought about protesting, but I was tired of that.

"This is my second time in," he told me between bites of food. "Ain't quite as serious as you, but serious enough."

He nodded his head toward the black that had pushed me. "That's likely the first, but he ain't going to be the last."

"Any advice on how I should handle it?" I asked.

Bryan shrugged. "You may or may not see him ever again, but you'll run into somebody meaner and tougher than him." He laughed and looked across the room at the young man. "So will he!"

"I've heard things," I told him.

Again, Bryan nodded. "Most of 'em true."

I hesitated, then asked, "I've heard that blacks don't mingle with whites, that Hispanics have their own groups—"

"Depends," he cut in, finishing the mixed vegetables on his tray, moving to the creamed chipped beef. "Don't be too much of a loner, and don't get too tied in with any one group. Some you stay away from. Always have something you gotta do, somewhere you gotta be." He paused. "You'll have to find your own way . . . that's all I can tell you."

"What about gang rape?" I asked, fearful of the answer.

He cocked his head, looking at me. "Could happen," he said. "You don't look runty or soft, so maybe they'll leave you alone." An enigmatic smile came across his face. "You already killed a couple—"

"I didn't!" I protested.

"Whether you did or didn't, it might be best now to let folks know you ain't to be bothered," he advised. "You put the scare into them, not the other way round."

"I don't want trouble," I told him.

"That's the kind that gets it," he said solemnly. "You may have to kill somebody. You'll do what you gotta do."

"Is it really that bad?" I asked plaintively. "Won't the prison officials—"

"Don't go to them about your problems," he interrupted, speaking softly. "Maybe they'll see, but you don't want to go to them."

I sat and ate my food, glancing at the clock from time to time, regretting the short time we had left.

"Why did you help?" I asked Bryan.

He pushed his tray back and folded his arms. "I read all about you. Rich boy, living in all them fancy places, now working at a lousy restaurant job." He chuckled. "Pissed me off, just thinking about you." He made a wide gesture to indicate the entire prison surroundings. "Then, I saw you in here and it come to me and I said, 'that boy ain't guilty of nothing'." He shook his head. "If I could see it, I wonder why the hell that damned jury couldn't?"

For the first time in months, I felt a rush of genuine pleasure. "You're a nice man, Charlie Bryan."

He laughed. "Shit, no! I'm a bad man. I'm a thief. I lie and cheat, I get drunk and beat up on people . . . hell, I'm somebody that you'd best not know."

Nonetheless, I liked him.

"You think we'll end up in the same prison?" I asked.

The laughter came out of his face as he picked up his tray, motioning with his head for me to follow him. "Even if that happens, Mathias, we probably won't see much of each other." He placed his tray on a conveyor belt, and I did the same with mine, both of us watching as they rode the belt into another room. "I run with my own folks inside and you'll run with yours." He made an apologetic gesture. "Don't count on being friends."

■ ■ ■

On Thursday of that week, I was escorted to the processing offices once again.

"You've been assigned," an official told me. "Medium Security, Mathias. I'd have figured you for Max."

"Single cell?" I asked, hoping the opposite.

"For a while," he answered. "Until they see how you're going to get along.

"When?"

"Right away," he told me, motioning me to accompany him to a semi-secluded alcove. "You take your shower, get your prison clothes here, then wait in there." He pointed to the holding cell, the same one I'd occupied when I'd first arrived. Inside, four other prisoners were sitting, waiting - two blacks, one Hispanic, and another Caucasian like me. They were already dressed in the gray-blues of the state prison. I was somewhat pleased that neither of the blacks was the young tough from the cafeteria, although disappointed that neither was Charlie.

"The bus will be here in a half-hour," the official continued. "Get going."

5

Prison for life is like being told you're dying,

Denial

Anger.

Bargaining.

Depression.

Never quite acceptance.

The prison bus rolled past the perimeter fences, through the gate of the thick, high-stone walls of the inner enclosure, and into the penitentiary yard.

Was I resigned to it?

The driver parked the bus at a drab concrete block building that jutted out from a more massive structure. It was a more recent building that had been added without regard for the architectural integrity of the original structure. The driver rose from his seat and, with the two sheriff's guards watching us carefully, unlocked the steel cage door that separated the rear space of the bus from the front.

"Get out!" the driver commanded. He descended the steps to join the other two men who'd moved out before him.

"Let's move!" shouted a deputy from outside.

Along with the four other new prisoners, handcuffed and shackled in leg irons, I stepped out of the bus and was led into a narrow outside passageway, one deputy in front, another behind us. It was sort of an elongated cage with bars above and on either side of us. As we shuffled along, a steel door at the far end opened, and we moved into a large detention room as the passageway door clanged shut behind us.

It was a room without furniture; no benches or chairs. In the center of the left inside wall, there was something like a teller's window. At the opposite end of the room, there were two solid-steel security doors with slotted observation windows. The deputy, who had led us in, walked toward the doors and leaned against the wall between them. Then, the right-hand door opened, and five prison guards entered. They were young, burly men in tan and chocolate-brown uniforms, each armed only with a long, wicked-looking hickory baton. A moment later, an older man in a custom-tailored uniform entered the room. He looked us over for a short while, and then turned to the sheriff's deputy and said, "Unlock them."

The deputy walked behind us, bending to insert his keys into the leg irons and handcuffs of the first man, then the second. He worked his way down the line to me, the last to be freed. He stood up behind us, kicking the leg irons well away before he bent again to retrieve them.

The officer nodded to us, a sort of greeting. "I'm Captain Underwood. I'm in charge of the security of this facility," he said in an almost friendly manner. "I have a number of things to tell you, some rules and regulations that you will be required to obey." He gestured to the window in the wall. "You'll pick up your bedding, and you'll be escorted to your assigned space. For a period of time, you'll be restricted to a single occupancy cell. You'll be allowed out of it for meals and for a limited amount of recreation. Later on, as we determine your behavior and attitude, you'll be reassigned and paired with another inmate. We are short on space and must make do with what we have. When you are reassigned, we will find work for you to do. For those of you serving lengthy sentences, you'll find that work is a benefit, not a punishment." He paused, and then went on, "Prison is not a nice place. We do what we can to rehabilitate those people who've made mistakes. However, our basic job is to protect society from people like you. Many of you are dangerous men, and you'll be living in a community of dangerous men. Therefore, our rules are strict. They have to be. You will obey them or else." Again, he paused, making eye contact with each of us as he continued, "What do I mean by 'or else?' I mean that we will take away whatever privileges you have, we will confine you, we will isolate you from whatever small pleasures that this facility may offer. We will do so until such a time that you can learn to obey those rules."

He began pacing. "Even so, the warden, myself, the guards, and the staff, we realize that even a community of dangerous men has societies of their own. We have African-Americans, Hispanics, Caucasians, Orientals, and we have race problems inside the facility. Some people get along, others don't. You're about to enter this community, and I advise you to be as careful as you can be. Be careful who you offend. Be careful in choosing a friend. Accept things as you find them. Don't ask too many questions, and stay out of things that don't concern you. We ask no one to be an informant. In fact, we really discourage it. Not only does informing put you in danger, it cuts no ice with us. We'll handle whatever comes. We don't want or need your help, but we *do* expect your cooperation." He glanced at his watch. "If you'll step to the window, we'll issue your mattresses and blankets. You'll be issued additional clothing and given shower schedules at a later time. That's all!"

He gave us a curt nod of farewell and walked out of the door as the supply window opened. Motioned forward, we moved to pick up our plastic-sheathed mattress pads and wool blankets, and then were led through the left-hand door into confinement.

A guard escorted me into and through the massive facility of criminal confinement with multi-tiered cellblocks. It was an older prison, built in the early 50's, when they had barred cell doors instead of solid ones. My escort took me to an isolated section to a cell where he locked me inside, alone.

Welcome to the big house.

6

Except for the age and appearance of the facility, my initial time in this new solitary occupancy wasn't much different than it had been at the county jail or the diagnostic center. My routine was very much the same; breakfast, lunch, dinner, and an hour to exercise, watch television, or just sit in an easy chair in a lounge area.

One day, my routine was slightly altered; a visit to the warden's office. Warden Carey was a tall, no-nonsense sort of a man, quite fit for his middle age. I'd been told that he'd worked his way up through the penal system, starting years ago as a guard in the Canon City facility. As I entered his office, with two guards accompanying me, he made no motion for me to sit, so I continued to stand.

"Mathias," he said, consulting his file. "How are things going with you?"

"All right, I suppose," I answered.

He nodded. "You've got a life sentence. Now, how are you going to manage that?"

"I don't know, sir."

"Early on, lifers tend to take out their anger on others," he began, something that sounded like a familiar topic. "That's why we keep an eye on you." He paused. "Are you angry, Mathias?"

I took a deep breath. "Yes, sir."

"At us? The prison personnel? Other prisoners?"

"I suppose so," I admitted. "Anything that has any part of the so-called justice system."

He didn't respond for a moment, and then asked: "Do you think you can get over that anger?"

"I don't know, sir. I think it'll take a while."

He chuckled. "Well, we've got plenty of time, don't we." He glanced down at my file once again and made a dismissive gesture. "We'll talk again one of these days."

Which, we never did. That was my one and only conversation with the warden.

The guards walked me back to my cell and locked me in.

It's funny how your mind can seize on one particular thing to wish for. I looked forward to the day that I'd be brought into the general prison population, anything to alleviate the continual boredom of living by myself. I lay on my bed and wondered with whom I'd be paired, and whether we could have meaningful conversations, whether we'd get along, be pals or detest each other. I looked forward with great desire to do some sort of work, to have something to do with my hands, something to occupy my days. I also dreaded change, knowing that I would no longer have the safety of my solitude. I thought about accounts that I had read and movies that I'd seen; where helpless men were turned into sex slaves, of crude blade thrusts in prison yard encounters, of gasoline-filled light bulbs exploding in cells.

Did those things really happen? What could I do about them?

One thing I did was to exercise, developing a rigorous routine. Not just a few minutes here or there, but entire mornings. After breakfast, I'd do pushups, sit-ups, squat walks, knee bends - any exercise I could remember and a few I made up.

■ ■ ■

By the third month, I was hard-muscled when they reassigned me. I was moved into a different section of the prison, the lower floor of an older cellblock where each barred cell contained bunk beds. Actually, they looked more comfortable than the ones found in the newer facilities. Since I was the newcomer to the accommodation, I got the upper bunk, and whatever space in the cell was left for my toilet articles and personal property. One new thing; there was a 13-inch television set mounted on the wall.

"Don't get your hopes up," the guard told me, seeing my interest. "We pick what you see." He closed the cell door, not bothering to introduce me to the other occupant.

My new cellmate was a short, chunky and chatty Puerto Rican named Christopher Munoz. He was a fellow near my own age, doing the second of seven years for drug trafficking. At first, he'd seemed a little more worried about me than I about him.

"Murder, huh," he'd said. "Man, I never did that."

I started to disclaim, then remembered Charlie at the diagnostic center.

Let them think the worst.

"Does it bother you?" he persisted, not too sure that he should have asked.

"Let's not talk about it," I said, hoping the gruff voice and stern attitude would do the trick.

"Hey, no problem," he said. "I never done that to nobody, so I just wondered about it." He paused, waiting for my response, then shrugged. "I was always a little uneasy, wondering if I'd do it if I had to . . . being in the drug thing, you know."

This time, I shrugged.

"I know you hear about how mean people are and all that," he went on. "Thank God, if it happened, it didn't happen around me. Me, I was in it not just for the money, and I didn't really get all that much . . . but it was for the fun of it."

From his chattering, I began to wonder if my months of single cell confinement might not have been so bad.

"You know, it was exciting," he rattled on. "We'd meet those guys from Columbia down there in Mexico . . . sometimes, some island down in the Caribbean. They'd laugh and joke around with us, drink with us. You know, it *was* fun. We'd pay them, and then we'd figure some sort of way to get the stuff back into the States."

"Cocaine?"

"Sure, cocaine, heroin, crack, marijuana, meth . . . whatever," he said, showing off his expertise. "Sometimes, we'd pack the stuff over the border, walking across at night. Sometimes, we'd send it by a ship. Maybe we'd hire some tourist to take stuff back in their suitcases." He laughed aloud. "Tell you what . . . the most fun was flying it back with Bruno Cady." He laughed again in delight. "Bruno is crazy; he can do anything with a damned airplane."

"Can he land in a prison yard?" I asked.

"Probably," Munoz said, taking my sarcasm with good humor. "He'd be crazy enough to try."

I didn't realize it at the time, but I believe that conversation was the beginning of my thoughts about escape. I will be the first to say that escape from prison is something that you read about, but it seldom ever happens. You see, the warden, the guards, and the state, local, and federal police all see those same movies, and read those same books. They just don't let it happen. If it ever does happen, it generally means that somebody screwed up and didn't follow procedure.

After the initial burst of nervous prattling, Chris turned out to be a pretty good cellmate. He was born in San Juan, Puerto Rico, but knew little of it. His parents had moved to Miami, Florida when he was a baby, and he grew up in the United States. He lived in Hispanic communities that included Puerto Ricans, Cubans, Mexicans, and other assorted emigrants. He'd finished part of his high school years, although not bothering to graduate. For a prisoner, most of the time, he was basically cheerful and good-natured. We didn't have a lot in common, but we developed a somewhat cordial relationship. I still did a lot of reading and he was usually considerate, only occasionally interrupting to ask a question or to make a brief comment. It was good to have him as a companion when we went to our meals, and when we got our breaks out in the yard. He brought me into the fringes of the various Hispanic groups where I was met with bare tolerance, but not outright hostility.

"Watch out for those motherfuckers, Kev," he told me in a low voice, giving a slight nod to indicate a sizable knot of Hispanic prisoners congregated at one side of the open area. "Street gangs outta LA . . . and there ain't nothing they wouldn't do if you piss 'em off."

Mainly from Chris, I found out about the composition of prisoners in our penitentiary. The majority was black with dozens of separate societies within that racial group. These factions ranged from aggressive to passive, but most all harbored a dislike for skin colors other than their own. Caucasians made up the second largest crowd, many with race-hate cliques and bully-boy clans. Hispanic men, mostly Mexicans, Cubans and Puerto Ricans, made a sizable group although Asians were beginning to rival them in size. A good number of all races, however, were loners like me; men who'd committed this crime or that, in prison for what they'd done as individuals, and not as part of some special group.

"See that guy over there?" Chris once asked me, pointing to a prisoner across the yard. "Big Mafia guy outta Philly or maybe Newark . . . I forget which."

I stared at the older man sitting on the yard's bleachers, surrounded by a small group of sycophants.

"Vincent Gianntana," Chris supplied the name. "He's what they call an Underboss . . . whatever that is."

I nodded, vaguely remembering the name from old newspapers. "What's going on with them?"

"Holding court," Chris pointed out.

"How come he's not in a federal prison?" I asked.

"Got him here on an accessory to murder charge," my cellmate responded. "Shoulda left it to the local wiseguys. Hadda come out here and oversee the hit. Got him on accessory charge."

I watched the group for a few minutes. "Does he get special treatment?"

Chris shrugged. "Some ways, yes. He's been here over ten, ain't ever going to get out. He can buy what he wants, up to a point. They don't treat lifers like . . ." He paused, suddenly remembering my sentence. "Sorry."

"He's a lifer?"

"Same as," Chris explained. "At least twenty to go, and he's late sixties."

I studied the man from our distance. He was more slim than fleshy, a bit of a pot at his abdomen, but not so bad for a man of his age. He was silver-haired above a face with deep lines and sharp features. He was talking with a member of his coterie in an easy, often-smiling manner; a seemingly pleasant man.

"Looks mild enough," I ventured.

"Pay him respect," Chris counseled. "He ain't what he seems."

"Anybody friendly in this place?" I asked with some bitterness.

"I wouldn't count on it," Chris responded with a laugh. "And that includes me."

"Have I done anything to piss you off?"

"Not yet," he replied, making sure I knew he was joking. "Please don't."

I nodded again at the aging gangster. "I always kinda half-figured the Mafia as Hollywood stuff."

"Oh, they're for real," Chris told me. "Not as headline as they used to be, I guess, but they still count. There's not too many in here with us, but we don't fuck with 'em. You bother one of 'em and, somehow, some way, you'll end up dead."

I turned away and faced Chris squarely. "There's something I've got to ask," I said. "How do I survive?"

He gave me a sad smile. "Man, I can't give you any pointers. It's a day-to-day thing. You just do whatever it takes to get through 'til the next day."

"Am I going to get killed?"

He shrugged. "You might. You don't look scrawny which is good."

"How about getting raped?" I asked; the thought of that worse than the thought of death.

He nodded. "They'll likely try."

I glanced around. "Who?"

Chris gave a hand-sweep gesture, indicating the entire prison yard. "Must be a hundred or more that would do it, if they catch you alone."

"Will anybody help if I'm not alone?"

"Not likely."

"Then what do I do?"

He sighed, and pointed to a band of heavily muscled, heavily-tattooed skinheads. "You could join up with a group like that, but they're likely to do it to you even if you're one of them."

"What about hanging with your people?" I asked.

He shook his head. "No way," he said. "You're Anglo." He stroked the side of his face, "Make yourself a weapon, and use it if you have to."

"What kind of a weapon?" I asked.

"Something that'll stick 'em or slice 'em," he told me, ending the conversation.

It was a sobering thought. I didn't have any idea as to how to make such a cutting instrument, much less how to use one. I dreaded even the thought of a knife. For one thing, I think I've always been in great fear of knives or other sharp-edged tools. Perhaps that's because we've all cut ourselves, one time or another, and we can relate to that sort of pain even from the slight wounds we've experienced. By contrast, since

I've never been shot, even gunshot wounds seemed almost preferable to cuts.

Despairing of the likely acquisition of any lethal weapon, I hoped that my hours of physical fitness would provide me with strength enough to take care of myself.

To stay undamaged and alive.

7

No doubt there are penitentiaries with license plate manufac-
turing facilities or with metal shops - places where you could
make something sharp and dangerous. Here, my first work
assignment was in the prison printing section. About the only
things sharp were the giant blades that were permanently
attached to large paper cutting machines. Or the spikes of
punching machines that drilled precise holes in ledger sheets.
Our prison produced a large share of the business forms for
our state government offices as well as for private industry.
Most of our work was menial, only a few inmate craftsmen
working in the facility. Most of the design and layout work was
done by outside firms; we did only the printing, packaging and
shipping. My first job was to truck large rolls and packets of
plain white sheet paper to various stations in the printing shop.
It wasn't particularly heavy or fatiguing work, but it was monot-
onous. After a learning curve of, say, ten minutes, it was a hell
of a boring way to spend the day. Conversations with other
convicts were not particularly condoned or sharply restricted,
but most of my associates seemed to go about their similar
jobs quietly. During breaks, we'd sometimes exchange a few
comments, but the talk was usually as bland as the work.
Much of it concerned either the arrival of letters from relatives
or the lack of the same, food in the dining hall, chances for

early parole, and reviews of the television programs that we were allowed to see.

I spent six months at this duty, and I really didn't appreciate the benefits of my situation. Most of my fellow workers were passive rather than aggressive, and I really didn't know how lucky I'd been in this circumstance.

"They're taking care of you, buddy," my cellmate confided one night after supper, bending over the sink to rinse his partial plate.

"How so?" I asked, surprised at the remark.

"Easy work," he said to me, turning to face me, a slight tone of derision in his voice. "Maybe 'cause you're a college boy."

I shrugged. "I didn't ask for favors. I'm in for murder. Why would they give me special treatment?"

It was his turn to shrug, fitting his plate into his mouth. "I don't know, but it's pissing people off." He crossed to the television set and turned it on, watching it glow to a 1950's western movie fed to us over the in-house TV system.

Again, I was surprised, and then angry. "Who's pissed off and why? I'm just doing what I'm told and trying to get along."

Chris sat down on his bunk, and I leaned over to look down at him.

"Other people think they ought to be getting soft duty, people who've been here a while," he said. "They think you ought to be getting the shit jobs."

"Should I volunteer?" I scoffed.

"Wouldn't hurt," he said, and gave all his attention to the western movie.

I thought about his comments for quite a while, wondering at the mentalities of these penitentiary societies, the jealousies and irrational perceptions. So far, it hadn't been too bad, boring as I've said, but not too bad. The fear of the unspeakable and the unthinkable had, to some extent, faded.

I had a sudden chill; possibly a premonition as dread returned. Perhaps if and when something came, it would be far worse.

█   █   █

Two weeks later, I was moved into kitchen duty. My managerial experience with a restaurant as a qualification, no doubt. In a prison facility, food is served cafeteria-style. There's a menu supervisor, kind of a lower level chef, hired from the outside to provide a somewhat balanced diet for the incarcerated. A couple of other cooks are paid employees of the penal institution, but the bulk of the work force is made up of inmates. Prisoners do some of the cooking, all of the serving, all of the sweeping of floors, all of the cleaning of trays, pots and pans, and all of the storing and procuring of food supplies. There are some choice jobs such as cleaning the grease traps in the plumbing system - one assigned to me on a regular basis. It seemed my almost daily chore to reach into the sludge of suet, gristle, and slimy fluids, to scoop out the mess, and leave the trap swabbed clean until the next onslaught from over a thousand prisoners.

As suddenly as I was shifted to kitchen duty, I was reassigned to shower room duty in a cellblock other than my own. My workday started not in the morning, but at one o'clock in the afternoon. As the men from different levels were escorted to the showers, my job was to stiff-brush the floors; to squeegee and mop between each group arrival, making sure that the soap suds, piss, and scum went down the drain. I would stand to the side and pretend not to see as, a common occurrence, a man would lather his penis and stroke it hard, spurting his semen into the spray that washed down over him.

Two weeks after I started, in the early evening, a group of five naked blacks came into the shower room, each one sculptured in ebony muscle. They came in, without the usual banter and joking of a bathhouse assemblage, and looked at me with singular attention.

I knew at that moment what was going to happen, what I'd feared.

There was no guard in sight.

"Take your pants down, white boy," one of the men said, stepping forward.

"No way," I said, fear in my voice apparent to all.

"Take 'em down for him, Jesse," another man said gleefully.

I backed against the wall and kicked at them when they came. Four of them swarmed, dodging my fists and feet, strong arms seizing me, pinning my arms against the wall, other arms clamping around my legs. They threw me face down onto the wet floor to spread-eagle me, hands tugging at my waistband, pulling my trousers and shorts to my ankles. A powerful arm reached under my stomach and pulled me up to a kneeling position as my head was forced even harder against the wet cement.

The shock of the penetration was excruciating, not only for the pain, but for the shame of it. With the thrusts coming again and again, I screamed in anger and anguish, my sounds turning into crying.

"Don't cry, honey!"

"Enjoy it, baby!"

"More where that comes from!"

"I'm next! I'm next!"

"What the hell's going on in here?" came a different voice.

The man on top of me pulled out, and I groaned at the relief, sobbing at the humiliation. I couldn't look up, couldn't make myself turn to see what was happening. I lay face down, only half-hearing the voices.

"Get away from him!" the angry voice commanded. "Get your asses out of here!"

There were sounds of shuffling and under-breath mutterings, and then of wet feet moving away.

Then, for a long time, there was silence.

A guard knelt beside me. "You okay?"

I didn't answer. I couldn't.

"They're gone now," he said, his voice gentle and consoling. "Let me help you."

I shook my head. "Just go away for a while," I managed to whisper. "Just let me alone for a while."

He didn't respond for a moment, then rose with a nod and left.

I don't know - maybe it was five minutes, maybe a half-hour later that I crawled to the wall and used it to rise. I scuttled along it, coming to one of the showerhead faucets. I turned it on full, more hot than cold, then stood under it to let the water sting and soothe my flesh. I soaped my anus and cried again into the spray of the shower, hoping to wash away the pain and the mortification.

Finally, I dressed, and the kindly guard took me out of hell.

8

"Sorry, man," Chris said, somewhere around dawn.

I didn't answer.

He'd heard me come in during the night, and I couldn't say anything. I had lain awake without a blink of my eyes, staring at the dark ceiling, seeing nothing but the shower room, and the faces of those I had actually seen. I'd relived the horror, the shame of it - each word, each movement of my limbs, every scratch and pain of it. I'd known Chris was awake with me, at least a part of the time, but he'd been wise enough, considerate enough to never utter a word.

When, at last, the morning call had come, when Chris was up and dressed and I'd shown some semblance of recovery, he'd dared to speak, to show concern.

"Don't be embarrassed about it," he said, trying to be of comfort. "It happens."

"Never to me again," I vowed.

I went to work that day in that awful shower room, dreadfully aware of the inquisitive glances that came my way, aware of a guard who stayed conspicuously nearby, of small smirks on some faces, curiosity on others. Whenever I heard laughter, I assumed it had to be about me. I watched for those who had assaulted me, but they didn't come on this day. I wondered what I'd do when any one or all of them appeared.

Finally, my shift was over and I returned to my cell.

"They paid the guard," Chris informed me. "You were lucky that the other one came by." After a moment, he added, "I 'spect the one guard will get canned if he ain't already." He paused again. "You want to identify who did you?"

I thought about it and shook my head. "That would be a mistake, wouldn't it?"

Chris considered and nodded. "Better let it go."

"Uh-uh!" I practically shouted. "I won't let it go. I don't know if you can, but let them know that I'll kill if anyone approaches me again. I'll find a way." I took a breath, and told the big lie. "I've killed before, and I know how to do it. Tell anyone that messes with me again, they're dead if they try."

From that day on, escape was ever on my mind. I knew I could never survive this prison, this waste of my life. Perhaps if I'd been guilty of anything, perhaps I would've accepted it. But, now, even if I died in an escape attempt, that would be just fine.

After the shower room horror, I'd been reassigned to the kitchen. Whatever job given me, my body performed, but my mind speculated as to any conceivable means of escape. When I lay in my bunk at night, the lights out and prisoners were sleeping, I examined possibilities, all of them irrational. My determination was ever there, but I couldn't find the answer.

Escape is a fairly common topic of discussion in prison. Everybody talks about it, but nobody ever does anything about it. You've got to give the jailers their due; they've thought about almost everything that you can think of. Even though it's a common subject of conversation, the talk doesn't last very long because most everyone realizes that it just isn't going to happen. Even so, it doesn't stop inmates from fantasizing about getting out, getting away to a new life.

"If I was on the run," Chris was saying to a small group of daydreamers including myself, "I'd get hold of old Bruno Cady and have him fly me outta the country. Go down to one of them South American countries where they can't get you . . ." He looked at me for the word. "Can't bring you back?"

"Extradite."

"Yeah," he nodded, resuming his narrative. "Where they can't extradite you."

"Who's Bruno Cady?" asked one young inmate.

"Damned best pilot you ever saw!" Chris declared. "Learned his trade way back in Vietnam, and kept at it when he came home."

"Running drugs?" another listener asked.

Chris nodded.

"What makes him so damned special?" a skeptic in the group asked.

"'Cause he don't never get caught," Chris told them. "Hell, one time, the DEA was on the ground at a drop site, waiting for him to come in, gonna catch him with the goods." He shook his head, showing his admiration. "He never came in."

There was silence from our group, waiting for Chris to go on.

"How'd he knowed they was there?" the skeptic asked.

"I asked him about that when he was telling the story," Chris told him. "Said it was nothing, but pure gut feeling. He knowed they was there."

"He didn't get tipped off?" asked another.

Chris shook his head. "He says not. He just got that feeling and headed off a couple hundred miles a different way.

Put that plane down in some damned field, walked away, and told his buyers where they could get their shit."

"Walked away from his plane?"

Chris laughed. "Hell, it wasn't his plane."

"This dude still operating?" another cynic wanted to know. "How come if the law knows about him, they don't put him away?"

"Hell, he don't do it every day," Chris told them. "He's got a legitimate business, runs a flying school out of a little old private field down there outside Baton Rouge. They know what he does, but they can't prove it."

Call me another of the fools, but I put Chris's information into my head for future use.

If I could find a way!

"You really tight with this Cady fellow?" I asked.

"Tight as a tick," Chris assured me.

"What's he look like?" I asked.

One man of the group hooted. "You gonna look him up?"

Chris, however, gave me a straight look, and a straight answer. "Hard to say. I ain't seen him in a while. He was tall . . . too tall to pilot in fighters, they figured. Skinny, but he was kinda turning to fat last time I saw him."

"How would you recognize him?" I persisted.

"By his eyes, man," Chris told me, an expression on his face that told me he was envisioning as he spoke. "Bruno can be a lot of fun when he's having fun, but when he looks hard at you, you kinda want to step back."

I waited until the group broke up, and then took Chris to one side. "You ever contact this Cady?" I asked. "Since you've been inside?"

He shook his head.

"Could you get word to him if you needed?"

Chris shrugged, his brow furrowed as he sought my meaning.

"If I ever get out of here, Chris," I began. "Would you pass the word that he might expect me?"

"Don't be crazy, Kev," he said softly. "There's no way out. You know that."

"Just supposing, could he get me out of the country? Would he do it, based on your say so?"

He shrugged again. "Sure, I guess so." He smiled. "Hypothetically speaking, of course?"

I laughed. "Big word for a jailhouse spic."

Chris shared the laughter. "Got my GED," he countered. "Keep me in here long enough, I'll have my Ph.D.!"

9

Spring came.

Summer and Fall.

During those months, I occasionally saw the men who had assaulted me in the shower room. The exact rapist, I didn't know. At least, I knew one or two. We'd stare in the yard, their faces cruel and mocking, mine showing my genuine hatred. Whether because of my threats or because of their lack of opportunity, I wasn't bothered again. Of course, it was known throughout the prison of my humiliation but, strangely, there had been a subtle change of attitude toward me, a sort of sympathy. My degradation seemed less important to others than my reaction to it. The inmates apparently believed I would now kill if provoked. In a bizarre twist, I'd gained respect.

Winter came with mild days in December and early January, and then turned bitter cold in mid-month although without snow. Our time in the yard was brief, all of us retreating to the warmth of the indoor recreational facilities. I spent as much time as I was allowed in the gym, doing weights, keeping myself strong and trim. I was still working in the kitchen at various jobs, everything from serving, to dishwashing, to supply inventories

On the third day of the big chill, I was working the late shift. I came to the kitchen a couple of hours before the evening servings, replacing those who'd been on the job since four o'clock in the morning. For the first time in my going-on-two-years, I was working with the Mafioso bigwig, Vince Gianntana. I was surprised to see him there, assuming his reputed importance would have exempted him from common labor. As a matter of fact, I learned he drew work assignments just like the rest of us. Energetic for his years, he did his work quickly and efficiently, making an occasional comment, and sometimes showing a surprisingly witty sense of humor. While not in the sense of a budding friend-ship, I did feel he was easy-going in his manner toward me. A couple of his remarks showed evidence of learning, and we spoke of interests other than crime and punishment.

On this Tuesday evening, in addition to a myriad of after supper chores, one of our jobs was to lug the many sacks and containers of trash and food scraps out to the big dumpster bins. Shivering in the near zero-degree darkness, wearing only our prison shirts and trousers, we carried and dragged out the refuse of over a thousand convicts, bucking garbage bags up and over the lips of the bins.

These large steel containers were at the side of the central avenue that stretched from the front gate into the heart of the prison. This central avenue is, of course, one of the most scrutinized security areas of the prison. Here, our supplies arrived, our products were loaded and shipped, commercial vehicles coming and going many times during the day and night. No truck, van, or automobile entered or left the avenue without a thorough inspection - inside, underside, and outside. A guard tower overlooks the street, and video cameras record the activities.

We were heading back inside when we saw the outsized trash truck clear inspection and move through the second gate. We rushed to pick up the last of the black plastic sacks, and then hurried back outside again to toss them into the last remaining bins. We watched as the truck's front-loading hydraulic fork lift raised one bin and dumped its contents into the open maw of its body. The sounds of different gears began as a compactor ram whined from the front of the enclosed bed, compressing the refuse, smashing it tight, and then whining back as the fork lift lowered. As the truck moved forward, the lift still descending to spear one of the other bins, impulse rather than reason galvanized me.

I vaulted into the last bin.

To this day, I have no idea of how it could have been possible. Perhaps the guard on the parapet had stepped into the warmth of the tower for a few moments and didn't see. Perhaps the descending lift obscured the driver's vision. Perhaps the angle of the truck prevented the cameras from recording what happened.

To my surprise, I saw hands grasping the lip as Vince Gianntana attempted to follow me. I grabbed him by the back of his shirt to pull him into the bin with me. A few moments later, we felt the jolt of the fork lift shafts stabbing into the bin's base apertures.

The voluminous contents of the bin slid and slithered over us as it was raised and inverted. Then, we were falling into the cavity opened by the retreating compactor. I tumbled into the waste, vaguely aware of Gianntana's body dropping somewhere to my left. I had no further thought for him as plastic sacks and loose refuse piled down upon me, driving me down into the depths of the truck's repository. I tried to swim upward through the trash, frantic at the sound of the compactor whining up again. Around me, sacks burst and garbage oozed over me, solid wastes squeezed against me, arresting all motion, pressing the breath from my lungs. Over the sound of the compactor, I thought I heard a cry of pain, but I couldn't be sure. I could think only of myself, of what a foolish and dismal way to die. I prayed the guards had seen me, that the driver of the truck would release the dreadful pressure, and that hands would dig me free of this terrible burial.

The whining ceased, yet the pressure remained.

Somehow, I flexed my shoulders and upper body just enough to inhale a shallow breath, then another. I heard the truck's hydraulics groan into remission, and then felt the surge as the vehicle turned, backed, turned again and moved slowly forward.

If I'd had sufficient breath, I would have screamed for help as the truck rumbled to a stop at the inspection station. Outside, I could hear the muffled voices of the driver and the guards complaining about the weather. I could hear them as they walked around the truck, and heard the knock of the pole-mounted mirrors against the undercarriage. After only a few minutes, the truck began to rumble forward again, gathering speed.

I managed to flex again and gained a little more space, not much, but enough to breathe a little more easily. The pressure was still painful, but I began to see hope in my situation. I knew we were outside the prison walls and moving at highway speed away. Even though I was squeezed almost as tight as an insect in amber, the surrounding trash and garbage was insulating me from the bitter cold. I couldn't move my arms or legs, but I could dig a little with my fingers. I began clawing down, trying to burrow an airway. At first, it was an inch or two, then four, then almost a foot. As the truck bounced along, the load was shifting a little, pressure easing ever so slightly.

It must have been no more than an hour, but, as the saying goes; it seemed an eternity before we stopped. I could hear the engine idle and heard the driver leave the cab, slamming the door. A few moments later, he returned and moved the truck ahead. Then, it turned about and backed, and a different sound of hydraulics began as the entire body began to tilt. Suddenly, the truck's huge burden thundered down, overwhelming me. Once again, the compactor began to whine and the heightened pressure became unendurable. I knew now I would die.

Suddenly, the pressure was released and I was falling, my body sliding with the trash and refuse out into the darkness. Then, I was bouncing hard, careening down a steep slope; a part of an avalanche of garbage pouring into a valley of rubbish, litter, waste, and debris. Above me, the truck literally shook itself free of its load, lowered the bed into its driving profile, and moved away.

For several minutes, I could do no more than to regain my breath and to work the numbness out of my arms and legs. Only gradually did I begin to feel the dreadful cold invading my inadequate clothing. I got up and moved around in the darkness, only able to see a little from the starlight. It was a clear night, beautiful yet deadly. As cold as it was now, with no cloud covering, it would be much colder later.

I remembered Gianntana and wondered where he was. "Vince?" I said almost in a whisper, and then realized there was no reason for that. "Vince!" I shouted. "Where are you?"

I listened carefully, but heard no sound other than a slight wind fluttering through the rubbish valley. I crabbed my way to the left, and then to the right, my hands touching into the dark masses, much of trash hard-frozen, some of it still moist and sticky. Four or five minutes I searched, finally touching what felt like flesh.

"Vince?" I exclaimed, bending down, not even sure then. "Vince?"

"Yeah," came a reply, as faint as the distant wind.

"Are you hurt?"

There was no answer.

I bent lower and tried to see. There was something protruding from his chest, and I could now hear a different sound - a nasty, bubbling sound whenever the man took a slight breath. "My God, Vince," I said in dismay. "I don't know what to do."

"Nothing," came a hoarse rattle. "Don't leave me here."

"What?" I asked, bringing my ear to his mouth.

"Clean," he whispered. "Clean earth . . ."

And he died with those words on his last breath, the bubbling exhale tapering into silence.

Some sort of a metal support had impaled him - a brace of a chair or of a table. Something had been broken and thrown into the trash. I made an effort to pull it out of his chest, but it was too firmly fixed, too short to get my hands around.

By now, I knew I was in danger of freezing to death. Not at all sure of what to do about Gianntana's body, I took his limp arms to drag him part way up the slope, out of the trash. I left him there for the time being, concerned about saving myself from the cold. I began searching through the refuse, looking for any material that might provide some warmth. I cried out in delight when I found a discarded bathrobe, ripped in places and frayed, but heavy enough to give some comfort. I tried it on, a little small, but not bad, not bad at all.

I had a sudden inspiration. I began to tear at the black refuse bags, opening them and dumping out their contents. I tore armholes and a neck hole in one, and then slipped it over my head and down over the ratty bathrobe.

Then, another and another.

I wandered through the wasteland, and eventually found a pair of jeans big enough to fit over my prison trousers. I wrapped other plastic sacks around my shoes and ankles, and fashioned a thrown-away tablecloth into a headscarf.

I was almost as wide as tall, and I stopped layering only when I found it would restrict my movements. Though the night was still bitter, I thought my motley garb might save me from freezing.

With comparative warmth, my worries returned. By now, every law agency of the land would know we were gone, and would be looking for us. By now, they'd have probably realized that we'd gone out with the trash truck, and they'd be on their way here.

Time to move, to get as far away as possible.

I started up the slope and stopped at Gianntana's body.

I knew what he wanted. Not to be found in the garbage. To be found in clean ground somewhere. I sighed and shook my head, trying to let him know I couldn't fulfill his last request, to carry that heavy body out of the dump and to dig into frozen ground. I also wondered if such a man, with a criminal history of theft, corruption, and murder, deserved something clean and pure.

"I'm sorry, Vince," I muttered. "They'll find you and give you a decent burial." I started to move on, and then reconsidered. It couldn't hurt to pull him up a little higher, further out from the garbage.

I bent down to drag him, the load heavier than I'd imagined.

When I got to the top of the incline, I pulled him up onto even ground and stopped to rest for a moment. Perhaps the night had brightened or my eyes had become more accustomed to star shine, for I could see the county dump was being excavating into new space in the surrounding earth. A bulldozer was parked where work had stopped; overhangs of topsoil had not yet tumbled into the landfill crater. All at once, I knew I could do something more.

I took Vince's arms once again and began to drag him. It was easier on level ground, and the distance was not so far. When I got to the edge overlooking clean earth, I started to ease him down into a depression. As I did, I touched something solid under his shirt. I ripped the shirt open, reached inside, and found the thick belt he was wearing around his waist. I found the buckle and pulled it free.

I knew exactly what it was - a money belt.

I took only a moment more to feel the thickness of its contents. I strapped it on under my clothes, and then lowered Vince's body into a pocket in the loose soil. It occurred to me it might be better if his body was not found too quickly. Such a find would likely give the hunters an advantage in narrowing their search area. I stepped down and brushed the surrounding soil over him, using my numb hands to dig him a shallow grave. As I climbed back up, some of the overhang gave way and covered him even more. I stood at the top of the excavation, touching his money belt with my hands.

"Something for something, Vince," I said as a benediction, and began walking fast away.

I followed the road to the padlocked entrance gate, climbed over the adjacent wire-strand fence, and started down the gravel road. It would've been prudent for me to stay off the roads, to make my way over frozen fields, but I knew I needed to get away from this area as quickly as possible. The road seemed the best choice for the time being. I needed to find a direction, and work my way to some sort of shelter and safety.

On such a clear night, I reasoned, I'd see the headlights of any car long before it would reach me. I could flatten myself, a trash heap, in a ditch or hide in the brush. I really was beginning to believe that the people at the penitentiary might not have realized exactly how we'd gotten out. If they'd immediately determined our means of escape and destination, the county dump would have been swarming with police by now. However, I wasn't fool enough to believe they wouldn't eventually come to that determination. Perhaps, I'd been given a little edge of good luck for a change.

Thank you, God! Maybe you're making up for getting me into all this in the first place.

I followed the road until it stopped at a blacktop highway, then considered my option; go right or left? I didn't know exactly where I was. To my right, the sky was starlit and dark. To my left, I thought I detected a very faint wash of light on the horizon. I knew it was far too early for dawn, somewhere near midnight. That glimmering could indicate some sort of a small village or town. The darkness to my right would likely be open country.

How long could I survive the winter in the open? Could I hide in ditches in bitter weather? Seek shelter in barns? Find wild game for food or steal it from a farmhouse?

I turned to my left and started down the highway, my feet on the pavement. I was very cold, my teeth chattering, my hands feeling as though they'd fallen from my arms. I trudged along, tucking them inside my rags to warm them. I had no idea of what distances I was covering or how far civilization might be. I knew only the exertion was generating some body heat, enough perhaps to keep me alive.

I knew that walking this highway would soon be a problem. Even at this late hour, there would be a few automobiles on the road and I'd have to watch for them. In a couple of hours, the traffic would increase. I'd have to get off the road well before dawn, and find a hiding place of warmth.

Several times, automobiles appeared in the distance, and I crouched low in the roadside ditch, wondering if anybody could have spotted this black-bagged scarecrow. Just as I had decided the authorities were looking elsewhere, two police cars came racing down the highway, heading, I presumed, toward the county dump road.

Time to get off the road, I reasoned. Flat in the ditch, I breathed with relief as they sped by.

I waited until they were out of sight, and then rose from the ditch to climb over a sagging fence. The ground was frozen hard and there was little chance I'd leave a trail. I walked deep into the dry stubble field before turning again toward my destination. From this considerable distance, I could see other automobiles moving at high speeds, probably more police cars following the first pair. As I crouched, moving not at all, I took comfort they would not likely see me either.

The manhunt had begun.

The cold, bitter hours passed as I continued my flight. In the open fields, I moved only when the highway appeared empty. I had crossed four fields, creeping under and climbing over fences, when the coming daylight became my enemy. As the sky began to lighten, I moved into a stand of barren trees, realizing it would no longer be safe for me to continue. Although I was sweating from my exertion, I knew the bitter cold would freeze me if I didn't find shelter.

In a small clearing, I came across a pair of slight mounds with sort of a dry gully in between. When the sun came up, it might shine down into this depression and bring warmth. I gathered leaves from various places and piled them high into the gully. When I had as many as I could find, I burrowed into them and covered myself with care. As I tried to settle in, I became aware of Vince's money belt, slightly constricting. I opened the zipper and, with nearly frozen fingers, took the bills out and, with only the faint light of the coming dawn to see by, started counting.

Eighty-two hundred and fifty-five dollars! Escape money!

Exulting over my fortune, I replaced the money in the belt and laid back, raking more leaves toward me, over me, covering my face completely, and then tucked my hands inside my clothes to warm them against my skin.

Exhausted, I slept, somewhat warm and almost comfortable, unaware of distant sirens.

10

The sound of barking dogs awakened me. They were far away, and I didn't know if they were tracking hounds or simply some farmer's pets yelping at squirrels. Somewhere in the distance, I thought I heard the faint beat of a helicopter. I wondered if they'd found Gianntana's body and wondered if, from planes or helicopters, they'd be able to see my trail through the fields. Perhaps they had heat-sensing equipment that would search and find me. Surely, they must have determined how we'd escaped, and surely the circle was closing around me.

I sat up, stiff and sore, wondering if I had suffered frostbite during my deep freeze sleep. My hands were the most affected, but they looked all right. The fingers seemed to work even if numb and barely bendable. I brushed away the leaves, loath to leave my bed, but I was worried over the dogs. Undoubtedly, there was a massive hunt underway - prison guards, state police, sheriff's deputies - all searching the roads and adjacent fields.

I stood up and walked around a bit, trying to get the circulation going in my arms and legs. Although there were clouds in the sky, the sun was still shining, and I estimated that it must be around four o'clock in the afternoon. The temperature seemed warmer than before I'd slept yet still too cold for comfort. I hesitated, reluctant to leave the concealment of the trees. There'd be a couple of hours of daylight left, and my black-bagged appearance would surely stand out against the brown and beige of the winter fields. As much as I dreaded the cold of another freezing night, I yearned for darkness.

I scattered the leaves, kicking them around so as not to show that I'd spent the night there. To my eye, when I left, there seemed to be no indication. I moved to the edge of the grove and ventured a few feet out into the open again. I could no longer see the highway, and I guessed it must have veered in a different direction. In the far distance, almost directly ahead, I could see a water tower and a few buildings. I wasn't sure, but I made a pretty good guess it was the small town nearest to the prison, a town of three or four thousand named Fairfield.

Probably the hometown of all the prison guards, Captain Underwood, and the Warden himself.

I estimated that I was, at least, six or seven miles from the town. I no longer heard any dogs, and I could see no pack of pursuers. Taking the time to make sure, I stepped back into the trees to reconsider.

Wait until dark, I told myself. *No use taking a chance. I can travel to the town during the night.*

I retreated deeper into the woods once again and walked around trying to keep myself warm.

I've been a fool to try to escape in this kind of weather. I'll likely freeze to death or, worse, lose a limb, and end up back in the pen, a cripple for life doing life.

An hour later, the sun went behind the clouds and the landscape darkened sooner than I'd expected. Impatient, I decided it was gloomy enough to take my chances. I started across the open field, trying to crouch and walk in the lowest, shadowed sections of the land. It seemed only a few minutes of dusk, then it was dark again and I felt a little safer. It appeared this night was going to be cloudy, possibly keeping the temperature above zero.

Thank God!

I skirted wide around a couple of farms, staying far away from the houses, barns, and outbuildings. I looked at the lights from their homes, envying them their warmth, comfort and food. Not only was I miserably cold and thirsty, I was desperately hungry. It had been over twenty-four hours since I'd had anything to eat or drink, and my exertions and the frigid weather were sapping my strength. Resolutely, I continued moving, head down, forcing one step after another across the fields. From time to time, I looked up to see the lights of town houses straight ahead yet so very far away. Doggedly, I bent my head down again and continued on.

What I would do when I got there, I didn't know.

Give up more than likely.

I estimated it must have been well past midnight, perhaps even two or three o'clock in the morning when I came to a farm fence. Beyond it was the small pasture of a town-edge farmhouse, with another such dwelling not far to my right. Beyond the farmhouses, I could see a paved road with streetlights and suburban houses on either side. No lights were showing in any window, either in the farmhouses or in those of the city resident homes.

I eased over the outer fence, knowing I'd have to pass between the farmhouses, closer to either one than I'd like. I walked along the left side of a line fence that divided the farm properties, trying to be as quiet as possible.

The fence gate was right next to the farmhouse on my left. From inside the nearest house, I heard a dog begin to bark, the sound muted but persistent. Then, from the other house, another dog added its yelps to the alarm. I opened the gate, went through, and closed it softly.

From inside the first house, I heard a man's shout, "Shut up, you damned mutt!" A light in the second house came on, but I was now out of the yard. I hurried across the street, and hunkered inside a dark cluster of evergreens at the street corner. After a few minutes, the light went out again. I stayed quiet for a few minutes to consider what next to do.

To have escaped at all was a fluke. To have evaded capture for this long was unbelievable. What to do now, I had no idea. All I knew was that I had to find shelter from the cold. I knew I had to have food and warmth. And yet, I realized I had freedom, and I knew I would never have this chance for escape again. I looked down the street at the silent, dark houses and wondered if I could invade one of them. I was a desperate man, an escaped convict, but how could I threaten anyone? I had no weapons.

Maybe someone old and weak, afraid of my youth and strength. I hated myself for that sort of thought, but it was the only one that made sense. *Maybe an old man or an old woman, helpless and afraid. Perhaps I'd find a weapon in the house. How long could I hold them? Long enough to get warm,* I thought. *Have something to eat and drink.*

I started down the street, hiding from the flare of the streetlights, looking at the houses. These were older homes, some built maybe back in the thirties or forties, nice-sized, mostly bungalows, a few two-storied.

Which one?

I came to a second corner, thick with juniper shrubs three and four feet high. I burrowed into them, thankful of their insulating qualities, thankful for the cover they provided for me to survey the neighborhood.

I don't know how long it was, an hour or maybe two, before a few lights began to come on in the homes. I'd see lights appear in small bathroom windows and in kitchens. An automobile came by, going down one side of the street, and then coming back the other direction, the driver tossing newspapers out onto the driveways. Porch lights would come on, and men and women would come out, in their heavy bathrobes and slippers, to take their papers inside. I didn't see anyone who looked particularly old or fragile.

Just as the gray of dawn began to lighten the sky, a man and woman, middle-aged from the look of them, came out of a bungalow, the third house to my left. They got into a Honda, parked in the driveway, and backed out into the street.

Going to work?

I hunched down into the evergreens as the headlight beams swept past, and then leaned out to study the house they'd left. *It was dark! People gone for the day,* I hoped. *This was better. Breaking into an unoccupied house, getting warm, stealing some food, maybe a heavy coat - and gloves!_*

I made up my mind fast, moving out of my hiding place and down the street to the house. I went around it, through a gate into a backyard. I went quietly up the three steps to the back porch, and looked in the window of the back door. There was a soft light from an electric range which gave low illumination to an old-style yet modernized kitchen. The silhouettes of two coffee cups remained on the counter next to the sink. Beyond the kitchen, the house interior was dark.

I stood very still and listened for a short time, trying to hear noises inside that would indicate someone still inside; a child, a teenager, an elderly grandparent.

I looked around on the porch for something to break the glass. I picked up a small gardening tool, a hand spade with a wooden handle. I hated to make the break, to make the noise. Perhaps the people next door would hear and cause someone to see. I tried the door and, as expected, found it locked. I shook it a little, and took hope from the certain looseness. There was a give that indicated old wood and ancient hinging. I put the spade back where I'd found it, and used both hands on the knob, shoving it, lifting it, feeling the door move just a bit in its frame. I shoved harder, straining against it, lifting it at the same time. The door came open, the bolt of the lock slipping past the talon notch with just a scratch of a sound. I stepped quickly inside and restored the door into a locked condition again.

Warmth! Wonderful warmth!

I stood still for some time, letting the heat of the home envelope me. I could feel my icy face, feet and hands turn to flame as the pain of blood began to re-circulate. I rubbed my hands, my face, my nose, and my ears. In the dim light, I looked at my hands, hoping the redness would disappear and that frostbite had not damaged them. I walked slowly to the sink and turned on the cold-water knob, cupped my hands full and drank, then turned on the hot knob to blend a warm stream. I kept my hands under it for several minutes, and then gingerly washed my face.

Foolish! I scolded myself. *If there's anyone in the house, they'll have heard!*

I turned off the water and listened intently.

Nothing!

I moved to the doorway and walked softly into a dining room. I came to an open entryway on my left that led to a central bath with bedrooms adjacent on either side. All doors were open, no one inside.

I continued into the living room, a large room with a flower-print love seat under the front window, a matching sofa, two wingback chairs with ottomans, and a simulated oak wood entertainment unit dominating a corner. Daylight was brightening through the window, and I could see the details of the room clearly. There was a large painting of an ocean vista in a walnut frame over the sofa. There were also smaller paintings of mountains and tree-shaded streams on the walls. Other furnishings included a couple of occasional tables, and a walnut secretary against the back wall. Nothing fancy, everything plain and simple, neat and clean.

Back in the kitchen, I found another door, opened it, and saw that it led to a basement. I took a few steps down, making sure that the lower level, too, was unoccupied. I went down the rest of the way to look around. A faint amount of daylight, coming from the window wells on either side of the house, gave dim illumination to a half-basement, cramped and unfinished. One side of the basement included a furnace, a water heater, a washer, a dryer, and a sink nearby. One crowded corner was devoted to a sort of home office; a computer on a metal desk, an office chair, some battered file cabinets, a television set, and a video recorder on a stand. There was a chest of drawers, a worn easy chair, and a pair of lamps. There was fishing and camping gear that appeared old and seldom used. There was an ancient eight-millimeter movie camera, an old projector, and a battered screen unit. Much of the rest was a catchall of seldom used pots, pans, dishes, recreational equipment, old books and magazines.

Anxious about news of my escape, I moved immediately to the television set and turned it on, tuning the volume low. I used the remote, looking for a news program, and found a regional station - the early morning news team talking about the murder of a prominent businessman. Our escape was the second story of the morning. In solemn tones, the attractive female half of the morning team told of a massive manhunt being conducted in the area surrounding the prison where noted mobster, Vincent Gianntana, and double-murderer, Kevin Mathias, had made their getaway.

The male anchor voiced the opinion that, in the minds of many, the mob had helped in the escape, taking the fugitives out of the state and probably out of the country. Experts, with knowledge of the Mafia, were exploring their sources, seeking information to confirm this speculation.

Nonetheless, the young woman cautioned her listeners to be wary of any suspicious people or circumstances. Citizens of southern Colorado, certainly the residents of Fairfield, were warned to be on the lookout.

Not encouraging news, but what did I expect?

I listened to a weather report, glad to learn temperatures were returning to more moderate seasonal norms. I tuned back to the original station, readjusted the sound, and turned the set off.

The news that the manhunt was continuing was worrisome, but I was pleased they hadn't found Vince's body. I chuckled at some nonsense about his mob helping us that was really being taken seriously. If I could elude them for a couple of more days, maybe they'd start looking elsewhere.

Laying the money belt to one side, I took off my rags, peeling away the garbage bags first, then the bathrobe, shirt, pants, shoes, socks and underwear. I stood naked in the basement, looking at the shabby discards, loathing them for what they were, loving them for having helped me survive. I didn't know what to do with them, but I knew what I wanted to do with me. I headed upstairs, bending low from sight as I passed through the kitchen. I went into the bathroom and shut the door. I pulled back the curtain on the shower and felt the water still beaded on the plastic wall. I reached over to touch the still-damp towels on the rack.

I turned on the shower, stepped in and pulled the shower curtain to enclose me. I found the still-slippery soap in a soap-dish inset in the vinyl shower wall. I lathered myself, washing my hair first, then the rest of me. I felt my body returning to normal, the bitter cold of two nights and a frigid day streaming away. I stayed in the shower for a half-an-hour, not really caring if the residents came home and found me like this. I couldn't get enough of the warmth, the pleasure, the luxury of that shower.

I suppose I always knew that to escape meant stealing to survive. When you're in prison, dreaming about getting away, you don't get to that right away - you figure you'll cross that bridge when you get to it. Now, as I stood in the shower, I realized I'd have to steal from these people - some of their food, underwear, shirts and pants, a warm coat with a hood or a hat - and gloves! Up until now, I hadn't really had the opportunity to think of what I was to do next. I wasn't a murderer, but I sure as hell was going to be a thief. I didn't like the idea, but there was no other way. I'd only take what I needed and be out and on my way again.

Another thing about stealing bothered me. Whatever I took, whatever trace I left of my being here, was going to give the law a lead on where I was, drawing the circle tight around me. As soon as these people came home and saw I'd been there, they'd call the police.

Leave no traces. Steal what they won't miss.

When I turned off the shower, I stood to let the water drip from my body, letting the air dry me for a while. Then, I stepped out and used both of the towels to finish drying, making sure not to get either one too wet. I re-hung the towels on the rack with care, trying to replace them exactly as I'd found them.

When the steamed mirrors cleared, I looked at myself carefully. No worrisome red or white spots on my face, no evidence of frostbite. Aside from needing a shave and something to eat, I was fine.

I moved back through the house and went into one of the bedrooms, the one with the bed hurriedly made. This was the one they slept in. It had a queen-sized bed, magazines on the nightstands on either side, a dresser with a mirror, and a small TV set on a stand. I checked a chest of drawers, found it full of women's things, and then moved to another in the room. In the third drawer down, I found shorts and tee shirts. I reached clear down to the bottom of the drawer, pulled out a pair of briefs, a size smaller than the ones on the top. A little loose around the middle, but okay.

I found socks in a drawer, took a pair that looked like nine or ten others, closed the drawer, and moved to the closet. I noticed the position of the partially closed sliding doors before I opened them all the way.

The man and woman shared the closet, her things on the right, his on the left. I looked at the man's clothes, a little dismayed at how few were there. There were two dress pants, three everyday slacks, two pairs of jeans, and a mixture of dress and casual shirts. Not only did they look too large, he'd probably notice in a glance that some things were missing. I decided against taking anything, hoping to find some clothing elsewhere in the house. I closed the closet doors just as I'd found them and left the room.

I checked the second bedroom closet and found it to be a storage area for a vacuum cleaner, folding chairs, and boxes of assorted keepsakes.

Doesn't everybody have old clothes? I asked myself. *Where in the hell do they keep them?*

Just as I started back down the basement steps, I noticed a dangling cord a foot above my head. It was only a few inches long, hanging from the stairway ceiling near the top of the steps. I knew immediately what it was for; an access to one of those stairways or ladders you pull down to get into the attic. I pulled the cord and watched the contraption unfold. It was the stairway model, steeply slanting up and down. I went up, feeling the cold of the attic on my bare flesh, already regretting the change from the warmth below.

The attic was too low to be used for anything other than additional storage, the roof supports angled up from either side toward the inside roof apex. The spaces between the joists were bulging with fiberglass insulation, overlaid with pine boards of difference widths and lengths that formed a random walkway down the center. Between the joists, plastic and cardboard boxes had been placed on other planks and, driven into the slanting rafter woods, large nails held coats, suits, and dresses. One long length of steel pipe had been fastened high across four rafters upon which, additional garments on hangers and in garment bags, had been lined in a row.

I moved along the walkway in the dim light from small vents at either end of the attic. What I could see gave me heart. All sorts of warm clothing could be found in this attic;

clothing the man of the house would not likely miss. Shivering in the chill, I examined the hanging garments and looked inside the garment bags. I found wool trousers inside one of the bags that might fit me. I took the trousers from the inside hanger and re-zipped the bag. I tried on the slacks and found the fit to be a little roomy, but wearable. I rummaged through a couple of boxes, and found a sweatshirt at the bottom. Even with the chill of the attic, now I was comfortable. My eyes now adjusted to the dim light, I looked around for whatever else might be of use to me.

Then, I had this idea.

What if I stayed here? What if I hide out here in this attic? Dangerous? Sure, but any more dangerous than being on the run out in the open?

Excited at the thought, I looked around the attic, looking for a place or places of concealment - and my excitement died as quickly as it had been born. Aside from the smaller boxes, there was only one of moderate size back in a corner and, even curled tight, I wouldn't be able to get into it.

Or could I?

The excitement began again, and I walked over to inspect the box. I opened the top and looked inside. Summer clothing, lighter weight shirts and blouses, slacks and shorts, windbreakers - put away for the winter. I closed the top and tipped the box to examine the bottom and the single plank it rested upon; a narrow board spanning the joists. I looked at the layer of insulation between the joists and considered the depth, grateful for the thickness of the fiberglass.

Not great, but it just might do.

I put the box back to an upright position and retreated to the attic opening. I climbed down and returned the stairway to its closed position. Staying low and away from the windows in the kitchen, I explored for something to eat. Behind a door, I discovered a small pantry, loaded with cans, jars, bottles, packages, boxes, and sacks of food.

I realized I'd have to make my meals from items that wouldn't be missed. I couldn't open a can or a jar. I could leave neither discards nor signs of disturbance. I took a couple of soda crackers from an open wax package, a couple of grahams from another. I took no more than two pretzels from an open sack, a marshmallow from another, and a scant handful of raisins from a round container in the refrigerator. I cupped my hands and drank water from the sink to finish my meager meal. I opened a couple of kitchen drawers and found a pair of scissors in the second.

I went back down to the basement and considered what to do with my old clothes and my trash heap accessories. I thought about washing away the stench from the clothes, but I didn't think it wise to run the washer. Chances were that no one outside could hear, but those were chances I didn't want to take. I held each item to my nose and rationalized the odor had somewhat faded. However, these were prison clothes and I didn't want them.

My disposal was simple. I took the bags and the clothing to the attic and buried each item under a separate layer of insulation between the rafters.

Then, I went to the box in the corner, took out the contents, and laid it on its side on the walkway. With the scissors, I cut a hole in the bottom of the box, being careful not to cut at the edges where it would show, but leaving an approximate two-inch border on all sides. I buried the cardboard pieces under other insulation. Next, I cut a small section out of the strip of insulation at a point that would be directly under the upright box, peeled a part of the roll back, and examined the ceiling material below. It looked relatively strong, but I wasn't about to take a chance. I found a number of empty wire coat hangers scattered along the clothing rod and took six. Using nails from the basement and, with a hammer I found, I tapped them solidly into place in facing joists. I untwisted the wire hangers and attached them to the nails, fashioning a sort of hammock seat suspended between the two joists. With this support in place, I lowered myself gingerly into position, pulled the insulation back over my legs, and gauged the depth critically. There was a slight bulge over my legs, but mashing it down would help level it with the layers on either side.

I replaced the clothing in the box, leaving out a number of items from the bottom of the box, laying them to one side for the moment. Repositioning the box, I sat on the hanger hammock, bent forward and wriggled my torso into the carton cavity I'd created, burrowing into the clothing. Then, I sat up carefully, bringing the box to an upright position. With my hands on the joists, I adjusted my position, and tucked the insulation back into place as best I could. I couldn't see my concealment creation, but it seemed okay. I was sure that it wouldn't pass a close scrutiny, but, with luck, I wouldn't even need it.

Satisfied, I reversed my actions and came out. Then, I hid the items of clothing from the box under insulation as I had the prison clothes and trash heap materials. I replaced the box precisely over the area I'd cut and looked over my handiwork. To my eye, it looked no different than when I'd seen it originally.

I went downstairs to replace the scissors and hammer where I'd found them. I checked each room I'd entered, as well as the basement, making sure I'd left nothing to indicate my presence. I revisited the bathroom and took the precaution of emptying my bladder and my bowels, using a few sheets of tissue from a box rather than from the toilet paper roll.

Thinking of what I must do to remain in hiding, I rummaged through the bottom of a trash container and took an empty, wide-mouthed glass bottle with me to the attic, something that I could use to relieve myself while the house was occupied.

For a long period of time, I sat in the attic, contemplating my situation. I thought of the time it would take for me to take cover should someone would pull down the steps and climb into the attic.

Ten seconds? Fifteen at the most? Another fifteen to thirty seconds to get into my concealment?

I edged closer to my hideout box. I couldn't remain in it, but I wouldn't dare be more than a few feet away. Perhaps, t wouldn't happen at all, but I had to assume that it would.

I curled up on the boards, more comfortable than in a sitting position, thinking of what was to come.

Today was Thursday; they'd likely work on Friday and be away all day. On Saturday and Sunday, would they be home? Could I make it silent and undiscovered through both days?

I'd have to try.

11

I woke to the muted sound of the living room television set. It bothered me that I hadn't heard a car in the drive, heard them come in with doors opening and closing, or heard the sounds of their voices. I had slept the sleep of the exhausted. Afternoon, evening, and night had come, and I didn't have any idea of the hour. I wondered if the television had just been turned on or whether I'd slept through several programs, unaware of occupancy in the house. I was over the front area of the house, and the voices on the television were sometimes understandable even though muffled. If I could hear what went on below, it was necessary for me to keep as silent as possible in my attic perch.

Stiff from sleeping on hard boards, I longed to get up and stretch a bit, but I was afraid a step might be heard or that a board might creak. So, I lay very still, considering my next uncomfortable few hours. The chill of the attic wasn't severe, not with the wool clothing I'd put on. I would have loved a blanket, and I gave thought to finding one later, perhaps after the couple had gone to bed. Maybe not a blanket, but something to put between me and the boards, and something warm over me. I had decided to stay awake during their occupancy in the house, and to sleep when they left. I didn't know how that would work out over the coming weekend, but it was my plan for, at least, tonight and tomorrow.

I wondered what the people below looked like. I had only that brief glimpse of them in their car in the early morning hours. Middle-aged, I'd presumed from my quick sighting. I'd looked through their closet. His things suggested medium height and a thickening waist, his girth progression shown in the increasing sizes in the attic. Her clothing seemed petite and constant; a woman who had pretty much retained her figure through the years.

What sort of people were they? Apparently, they were a working couple, perhaps never with children or, now, empty nesters. I wondered what the man did for a living, what she did. On occasion, I could hear a man's voice that I thought came from other than the television, but I couldn't hear hers. Perhaps she had a soft voice or spoke very little. Perhaps it was the sound damping quality of the attic insulation, but it occurred to me these people had little to say to one another.

I was afraid to move. I listened intently to anything that might signal that they had come aware of and alarmed by my presence. I thought of every action that I'd taken in the lower part of the house, and wondered if I'd left something to betray my intrusion. I'd been so careful yet it nagged at me that my fatigue might have caused a mistake, some frightful and obvious blunder that they would be sure to discover. I listened for outside sounds; imagining each passing car to be the first of converging police units. In my fear, I pictured patrol cars blocking the streets, and even thought I heard footsteps of lawmen surrounding the house.

Minutes passed, and I relaxed.

Finally, the house below was nearly quiet. The television was turned off, and I heard only the occasional sounds of the occupants in the bathroom preparing for bed. This would be the time I would have to be most careful. In their moments before sleep, as the couple settled down into their own silences, they would be acutely aware of the sounds of their house, noting the familiar, sure to question any differences. I lay as still as I could, yearning to stretch, not daring to flex a muscle. It was essential that I should stay awake during their time in the house. I only hoped I could stave off the sleep that I still needed.

After about an hour, I moved a little, not rising, nothing drastic. I just did the stretch I'd been longing to do, extending one arm, then the other. Very carefully, I rolled onto my back, and felt the relief of a new position flow through me. I lifted one leg and bent it, rotated the ankle, lowered it, and did the same with the other.

I stared up into the darkness of the attic and, for the first time in my flight, I began to plan. Up until now, my escape had been impromptu actions, desperation goading me, sheer luck favoring me. My mind had told me only to get away from that prison place and get to another place - any other place. It hadn't told me what I'd do when I got there. All my actions had been ad-lib, my instincts guiding me. I realized that I'd reached a sort of limbo state of my escape, and now had entered a plateau of passivity, hiding in an attic. For a few more hours, maybe a day or two or even more, I might be safe. I might be uncomfortable, but I wouldn't freeze. If I kept quiet, I might just make a real getaway.

How to get out of here? How do I get out of this town?

■ ■ ■

I woke with a start, mad at myself for sleeping again, hearing the sounds of the couple up and getting ready for the new day. I could hear their voices now, not every word, but several uttered with the strength of disagreement. The man was angry about something. I could hear his swear words coming up loud and understandable. Her responses were higher in pitch; her voice seemed strange and foreign, the tone and the discernable words sounding defensive. From what I could make out, the argument had to do with money, something he wanted to buy, something she apparently felt they couldn't afford. They kept on during breakfast and were still at it as they banged out of the back door. I waited for a few minutes, even after I heard their car start up and move out of the drive. Then, I rose and stretched as well as I could in the low headroom of the attic. I moved about a bit to limber up, and then let down the attic steps and descended into the comfort of the warm, dark house. I raised the stairway, not wanting to let the attic chill down into the main floor, and I relished the delicious opportunity to now have the run of the house.

The kitchen stove clock showed the time to be almost four o'clock. I kept to the shadows, concerned that even the low-level glow of the electric range might reveal me to an early riser in an adjacent house, or to the chance glance of a passerby on the street.

I went down into the basement, turned on the small television set, and set the volume to a barely audible level. I searched the channels until I found a dawn-time newscast at the top of the hour. Our escape had been dropped to a fourth position, less important than a bus crash in Greeley, a drastic stock market fluctuation, and the indictment of a well-known sports personality for using a performance enhancement substance.

Concerning our escape, authorities were still searching the area for Gianntana and me, although speculation had it that we'd made it out of the state. There was now a nationwide manhunt with air terminals, bus and train stations under surveillance.

I returned the television to its original channel, reset the volume, and turned off the set. I went back upstairs into the kitchen, wondering what I could find to eat. I worried about loading up too much - whatever I took in, I'd have to let out. With the weekend coming up, I didn't know but what the couple would be home over the weekend. I settled for food items that would likely not be missed - a stalk of celery, a few more crackers, and a carrot.

I checked out my appearance in the bathroom mirror. My beard was growing and I used the mister's electric razor to trim it up a bit. It wasn't much of a growth yet, but it was dark enough to give me a different look. As long as it didn't look scruffy, it might be a decent disguise. I'd never seen myself in a beard before and I liked it. It gave me more of a mature look. A few more days, and I thought it just might do.

With the light of early day brightening the house, I prowled. I carefully examined the personal contents of the home, nosing into the papers and possessions of my unsuspecting hosts, trying to discover something about them. In the secretary desk, I found a number of saved and bundled envelopes that identified them as a married couple; Tom and Kim Palmer. In another drawer, I found ample evidence that this man and wife had their own business; invoices, business correspondence, cards, and receipts showing that they operated a doughnut shop in downtown Fairfield. No doubt this was the reason they hightailed it out each morning before dawn, getting to the shop to make the doughnuts and prepare for a breakfast business. I was enormously pleased at my discovery; this would mean that they'd most likely be out of the house both days of the weekend. I did a quick check of other drawers and, in one, found a ledger book that indicated that business was not too good. From a cursory glance, it appeared they were barely ahead.

There were no pictures of children, but there were a number of photographs of the man, mostly in uniform in his younger days, wearing the stripes of a U. S. Army sergeant in tropical ports of call. I found what appeared to be a recent photo of the pair. The wife, an Oriental, was considerably younger than her husband. In this formal portrait, he had filled out considerably since his Army days, now big around the middle. I judged him to be around his mid-fifties, just this side of ugly. His much younger wife, however, was surprisingly attractive; a petite figure, a pretty face framed by her lustrous black hair. Perhaps it was too many months in prison that stirred me, but I felt it a shame that a nice looking woman like this was spending her life with a man like that. Passage to a life in the United States, I supposed.

Hell of a price to pay, I considered.

I was reluctant to leave the comfort of the main floor, but I knew it was too risky to stay downstairs. Even though I was careful about windows, staying low and close to interior walls, I worried that I might be seen. I took a precautionary pee in the john and headed back up to my attic. I hadn't been there more than three minutes when I heard cars arrive outside.

My God! I've been seen!

In a few moments, I heard the front door open and the sound of voices - male voices. I crawled to my hiding contrivance, tipped the box forward, and lowered myself carefully onto the coat hanger seat. I squirmed into the box and sat erect, hoping the appearance would be fine. I sat as still as possible, for what seemed to be ages, and then heard the attic steps swing down. *I'm going to be caught,* I told myself, despairing, fearing what they'd do to me, and dreading the inevitable return to the prison.

"Stay down for a minute, Mr. Palmer!" a strong voice commanded. "Let us take a look first."

"I don't see the need for this!" Palmer's voice complained.

"Routine house-to-house, sir," the strong voice responded. "Won't take long."

I heard them come up into the attic, a couple of them from what I could discern, their heavy shoes scuffing along the central boards, moving toward me.

Near, very near, I heard them stop.

For a long time, I heard nothing at all.

"Nothing up here," a different voice said.

"Mr. Palmer!" the first voice shouted. "Can you come up with us?"

"I told you this was a goddamned waste of my time! There warn't nothing wrong down in the basement, and ain't likely nothing wrong up here!" Palmer's voice complained as its owner climbed up the steps. "I gotta get back to my shop!"

"Won't take but a minute," the strong voice assured him. "Take a look around. See if anything is out of place."

"No, goddamn it!" Palmer's voice grumbled. "It's fine! Now, let's get out of here."

"Take your time, Mr. Palmer," the strong voice suggested. "Anything missing?"

There were a few moments of silence, only the faint shuffle of Palmer's feet as he ventured further into the attic. "Nothing

I can see," Palmer snapped. "You're wasting your time! Those damned jailbirds are clear outta the area by now. You're just wasting your time . . . and mine!"

"Have you missed any food? Any sign of anyone inside the house?"

"No!" Palmer was obviously irked. "It's cold up here, let's get outta here."

"What about that box?" the second voice asked.

The man with the strong voice laughed. "He'd have to be a midget, Bernie. Let's go."

I heard them walking down the centerboards, walking away. I heard their shoes on the steps as they descended, and then heard the attic stairway swing back up into the raised position.

"Sorry to have troubled you, Mr. Palmer," I heard the now muted strong voice say. I couldn't hear the response, but I heard anger in the slamming of the front door.

I stayed in the box for at least fifteen minutes, afraid to come out. When I did, I kissed my fingers, and laid them on the box that had successful hidden me.

It wasn't likely they'd be back.

12

Saturday seemed to be a repeat of the other days and, assuming there would be no further house searches, I felt much better about my chances. Again, the Palmers left the house before the break of dawn, and I spent much more time downstairs. I took another shower, admired my growing beard, and ate a little more than before, still being careful not to take obvious foods. I'd grown a little bolder, smug now over my success in eluding capture. From the basement television, I found great satisfaction in that the search had all but been abandoned in our area, the authorities sure our getaway had been orchestrated by Gianntana's mob. I got the impression that the search had diminished in the immediate vicinity, and had broadened to other areas of the country. The newscaster assured the television viewers that airports, train, and bus stations had been plastered with pictures of Gianntana and me. Such surveillance was disconcerting, but I found relief in that the manhunt was general rather than focused. I took interest in other parts of the news - continuing warfare in the Mid-East, militia outrages in the Northwest, a drive-by shooting in Denver, the continuing aftermath of the Super Bowl and, most of all, the change in the weather. The cold spell had disappeared and was now being followed by a stretch of unseasonably warm temperatures. Highs were in the upper fifties and the coming week might even touch sixty degrees or slightly more. I stayed with the television for a few minutes past the early news, watched a game show, then turned it off reluctantly and moved back to the main floor. I thought of going back into the relative security of my attic, but I thought it to be safe enough to lounge a while longer in the living area. The man of the house, Palmer, had left the newspaper sections strewn about his chair, and I hungered for something to read to pass the time. I found the living room carpeting to be a warm and comfortable resting place, my prone position on the floor keeping me well out of sight of neighbors and passersby. I lolled in contentment, turning pages, telling myself that I was being as watchful and cautious as ever. Soon, very soon, I'd head back up to my refuge.

My complacent foolishness nearly got me caught.

I heard the car slow in front of the house, but thought nothing about it until I heard a car door slam. I knew instantly that someone was coming to the front of the house and I had no time to get to the attic stairway, much less open it, climb it, and close it. Instead, I scuttled across the room in panic, turning into the little hallway between the bedrooms as I heard the key in the door. Frantic, I considered the bathroom, but dashed, instead, into the spare bedroom. I heard the front door close, and I settled for the most banal hiding spot imaginable. I dived under the bed, pushing my way into the boxes and sacks that had been stored there. Even though I couldn't see her, I knew it was the Palmer woman and that she apparently was alone. Her tread was light as she crossed the floor; she was humming a little tune, nothing I could recognize, but she seemed happy, glad to be home.

I couldn't help but feel sorry for her if she discovered me. She'd be scared to death, home alone facing an escaped convict, a murderer by reputation. She'd likely panic, and that could be dangerous for both of us.

If she tried to run or scream for help, what would I do?

I didn't think I would hurt her, but I didn't know how far my self-preservation would take me. I was in a terrible situation and sure to be discovered.

What would I do?

I heard her go into the kitchen, open the refrigerator to put something away, then come right back out again. She headed for her bedroom and, from my under-bed view into the hallway, I caught a glimpse of her as she passed by. She was wearing some sort of a food service outfit, mostly brown with a white trim - something appropriate for the donut shop, I suppose. I heard her moving around in that other room, and I gave a thought of trying to move past her door without being seen, but dismissed the idea immediately.

Better to stay hidden as long as possible; she might go out again.

After a couple of minutes, I saw her again, coming out of her bedroom, wrapping a white robe around her as she headed into the bathroom. She was still humming, and then the slight tune was overwhelmed by the sound of the shower. Relief swept over me: She'd be showering in just a few moments, and I'd have a chance to sneak back to my attic. Praying that she wouldn't hear the squeaks of the stairway mechanism over the sound of the spray, I rolled out of my concealment. I came up cautiously to a crouch and, for whatever fortunate impulse seized me, I froze and stayed very still.

She came out of the bathroom and paused for a moment in the small hallway. She opened a linen closet in the hall, stretched to an upper shelf and took out a towel. I had a perfectly clear, full-frontal view of her nudity. Had she glanced my way, she'd have seen me, too. Then, she was out of sight as she went back into the bathroom and closed the door.

I waited until I heard the sounds of her in the shower, and then I moved in stealth out into the hall, through the dining room, and into the kitchen. I pulled the attic stairs down as quietly as I could, the metallic sounds seeming much too loud. I went up and closed the contraption, cushioning the ceiling panel softly into its final position.

I waited anxiously for several minutes, listening intently for anything that would indicate panic or alarm. The telephone began to ring and continued to ring unanswered, then stopped just before I heard her shut off the shower. After a while, I could hear faint sounds as she moved around the house, working in the kitchen, a radio playing.

I breathed calmly. Safe again, but it had been a close call.

The woman was more than I had imagined. Much more. Her face was pretty, a trim body with full breasts and a narrow waist. My mind focused on that triangle of pubic hair! To me, she was beautiful! You'll have to remember I'd been in jails and the prison for over three years, and my sex life with Gloria was well over months before that. To say I desired that woman would be to put it mildly. I was angry that a woman who looked like that could belong to a pudge of a man and I marveled at the injustice of it. I was angry with myself for my desire, knowing that escape was what I should have on my mind, not carnal yearnings.

I had added another complication to my flight.

I had to leave as quickly as possible. I had to get out of this house!

Tom Palmer came home about eight o'clock that evening, drunk and abusive, slamming the door, shouting loud enough to be clearly understood. "You damned cunt! What the hell you been doing all goddamned afternoon?"

I couldn't make out her response, but it had the tone of plea and fright.

"You wasn't home! I called, and you wasn't home!"

"Maybe I was in shower," I heard her say, her voice rising in her defense; her words were clear although with choppy expression.

"You damned gook!" Palmer accused. "You were out with somebody!"

"Tom, I home all afternoon," she responded. "You get when drink. You know I—"

I hear the sound of the slap and the sharp outcry of pain.

It was hard to stay in the attic.

"You leave me down there in the store all by myself!" Palmer's voice accused.

"We not busy, Tom!" the woman countered. "You say I could go."

"Well, we got busy!" Palmer said loudly. "You shoulda been there!" There were a few moments of silence, and then, "Where in the hell is the beer?"

"We don't have, Tom! You promised—"

"I ought to kick your ass outta my house, you damn slut!" Palmer yelled. "I don't need any damned slopehead telling me what I can or can't do!"

"I got no place to go!" she whimpered. "Please, Tom!"

I heard another slap and another wail of injury.

Escape or not, I didn't know if I'd let him hit her again.

I listened intently and, finally, I decided it was over. I wondered if Palmer had gotten control of himself, passed out or just become passively sullen. I supposed the woman had retreated into some lonely corner of the house, to cry away her bruises and anguish.

Why didn't she leave the sonofabitch? Probably because she knows only the life she'd found in a foreign land, and knows nowhere else to go or anyone else to turn to.

The night deepened and I seethed with my anger for a while, then gradually cooled down and convinced myself that whatever happened between the two of them was none of my business. It was their lives and, if she wasn't strong enough to walk away, there was no reason for me to risk my life.

Nonetheless, I felt a sense of cowardice.

I had to get out of this house!

■ ■ ■

Sunday was the hardest since the couple below, to my surprise, apparently didn't open their shop on that day. I was cooped up continually, unable to move about in the attic, afraid to make a sound, acutely aware they were downstairs for the morning, afternoon, and night. I used the bottle, afraid they could hear the sound of pissing. I heard no sounds of continuing violence, only the subdued sound of a radio in one room - probably the woman in her kitchen. I assumed the man was nursing a hangover and was sleeping it off. Late in the afternoon, I heard the gruffness of his voice, but it sounded more weary than belligerent. The day passed in a quietude that surely was the guilty aftermath of the night before.

Night came, and I made my plans.

I would leave the house in the morning after they'd gone to work. It would be risky, a chance I'd be seen and reported; a stranger walking through the early morning darkness, but I couldn't wait for daylight. I'd already located a winter coat among Tom Palmer's stored belongings, a wool overcoat that didn't seem appropriate for the man, something he probably had seldom worn. I'd found a cap with fold-down earflaps. It didn't particularly complement the coat, but it was warm. To my dismay, I found no gloves.

Chances are these clothes wouldn't be missed for months.

I curled up on my boards, pleased with the upcoming end of my strange new confinement, looking forward to the coming dawn.

Tomorrow, I'd be on my way . . . somewhere.

13

I was awake long before they rose, excited at the prospect of being on my way once again. I knew it was dangerous outside, and I was loath to leave what had become sort of a sanctuary. However, I knew it was only a question of time before I made a noise or made some sort of a mistake that would reveal my presence. I was also worried about causing harm to the woman, certainly not to the man, if they discovered me. Besides, I felt the time was right. I'd spent a week in hiding, and it didn't appear the search was still centered in this area.

I heard them up around four o'clock in the morning. There were the sounds of the shower and other bathroom activities, closet doors opening and closing, and so on. As usual, their conversation was minimal, only a few stern complaints from the man of the house, and a few faint responses from the woman. At a little before five, they left the house, closing the front door loudly, then driving away into the winter darkness.

I came down from my hideaway, dressed in my stolen clothing, and headed into the bedroom to check out my appearance. I'd lost several pounds and I looked a bit on the gaunt side. However, my beard was grown out enough now to look planned rather than scruffy. I thought the hat and the overcoat looked okay, not appearing to be overly out-of-date or unusual. Perhaps a shorter, mackinaw-style coat would've been more in keeping with a small town resident, but I had little choice. I looked around carefully for anything else that might be of use, and then spent a few minutes in the bathroom to take care of nature. Before I left, not knowing exactly why, I copied down the name and address of the Palmers; a silly thing to do.

I stepped out onto the porch, closed the front door, and let the latch lock after me. I was worried about the light beginning in the eastern sky. I'd rather have left earlier in the darkest part of the night, but that would have been impossible. Resolving to make the best of whatever circumstances dictated, I walked down the residential street while watching the dark houses carefully. I took even more care where lighted windows showed their occupants to be up and about. As I passed one house, the porch light came on, bright as hell, and a portly man in a plaid bathrobe came through the front door. In a moment of inspiration, I reached down to pick up the morning paper from the driveway, and tossed it onto the porch right at the man's feet.

"Supposed to *lay* it on the porch!" the man groused loudly. "Not throw it!"

"Sorry!" I sang out and hurried on into the darkness.

I walked seven or eight blocks at a fast pace and came to a broad avenue which appeared to be the main drag through the town. I took a few steps to a sign that identified the street as the business route of a highway. To my right, in the distance, I could see a cluster of neon signs marking the center of the town. I turned and walked in the other direction, hoping I'd find what I was seeking at the edge of town. Caution was even more important now since cars were on the road, their lights sweeping past, driving me to cover almost a dozen times. I continued to walk as fast as I dared, hoping that no one might see and consider my haste suspicious. I was terribly conscious of the coming of dawn, the darkness turning to various shades of gray. I loped along as I moved past the dark outskirt buildings; those edge-of-town businesses that repaired lawnmowers, installed window glass, mended crumpled fenders, and sold used appliances.

Suddenly, I was very tired and dismayed at the toll my exertion was taking. Maybe it was the lack of food, maybe the prolonged exposure to cold even in the attic. I stopped for a few minutes, trying to find some strength somewhere in my body, but the truth of it was exhaustion. I was just plain worn out. I rested far longer than I wanted, and it took all of my resolve to get going again. I moved slowly, like an old man, more shuffling than walking.

In another half-mile, my hopes were buoyed by the blast of light up ahead. Some place up there was using halogen lights to flood an area, and I thought it just might be what I was seeking. After a few minutes more, I eased into the gloom of an abandoned Sinclair station and peered ahead from the shadows.

There it was, but I was disappointed.

I'd hoped to find a major truck stop, some place where there would be a variety of different vehicles, some one of which might provide my way out of the area. There was a truck stop all right, but it was a small complex with a gas and diesel station and an adjacent diner. On the modest-sized tarmac, only one tractor-trailer rig and three pickups were parked near the diner. The big truck had a closed refrigerated trailer and even from where I stood, far from the edge of the brilliant lights, I could see that the roll-down door was padlocked.

I don't know what I had expected to find. In those tedious attic hours, I'd thought of auto-carrier trailers with unlocked sedans, of moving vans with easy access, of delivery trucks with boxes and crates, and even open bed trucks with materials or substances in which I could hide. I don't know whether I'd considered hitching a ride or actually stealing a car. As I've said before, my escape plan had been no plan at all. I could do only what the moment and the circumstances provided.

I stood against the wall of the abandoned service station, the daylight brightening around me. I waited in vain for some sort of an escape vehicle to arrive, but whatever I hoped for wouldn't come. The big truck pulled out, then two of the pickups. As the sun came up, I could see the nearby two-lane highway, now with a regular flow of early morning traffic, some vehicles still with their headlights shining, others running dark.

Four passenger cars came off the main highway and approached the truck stop, pulling in and parking in front of the diner.

What am I doing standing here in the open? I asked myself. *How soon will a call to the police be made from a cellphone? How soon will a patrol car come to investigate this lurking, suspicious man?*

Perhaps it was the exhaustion, perhaps a cold sense of reality. Whatever, I decided, maybe it was over. In a strange way, I was almost glad.

No, not really glad. More like resigned.

I'd been under such stress, such tension for almost a week, fearing discovery at any time. Even when I had slept, even when I'd thought myself secure, there had always been fear. There had always been dread.

I looked at the diner.

Damn! I was hungry.

I hadn't had a decent meal in days. I was light-headed from my near-starvation, from my exertion, from the still-sharp cold of the winter morning. I reached inside my shirt and fished a twenty out of Gianntana's money belt.

"To hell with it," I said half-aloud, angry at my weakness, realizing I really didn't give a damn. "If it's over, it's over."

I stepped out of my poor concealment and started toward truck stop. As I reached the parking lot, I followed a pair of young men moving toward the diner from their expensive car - a couple of cocky, swaggering dandies in pricey casual clothes. I caught the door and moved right behind them as they entered and walked to the counter. My hope of escape returning, I thought it better to saunter in as a possible part of a group, rather than as a loner. I took the adjacent stool and sat next to them. Whether they noticed me or not, I couldn't tell. I was close enough to hear their conversations, and I was a bit sorry I'd edged up to them. Their dialog consisted of sly, sarcastic comments about people they found less perfect then themselves. They apparently thought little of the diner, and I wondered why they'd chosen to stop there.

The chubby young woman behind the counter gave us a friendly, welcoming nod; her smile fading at the indifference of the pair as she started taking orders.

"Separate checks?" she asked as she came to me.

"Yes, please," I answered.

One of the two men, a supercilious blond fellow, gave me a withering glance, apparently irked at the hint of any association. He turned back to his buddy to resume whatever the hell they were talking about.

The young server hadn't missed the hostile glance, and decided she wanted to be on my side. "What'll you have?" she asked with a friendly nod.

I grabbed for one of the menus and gave it only a couple of seconds. "Harvester breakfast," I said with an appreciative sigh. "Eggs well scrambled, pancakes with butter on the side." I paused, and then added, "Sausage and bacon . . . do you have hash browns?"

"Yes, sir," she answered, writing it down. "Coffee?"

"You bet. Black."

She smiled. "You act like you haven't eaten for a week."

"Feels just like that," I told her.

There was a mirror behind the back counter and, as I waited, I glanced at it from time to time, hoping that I'd find some sort of a ride out of town. I felt my optimism rising, and I mentally kicked myself for taking such a risk, coming out into the open like this.

Maybe things won't go bad, I thought. *I've been lucky so far, maybe my luck will hold.*

When the food came, I tried to eat slowly, but the fork gained speed, flashing from plate to mouth as I ate ravenously. The server gave a smile of amused wonderment, as I wolfed down the meal. I was finishing the last of the hash browns when I heard a distant noise, something outside, a faint sound of glass breaking. I was so engrossed in my meal that I focused just on what was in front of me. I looked at my well-mopped plate with dismay, wondering if I shouldn't order a second breakfast.

I was touching my lips to a refill of hot coffee - my fourth or fifth - when I felt a light touch on my shoulder.

"That your Beamer outside?" a voice asked, nothing friendly about it at all. I glanced up. The mirror behind the counter showed me two uniformed men, sheriff deputies. One, big and burly, stood close with his hand near my sleeve, while a slender one was watchful at the door. I'd been so intent on feeding myself that I'd forgotten to watch for trouble - and it was here, standing right behind me. I started to turn, the coffee cup masking the lower part of my face, when the young blond man next to me swiveled around, his manner challenging and insolent. "My car, officer," he said crisply. "What's the problem?"

I turned back away, the coffee cup still partially hiding my face. I kept it there as I watched the unfolding drama reflected in the mirror.

"We got a call from the State Patrol," the heavyset officer behind me explained gruffly. "Somebody in a blue car . . . something like that Beamer . . . damned near put a woman and her kids in a ditch back down the road."

"We've been here eating," the young man said smoothly, gesturing to me. "Ask anybody here."

"You with him?" the deputy asked me, making eye contact in the mirror.

I shook my head, my eyes straying to the reflection of a large over-the-road truck pulling into the parking lot, hauling something in an open stake-bed. I couldn't make out the cargo, but the sight gave me heart. The nearness of the law officers, however, seemed to dash that hope.

"Anybody hurt?" the young man beside me was asking casually, just a touch of mockery in his voice.

"No thanks to the other party," the officer responded gruffly. "Guy was speeding, trying to pass a truck, ducked back when he saw he wasn't going to make it." He paused. "Forced her off the road . . . she had to go in and out of the ditch. Lucky they weren't killed."

The door opened and the stake truck driver came in. He hesitated, curious at the sight of the officers. He walked down to the far end of the counter, seated himself on a stool and picked up a menu.

"Must've been somebody else," the young man told him, feigning concern. "Lots of blue cars out on the road."

"With a broken tail light?" the deputy said with a degree of satisfaction. "That might tie it down."

The young man lost his arrogance abruptly. "What tail light?"

"You're missing one," the deputy told him. "Maybe we'd better go take a look at that."

"There's nothing wrong with my car!" the young man insisted angrily. "At least, there wasn't when I came in."

I decided it was a good time to pay my bill. I motioned to the server, got up and walked to the cash register at the end of the counter, showing her my twenty-dollar bill.

While she made change, she kept glancing at the argument between the two young men and the lawmen. She leaned over and handed me bills and coins. "I saw Harry bust that kid's tail light," she whispered conspiratorially, nodding to the cops and the young men who were going out the door. "Should I say anything?"

I counted my bills, handed her three one's as a tip and shrugged.

"I don't like them," she confided. "Snotty rich punks. They could've killed that woman and her kids." She shrugged. "Maybe I ought to just stay out of it."

"Probably," I agreed. "You have a restroom?"

She nodded and tilted her head. "Through the side door, outside."

"Need a key?" I asked.

She shook her head. "Come again."

I went through the side door and headed for the rest-room. I went inside and into the single stall, got rid of some of the coffee, and then sat on the stool for a few minutes. I ignored the strong smells and the litter on the floor, trying to decide what next to do. I wondered how long I should stay in there, wondering if it was best to go out now while the cops were busy with the Beamer boys or wait 'til they were gone. I lingered a while, and then had a dreadful thought: *What if the truck driver was only stopping for a quick donut and coffee?*

I decided I had to make my move now and take my chances.

I came out of the restroom, took a peek around the cor-ner, and saw the two officers and the two young men arguing heatedly beside the BMW. The young driver was belligerent, gesturing at the taillight, making some sort of an accusation. Both officers moved in quickly, the big one grabbing the driver roughly by the front of his jacket, his partner squaring off in front of the other guy.

Now, the burly deputy was shaking the driver violently while his cowering companion was plainly showing his fright. It was an intense situation and all eyes, outside and inside the diner, were focused on the cops and the unfortunate young offenders. I took another look at the truck and saw a jumble of tires ris-ing above the sides of the trailer. A barely readable sign on the cab door identified a recycling company, but didn't show from where. I walked casually toward the truck, acting as though I was searching for my car keys, hoping neither of the busy officers would remember that there was no car beyond the truck. I glanced at them out of the corner of my eye as I strolled across the pavement. They either didn't see me or didn't care; they were intent upon the intimidation of the two young men. I went around the front of the truck, relieved to be out of their sight. I crouched low and looked beneath the truck, seeing only their legs. No one had turned in my direction. I stepped up on a rear tire of the truck and hoisted myself over the side, head and body low, rolling into the cargo of odd-sized used tires. Most were large tractor and heavy machinery tires. Some were stacked vertically, others lined in a canted and horizontal rows. In addition, many smaller tires were jammed in between the rows. I found myself a tunnel of tires and squirmed inside, feet first, delighted with this "cave." Even now, the rubber around me gave me insulation against the cold. Still, there was a possibility that I might have been seen. With some degree of apprehension, I lay tense for a few minutes, waiting for the command to come out and surrender.

I wondered what had happened to the Beamer duo. Had they had talked their way out of trouble or been taken away by the deputies? Then, I decided I really didn't give a damn. About that time, I heard one car leave, followed closely by another. Probably the first was the BMW with the patrol car right behind, herding it into town. They'd be taking the smart-mouth and his friend to do a little repentance in the local jail-house.

Even as a jailbird, I felt no pity for them.

After a time, I heard footsteps approach, then felt and heard the driver's cab door open and slam shut. The engine started up and the truck began to move, the cargo around me vibrating and jiggling as the vehicle changed gears and rumbled out of the parking lot, heading toward the highway. Two minutes later, I felt it turn onto the thoroughfare and, as it gathered speed, the load around me shifted slightly, then settled into a gentle oscillation. Was I heading east, west, north or south? I really didn't know. Wherever it would take me would be fine. I lay down on my side, cradled my head on my arms, and closed my eyes.

14

I awoke sweating. Even in the depth of winter, the sun had been shining down on these black tires, radiating heat into the cargo. I struggled out of my vulcanized cocoon and shoved up to daylight, feeling the cool air whipping over my face. I was still mostly submerged in the clutter of tires, and I eased my way slightly higher - high enough to stay warm without being baked. I looked up at the blue sky of midmorning, watching the tops of telephone poles flashing by. The sun, threatened by only a couple of small clouds, was beaming down on me as I rode to freedom.

We stopped once as the driver took nearly an hour for lunch, during which I burrowed back inside the tires. From the sounds I heard, it seemed to be one of those really big and busy truck stops, with many rigs coming in and going out. There seemed to be a lot of people moving around the area; I could hear their chatter and laughter. After a while, I felt the truck body move slightly, and I assumed the driver had stepped up on the bed to check his load. I lay as still as possible, hoping that no part of me might be visible, hoping he wouldn't decide to do something like rearranging the load.

Then, I heard the cab door slam and, once again, we were on our way to wherever. I came up out of my shelter and stuck my head up through a tire to breathe. I was tempted to crawl out further, to look over the side of the trailer to see if I could get an idea of where we were, and where we might be going, but it wasn't worth taking a chance. It seemed logical that the driver would have some sort of a reflected view of his load, and it wasn't sensible for me to come out of hiding.

Better I play prairie dog than to risk discovery.

By my estimate, a couple or three hours later, the air began to turn uncomfortably cold again, and I moved back deep into the tunnel of tires. I slept once more, snug in the warmth, lulled by the droning of the truck, affected by my fatigue as well as by boredom.

I was awakened by the clash of downshifting gears, the truck slowing to a stop. It moved forward at a modest speed, then slowed and came to another stop, and then another. I worked my way up through the load into the night, seeing traffic lights, streetlights and neon signs, warehouses, and large commercial buildings. I was in some sort of a town or even a city. I pulled myself up on top of the load and saw that it was more than a small town.

I saw a sign on a building as we swept past; I was in Salt Lake City.

In a stretch of closed-for-the-night buildings in an industrial area, I waited for the truck to slow for a stoplight. As it stopped, I swung over the back end of the truck bed and stepped off onto the street. I moved to the sidewalk as the truck drove away and, smelling slightly rubberized, I started walking, not knowing exactly which way to go, not knowing what I should do next.

In contrast to my earlier fatigue, my long ago breakfast and the day of rest had rejuvenated me. I felt good, actually exhilarated. I was far away from the prison territory, hundreds of miles from the area where police might still suspect my presence. There was danger here, of course, but not as severe as before. Still, I'd have to watch my step and not let complacency or carelessness betray me.

I walked for ten or maybe eleven blocks, coming to a major street of the city; a broad avenue well lit with overarching streetlights. I walked to a bus stop, wondering what was the time, and if the city buses were still running. Almost immediately, a bus came around a corner and swooshed up beside me. Fishing some change from my pocket, I stepped up into the bus, paid the fare, and looked back into the bus. There were five people aboard.

"You got the time?" I asked the driver as we accelerated away from the curb.

"About nine-thirty," he said, not looking at his watch.

"Closer to ten," corrected a hefty old woman, sitting several rows back.

"We going downtown?" I asked.

The driver shot me a look. "You just wake up or something?"

I shrugged and took a seat behind the time-correcting woman, close to the exit door in case I needed off in a hurry. We cruised for a block or two before she turned around, somewhat of a chore considering her bulk. "You new in town?" she asked.

"Somewhat," I answered.

"Whatcha going to do downtown this time of night?" she persisted.

I shrugged. "It's not that late."

"It is in Salt Lake City," she told me. "Ten o'clock, they roll up the sidewalks."

"Well, I'm just visiting friends," I improvised. "I needed to get out of the house for a while."

"Well, you'll likely walk around down there for a few minutes, then get right back on the bus to come back again," she told me. "I gotta go down there to work."

I nodded.

"I clean up them office buildings," she told me. "Work for a janitorial service."

"Keeps your days free, I guess," I responded.

"Oh, I work days, too," she informed me. "Take care of some young 'uns while their moms are working days."

"Get any time off?" I asked, not particularly wanting to encourage her yet not wanting to be impolite.

"I ain't complaining," she answered. "I can watch my soaps and the kids at the same time. Money's not bad, neither."

"That's good," I said, wondering whether I should continue the conversation.

It wouldn't hurt to appear a convivial citizen, rather than a suspicious and silent stranger.

"There's no bars downtown, you know," she told me.

I nodded. "Yeah, I know. I'm not much of a drinker anyway."

"Might be a couple of restaurants still open," she ventured. "You could get some coffee and pie." She paused for a moment. "'Course, they don't much go for coffee either."

"They?"

"Mormons," she answered.

"You're not Mormon?"

"Jack Mormon," she replied.

"Which is?"

"Someone who used to be a Mormon, but isn't much of one anymore," she told me. "'Course, the Tabernacle Choir is something else. You heard them?"

"On the radio and television, a few times," I replied.

"They practice during the week . . . I don't know exactly which night . . . but you ought to get over there and hear them sing," she said, nodding wisely. "It don't cost you nothing to go listen to them practice."

"I'll try to catch them," I told her.

Apparently out of small talk, the woman gave me a smile and turned back around. I sat in silence, looking out through the bus windows as we moved into the business district of the city. I'd been to Salt Lake City once before, and I was somewhat familiar with it. In any other city, there'd be all-night bars, plenty of places to go to spend the hours until daylight. I just couldn't stand the thought of another night out in the cold.

With Vince's money, I could go to a hotel.

No go. They'd ask questions. They'd wonder about the lack of luggage, and they'd want identification when I registered. I thought about bribing someone just to let me stay the night, but that would be a sure sign I was on the run.

Another frigid night seemed probable.

I got off the bus when I saw the neon of a restaurant. I was starving again, and I knew I'd better get something in me before the lights went out. I walked into a restaurant, joining only a half-dozen other late customers in the dining area. The woman who came to wait on me looked tired, but she tried to be pleasant as she handed me a menu.

"Something to drink?"

"Coffee."

"With cream?"

"Black"

She waited for my order.

"Roast beef dinner," I told her, touching the illustration of the pot roast, knowing it wouldn't look or taste that good.

She nodded and strolled into the kitchen.

When the food came, I was surprised. It looked good and tasted better. I lingered over the meal and coffee, used the restroom, and left a little after eleven o'clock; the manager and waitstaff hoping I would go. I walked a couple of blocks considering my options. The weather was getting colder, and I had to make some decisions. I figured the city buses would stop operating around midnight. I considered going to the bus station, but I remembered that posters with my face and description were up in every transportation hub.

The solution to my problem staggered into me.

"Whoa, there," I exclaimed, reaching out to steady the teetering man who was ready to take a fall from our collision. "You okay?"

He was a thickset man of an indeterminate age, a street person dressed in an assortment of mismatched and, probably, donated clothing - much of which had been saturated with dribbled food and strong beverage. To find him on a street in teetotaling Salt Lake City was a surprise.

"Okay," he acknowledged, blowing his reply with the sour breath of an alcoholic evening. He swayed a bit but regained most of a balance as he tried to focus on my face. "Sorry, mister."

"No harm done," I assured him. "You want me to help you find a place to sit down for a while?"

He shook his whiskered head. "Lay down when I get there."

"Get where?"

"Place where I lay down," he said.

"How far is that?"

"That way," he pointed, the movement nearly sweeping him off-balance again.

That's when the idea came to me.

"Perhaps I can help you along the way," I suggested.

He peered at me through his haze, trying hard to understand.

"That'd be okay," he said finally. "You got any money?" He waited for my answer. "We could get a bottle and split it."

"Maybe later," I suggested. "After you've had some time to lie down for a while."

He was disappointed, but allowed me to take his arm and guide him in the direction he'd indicated.

"How far is this place?" I asked.

"I don't know," he wheezed, the effort of walking erect taking most of his concentration. "Not too far or I couldn't get there."

"What kind of a place is it?"

He shrugged, slowing his weaving pace to a shuffle. "Good place. Nice people."

We walked very slowly for a couple of blocks, my companion subconsciously aware of the correct path; no doubt a fuzzy recall from numerous prior experiences. We turned a corner and found an old brick building with an overhead exterior light illuminating a doorway, and a simple sign identifying it as the *Amazing Grace Shelter*. As we entered the door, a slim, energetic young man, with a benevolent manner, gave his arm to support my weaving comrade.

"Hello, John," he greeted the man with familiarity. He glanced at me for a moment, then returned his gaze to follow John's unsteady progress into a large open and crowded room. It was populated by homeless men, almost all prone on their cots, a few sitting up and holding their heads in their hands. John found a cot and flopped upon it, instantly motionless, falling into an alcoholic coma that would likely last until late the next morning.

The young man looked at me, his expression showing curiosity.

"I found him on the street," I explained. "And I brought him here."

"John knows the way," the young man told me, a bit of something in his voice that indicated that my help had not been needed. "Were you drinking with him?"

I shook my head. "No, I just thought he needed some help. He was pretty drunk . . . falling down, you understand."

The benevolent look came back into the young man's face. "Well, that was very kind of you. John has, on occasion, gotten so drunk that he's passed out on the street." He sighed. "One of these cold nights, he'll probably freeze to death."

"Where do they get the booze?" I asked.

"Lord knows," the young man responded.

"And so do they," I said, nodding my head toward the room of inebriates. "I'm surprised to find so many in this city, this state."

"Tim Nelson," the young man said, offering his hand.

"Harris," I responded, making up a name as I shook his hand. "Dave Harris."

He was looking me over, sizing up the somewhat dated overcoat and the rest of my clothing. "You need something to eat?"

"No, I'm fine. Matter of fact, I was just finishing dinner when . . . ah, John bumped into me."

"You live here?"

"Passing through," I told him.

"Well, thank you for bringing John," he said, assuming that I'd now be on my way.

"Is this a Mormon shelter?" I asked.

"Interdenominational," he answered. "Our volunteers are from several different churches in the city."

I scanned the room, looking for volunteers. "You seem to be by your lonesome tonight."

He nodded in agreement. "Sometimes, I have help, and sometimes, I don't."

I nodded to the large room. "Sleep about twenty-five, thirty?"

"At least for the men." He waved his hand toward a far wall doorway. "We have some private rooms for families and for a few women."

"Families?"

"You'd be surprised," he told me. "Not everyone is here because of an alcoholic problem. Times being what they are, there are more and more families down on their luck."

Our conversation was interrupted by the simultaneous arrival of another boozer, and the loud sound of retching vomit at the rear of the room.

"Could you use some help?" I asked.

"Don't you have to be somewhere?" Nelson queried, not at all sure that he should take my offer.

"Not until morning," I replied. "And it's one of those nights that I can't sleep."

Another man entered the door, and Nelson gave me a quizzical look, then a shrug and a nod.

"I'll take the guy in back," I told him. "You take care of the new guests."

I'm reasonably sure Nelson had misgivings about letting a stranger tend to the aimless and homeless, but we worked through the night, helping as we could to minister to the needs of the ailing and mostly destitute men. A middle-aged woman, Vera, came out of the back rooms of the facility a few times to share coffee and small talk. There were no single women in the shelter this night, but there was a family trying to make it home to Iowa, low on cash, food and gas. I dug two fifties out of the money belt and donated it to their cause. After that, Nelson and Vera seemed to think I was all right; a man with his heart in the right place.

I'd like you to think that my night of care for the downtrodden was a humanitarian gesture, but it was more a survival effort; a little bit of do-gooding to buy me warmth. I had some anxiety about being in that shelter, thinking it a most likely place where police would seek criminals hiding out among the unfortunate, but no one came to search and arrest.

■ ■ ■

A little after five in the morning, I bid Nelson and Vera goodbye, accepted their thanks, and headed back to the main streets of the city. It was way too early for the business district to come alive, only a very few men and women trudging through the frosty air to office buildings. I looked around and saw only a couple of retail shops, nothing near that would offer what I needed.

I hailed a cab.

"Got a good shopping mall somewhere?" I asked.

The driver half-turned, a frown on his face. "Sure . . . but it'll be ten this morning before the stores open."

"Any of 'em with a restaurant where I can get breakfast?"

He turned back to start the cab moving forward. "Sure, but it'll sure be a long breakfast."

He drove me to a shopping mall which included a *J. C. Penney's*, a *Sears,* and, wouldn't you know, a *HappiTimes Restaurant.*

It was six o'clock when I entered the cafe.

I dawdled over my breakfast, drank a zillion cups of coffee, and then finally decided to enter the mall. All the shops were still closed, a couple of hours before they would open. The only people around were a few exercise-conscious elderly men and women doing quick-step walks, up one corridor, down another, round the entire facility, and back again.

I took off my topcoat, laid it on a concrete bench, then joined them, doing laps.

At nine o'clock, I needed and found another restroom. I took a look at my face and decided the beard was really doing a job. I didn't look at all like me; I looked like a refugee from the Balkans. What I needed was something to trim the beard, some instrument to clip the stray hairs that twined long out of the shorter stuff. And, I decided, a haircut wouldn't be bad either.

I spotted a drugstore in the mall and decided it would be my first stop.

At ten o'clock, all the lights in all the stores came on, and all the doors opened for business. A cinnamon bun counter began to waft warm sweetness down the wide aisle, and a CD outlet store began to play country music proudly and loudly. I went in the drug store and drifted down one aisle, then another. I found a hair and beard trimming kit, some toothpaste, a toothbrush, deodorant, some hair stuff, and a small plastic case to carry all of it. At the cash register, I found a morning edition of the *Deseret News* and bought it along with my other purchases.

Sitting on a hard bench in the mall, I went through the paper, looking for the latest on our escape. On the third page, I was literally shocked to find two pictures of myself. One, as I looked before going to prison. The second photo was a retouched image showing how I'd look with a beard.

Exactly as I looked right now!

I looked around in panic, wondering how many people in the mall were also reading the *Deseret News,* looking at my picture, then at me, comparing, trying to make sure.

I returned to the restroom and, thankful that I was sharing it with no one, I took out the hair and beard trimmer, and went to work.

Fifteen minutes later, I was wearing sort of a rough Van Dyke on my chin and a clumsy version of male pattern baldness on the top of my head. I hoped the missing hair hadn't stopped up any of the stools.

At least, I didn't look like any of my previous pictures.

My next stop was the men's department of *J. C. Penney's.* With cash, I bought an insulated winter coat, three shirts, two pairs of jeans, packets of shorts and tee-shirts, a cap with fold down ear flaps, socks, and gloves.

And a sports-style duffel bag for carrying.

I found a pay phone and sat down near it to look in the classified section of the newspaper.

"You have a car for sale?" I asked after I'd dialed, looking at the ad in the paper. "Ninety-six Saturn? Runs better than it looks? Twelve hundred or make offer?'"

"Yeah," a man's voice answered. "Want to come look at it?"

"How about meeting me?" I countered. "Southtown Mall?"

"Je . . . hoshaphat," the man nearly swore. "That's cross town from me."

"I can pay cash," I told him.

"Twelve hundred?"

"That depends," I hedged. "You sure it runs good?"

"Runs fine," the man said, sounding defensive. "I wouldn't have put it in the paper if I didn't mean it."

"You never know," I responded.

"Look," he said, turning a bit testy. "The paint's oxidized in places, and it's scuffed up in a couple more, but that engine ain't got but ninety thousand original miles, and the tranny's good. I had it fixed five months ago."

"Meet me in front of this store, and bring a bill of sale."

"You going to buy it?"

"I'm convinced you're an honest man."

"We'll have to get it notarized," he told me.

"No problem," I lied. "How long 'til you can get here?"

"About an hour," he replied. "Can you drop me off at my wife's work afterwards?"

"Where's she work?" I asked.

"Downtown," he told me.

"That'll be fine," I assured him. "Don't forget the title."

An hour later, I did some bargaining and gave him eleven hundred dollars.

"You're sure you'll get this thing notarized," he said doubtfully. "I really ought to take off the plates."

"I'll take 'em off and put on my own . . . and my sister's a notary," I lied again. "Just leave it to her."

"Is that legal," he asked, obviously no more sophisticated in auto buying and selling than I was.

"Hey, who's gonna know the difference," I said with a nonchalance I hoped would soothe his anxiety. I had one more thought. "Buy you a beer?" I asked. "To celebrate the sale?"

He gave me a sour look, and then turned it into a smile. "Yes," he responded. "I am Mormon and I'm honest. The car's okay." He paused, then added: "And there's no place you can buy a beer this early in the day in Salt Lake."

I dropped him off at a downtown florist shop and waved goodbye as he headed inside. Claims to the contrary, he hadn't been entirely truthful about the car. It was a four-door sedan that had once, long ago, been a bright shiny red. Now, it was more the color and the condition of rust. Not only was it rough looking on the outside, the upholstery and the floor carpets showed a lot of hard use. The odometer showed close to ninety thousand miles, and I hoped this wasn't the second time around. Still, the engine sounded pretty good, and the transmission seemed to shift through the gears without a shudder or alarming sounds. I drove the Saturn tentatively for a few miles through the Salt Lake City traffic, not wanting to attract any attention by erratic behavior in a totally unfamiliar car. I followed the highway markers on the city route and found an interstate entrance. Instead of moving onto the highway, I pulled into a parking lot of a grocery store to do some thinking.

I knew where I was going.

Louisiana - to find Bruno Cady, the crazy flyer who could fly you anywhere and not get caught.

15

The quickest route, I considered, would be a drive through Colorado, back through Denver. However, that would be where the police would likely still be concentrating their manhunt, figuring I'd be stupid enough to head back home. I reckoned my best bet was to take Highway 80 across Wyoming, through Nebraska, and then cut down through Missouri on my way south.

While I was pondering, the passenger door opened, and a young, scraggly-bearded face leaned into the car. "Thanks for stopping, fella. Damned if I thought anybody would."

I hadn't noticed anybody when I'd pulled into the lot. The scrawny young man surprised me as he opened the door further and sat down beside me. What surprised me even more was the coatless young woman, carrying a grocery bag, who came in through the right rear door and closed it after her.

"Wait a minute!" I exclaimed. "I'm not taking—"

"Appreciate it, mister," the young man interrupted, slamming the passenger-side door. "You're doing a kind thing, taking me and my girlfriend where we're going."

"I'm sorry," I said firmly. "This is a mistake. I didn't stop for you—"

With an almost apologetic smile, he showed me the revolver he'd kept under his ragged coat. "Mister, it ain't smart to pick up hitchhikers."

We stared at each other for a very long time.

"Where do you want to go?" I asked finally.

"Which way were you heading?" he countered, glancing over his shoulder, looking toward the grocery store.

"Wyoming."

"Sounds good," he said, waving the barrel of the revolver toward the highway. "Best we get going. We just robbed that supermarket."

"Shit!" I said, and put the car in gear. I pulled out of the parking lot at a moderate speed, looking behind me, dreading that I might see a cop car speeding after us. I could see no police cars speeding near, and I didn't see any alarmed citizens running around pointing fingers at us.

A few minutes later, we were on the highway heading toward a distant Cheyenne, nearly three hundred miles away. Nobody talked. Nobody asked questions. We just rode along in silence, three criminals in a rusty Saturn fleeing the wrath of the law. I tried to estimate their ages - the gunman maybe twenty or so, the girl no more than seventeen or eighteen.

"Piss-poor car," the young man said, looking around at the faded seats and the scratched, cracked dashboard.

"Robbers can't be choosers," I said with a flippancy I didn't really feel.

The young man didn't seem to take offense. "Hell, if the damned thing runs, that's okay, I guess." He paused. "Does the heater work?"

I nodded. It was the first question I'd asked of the past owner.

"You know how much we got?" the girl suddenly asked, leaning over the seat to speak. "Nine hundred dollars! Just about." She reached into her grocery sack and pulled out a handful of bills. "Want to see it?"

"Didn't you have a car of your own?" I asked.

"Naw," the young man answered. "We took a bus there."

"How were you planning to get away?" I asked, incredulous.

"Finding somebody stupid like you," the girl answered this time.

The young man looked at me critically. "You got any money?"

I thought about the money belt.

"Do you think I'd be driving a junker like this if I did?" I said, hoping to sound convincing.

"You look like you're doing okay," he went on. "Clothes are pretty nice." He looked at the girl in the back seat. "Think they'd be too big?"

I had a sudden picture of myself in the nude, stranded and freezing in the snowy Wasatch Mountains or on the vast winter plains of Wyoming. Or, lying colder still, face down with a bullet in my head.

We drove for a time without further conversation, me with my thoughts and fears, they with theirs. A strange pair with neither intelligence nor conscience, I decided that they were deadly, and I believed I had little time left. On the next side road, or the next, or the next, the young gunman would direct me off the highway and put an end to me. Right now, the highway was busy with traffic, and I was fairly certain he wouldn't want to do any shooting with so many possible witnesses.

I took an inordinate interest in the rear view mirror and began to slow down, pulling over to the side of the road.

"What are you doing?" the young punk demanded.

"State Patrol," I told him, jerking a thumb back over my shoulder.

He looked back in panic, and that's when I hit him, jamming on the brakes at the same time. I don't know what stunned him the most; my fist to his jaw or his head slamming against the windshield. I heard a gasp of surprise from the girl in the back, but I wasn't concerned with her at the moment. I hit the youngster three more times while, at the same time, I clawed at the gun with my left hand and pulled it away.

Several cars whizzed by as I got out of the car, careful to take the ignition key with me. I went around to the front passenger door, opened it and pulled the groggy young man out. I opened the back door, and motioned for the young girl to come out. She came, clutching her grocery sack of money.

I sat them down on the shoulder of the road and stood with my back against the Saturn, holding his gun on them.

"There warn't no State Patrol," the young man said angrily.

"No, but there will be," I assured him.

"You want the money, mister?" the girl asked, offering the sack.

"You keep it," I told her. "Try explaining it."

"You damned near killed me," the young man whined, holding his head.

"Always wear your seat belt," I reprimanded.

"What are you going to do with us?" the girl entered her whine.

"Nothing at all," I told her. "I'll just be on my way."

I took the precaution of searching each for additional weapons, but found nothing. The girl giggled when I patted her down, and the young man cursed me with every foul word in his limited vocabulary. I looked in the bottom of the grocery sack and found nothing remotely lethal. I presumed the revolver had been the only weapon for the pair of robbers.

I drove away, looking at the forlorn pair in my rear view mirror. Perhaps I was putting other drivers at risk by leaving them on the loose, but hitchhiking these days was generally recognized as foolhardy. They had no weapons, and the young man was too slight to be of much threat. I had their gun, and they didn't seem physically able to do much damage without it. More than likely, a highway patrolman would soon find them and, with a bag of money to explain away, I was sure they'd be hauled off to the nearest pokey. I looked at the revolver and wondered what to do with it. It was one of those with a short barrel - snub-nosed, I think they call it. Handling it carefully with one hand while I drove with the other, I broke open the cylinder and examined it.

Five bullets.

Weren't there supposed to be six?

Had one been fired?

I put the revolver up to my nose and sniffed; indeed, it had been recently fired.

Great! Here I am with another damned smoking gun!

I turned on the radio and dialed through the local stations, picking up a strong Salt Lake City signal. Sure enough, the announcer told of a supermarket robbery where a pair of youthful bandits had made off with a sack of money. No one was injured in the incident, even though a shot had been fired into the ceiling. Breathing a sigh of relief, I turned off the radio although I was still concerned with my possession of the gun.

Toss it out the window?

I decided that Highway 80 was far too busily traveled to allow me to merely sling the damned thing out. With my luck and dexterity, I'd probably drop it on the hammer, sparking a shot into an innocent passing motorist. Then, too, I wondered if it just might be something I should keep just in case of trouble down the road.

I got off at Park City to fill the tank with gas, taking just a few minutes to check under the hood. The engine seemed fine: The oil supply wasn't running out the bottom, and the windshield fluid was full. I paid for the gas in cash, buying a supply of candy bars, boxed donuts, a huge bottle of Coca-Cola, a loaf of Wonder Bread, and a tube of summer sausage.

I was pulling back onto the highway when a late-model, top-of-the-line silver Buick flew past with a familiar grocery sack stuck up in the back window. A stream of cars and trucks went by before I could ease into the line of traffic. I passed each car separately, cautiously, trying to move up on the Buick to confirm what I suspected.

I could see the blonde head of the girl leaning forward from the back seat, and I thought the driver was driving in an abnormally stiff position. From what I could see, I surmised that young Bobby, who I had believed to be of no threat, was holding something at the man's throat. I cursed myself, wondering if I'd searched the young thug carelessly.

A pickup truck, the driver angry that I'd passed him, came around me and crowded in between my car and the Buick. It was just as well, I decided. I didn't want the dastardly duo to see and recognize my car.

I followed them for several miles, now sure of the pair's lethal intent, and saw the Buick turn off at a nowhere ramp that led to some dry land desolation. I eased off the highway, at a much slower speed, and let the Buick get some consider-able distance ahead yet keeping it in sight.

About a mile up the road, I saw a slight swirl of dust as the big car turned onto a gravel side road. Moments later, I caught a glimpse of the Buick as it twisted through a turn in the rocky hills. I followed carefully, catching sight here and there of the silver car, and seeing an occasional kick-up of dust when the car slithered on the gravel.

I suppose it was instinct that brought me to a stop at the beginning of a curve. I pulled to the side of the road and cut the engine. I got out of the car, the revolver in my hand, and walked as quietly as I could down around the bend. I stopped at the sight of the Buick parked in a rocky cut. I crouched down and moved to the shelter of a rock outcropping. From this vantage site, I watched the young man forcing the short, stout, business-suited older man from the car. The rear door of the Buick flew open as the girl got out to watch. I saw the flash of the knife at the man's throat, and I knew that I didn't have time to be careful any longer.

"Freeze!" I shouted, running toward them at full speed

It was like they became statues.

"Sonofabitch!" the young man exclaimed.

"Sonofabitch!" the girl repeated.

"Drop the damned knife!" I shouted, moving within fifteen feet of them.

Instead, the youngster locked an arm around the small man's shoulders and turned him to me, hiding himself none too successfully behind the diminutive stature of the terrified hostage. "I'll cut him!" he shouted. "Back off or I'll cut his fucking head off!"

The short man's face was red yet with blotches of white, a coronary not far from happening. In spite of the cold, sweat was beading on his forehead. His eyes pleaded with me, seeking a savior.

"Where'd you have the knife?" I asked loudly. "I searched you! Both of you!"

The girl patted her jeans pocket near her crotch. "You sissy! You didn't look hard enough."

I took the wide stance and steadied the revolver with both hands, aiming at the young man behind his struggling captive. "Hold real still, mister," I said to the short man. "I'm going to shoot him."

"I'll cut him!" the boy shouted in alarm. "I really will!"

From what I could see, Bobby was holding a folding pocket knife at the man's throat. While not exactly a Bowie knife, even the three-inch blade could do some serious damage. Even so, we were getting nowhere with our mutual threats. I decided to see who'd chicken out. "You may get a little hurt, mister," I said as calmly as I could. "He'll be dead before he can do much damage."

"Damn, Bobby!" the girl said, her voice rising. "He's going to shoot you!"

The captive found strength and a hoarse voice. "You good with that gun?"

"Damned good," I lied. "Good enough to get a piece of him any time he peeks around."

"I'll cut him!" the boy shouted, his voice nearly as high as the girl's.

I didn't really realize that I'd put any pressure on the trigger but, suddenly, the gun bucked in my hand and the sound startled me. The young man yowled, clapped his hand to the lobe of his left ear and danced away. He dropped the knife, panicked at the sight of blood on his hand. The short man staggered away, and then moved as fast as he could to stand just back of me. He was breathing hard, trying to catch his breath.

"You shot him, you sonofabitch!" the girl screamed, her voice echoing from the surrounding rock walls.

Bobby was still prancing around and holding his ear, but he seemed less agitated now, probably realizing that he wasn't going to die. He went to his knees and sort of rocked back and forth, moaning. The girl hurried over to him to assess the damage, peering at his ear.

"Anybody got a hanky?" she asked.

Neither the short man nor I answered.

Flustered, she pulled up the tail of her blouse to dab at his ear. A few minutes later, she stepped away and stared at her bloody blouse in dismay.

"Lord, Bobby," she scolded. "You ain't hurt hardly at all . . . and look what you made me do to my blouse."

"He shot my fucking ear off!" Bobby wailed.

"Just a little piece of it," the girl responded in a huff, trying to rip off the bloody section of her blouse.

Beside me, the little man had regained a normal breath and a normal color. "Thanks, guy," he said in near worship. "You saved my life."

I didn't answer, feeling guilty for getting him into such trouble.

"How'd you know about this?" he asked.

"I picked them up earlier," I confessed. "Little shit jumped into my car in a parking lot, pulled this gun on me, then made me drive them out of town." I paused. "I got the jump on him and kicked 'em out."

"You didn't take them to the police?" he asked incredulously.

"My mistake," I admitted. "I figured the police would pick them up on the highway."

"Guess I shouldn't give you any blame," the man acknowledged. "I should've known better myself. I thought maybe they'd had car trouble."

"You see any car?"

The stout little man looked chagrined. "I guess it was the little blonde that took my eye," he confessed. "Funny, I don't think of myself as a horny old goat."

By now, the girl had her blouse off and was rubbing it on a stone, trying to get the blood out. She wasn't wearing a bra and her ample breasts jiggled as she labored.

"Put the blouse back on," I told her. "You and Bobby get over here."

She acted like she wasn't going to mind, but she fussily obeyed when I took a threatening step toward her. Bobby took a few moments longer, but then came submissively to join the girl.

"What are you going to do with us?" the girl demanded.

Shorty repeated the question. "Yeah, what are you going to do with them?"

"Put them in the trunk," I said to all of them.

"Whose trunk?" the man asked apprehensively, looking at the back of his new Buick.

"Yours," I told him. "Bigger'n mine."

"She's all bloody, and so's he," he complained, and then looked sheepish about it.

"Rather have them up front with you?" I asked.

He shrugged and moved to the rear of the Buick to open the trunk. "Looks mighty cramped."

"Rather have them up front with you?" I repeated.

"I ain't getting in there with Bobby," the girl declared indignantly.

"How about you take one in yours, and I take one in mine?" the man suggested.

"You take 'em both," I instructed. "I'll follow."

"I ain't getting in there," the girl repeated.

I grabbed her by the hair and guided her, struggling and trying to swing at me, to the back of the Buick. "You can get in by yourself or I'll put you in," I told her, releasing her hair. "You'll get a little scuffed up if I have to do it."

She gave me a last wild swing, which I avoided, and then awkwardly climbed in.

"Get in, Bobby," I told the youth. "Spoon position ought to work just fine."

Still nursing his ear, Bobby came to the car reluctantly yet hesitated before climbing into the trunk. I bent his head forward, grabbed him by the seat of his pants and pushed, only peripherally seeing that something had fallen from his hip pocket. I glanced down, saw the billfold and, with only a vague idea of what to do with it, I kicked it under the car.

I was reasonably sure that no one, other than me, had seen his loss.

Awkwardly, Bobby crawled into the trunk and tried to snuggle up next to the girl. She hit him on the back of the head for his trouble.

"Be nice," I told them, my hand on the trunk lid. "Watch your fingers."

I slammed the trunk lid down.

"Think they'll smother in there?" the Buick owner said, worried.

"You should care if they do," I replied.

"What are we going to do with them?" he asked.

"There's a town about ten miles up ahead," I informed him. "Ought to have some sort of a jail there. You go on with them, and I'll be right behind."

The man considered, shrugged, and stuck out his hand. "Clyde Faulkner," he introduced himself. "I sell sump pumps."

I shook his hand and gave a name. "Fred Mason."

"Fred, you've saved my life," he said, almost gushing about it. "I won't forget it."

"One of those things," I said nonchalantly. "Shall we get going?"

"Oh, yeah," he said, glancing at the trunk. "Think they can bust through the back seat?"

"Let's don't give 'em a chance," I suggested, pointing toward the highway. "I'll be right behind you."

He gave me another fawning smile and got into his car. He started moving it slowly forward, then turned it sharply to head back toward the highway. I reached down casually to retrieve Bobby's billfold and stuck it in my pocket as I started toward my car. He paced his drive at my walking speed, waiting for me to reach the Saturn, and then stopped the Buick as I turned my junker around. We set off in our two-car caravan, back along the gravel road and onto the highway. We drove at a moderate speed until we reached the next town, a little settlement with a city sign that boasted of 1355 good Mormon neighbors. I stayed with him as he took the exit into the side road that turned into the main street of the small town. I came to a stop about a half-block away as he parked in front of a concrete-block building with a prominent *Police* sign painted across its upper facade. I waited until Faulkner hurried into the building, and then I took off and headed back toward the highway.

Once on the main highway again, in my mind's eye, I pictured the local sheriff and his deputy hauling the two pubescent robbers out of the trunk, and into a cell. I gave some worried thought as to how the Buick owner and the pair of dunderhead dolts would tell of my part in the capture. Hopefully, it would take quite a bit of time.

I stepped on the gas pedal and hurried on down the road.

16

The ride went fine through Wyoming, the battered and scaly Saturn performing beautifully with the heater doing a good if noisy job. I swung down through Nebraska, spending my first night in a real bed at a motel whose elderly clerk gave me and Bobby Fowler's billfold identification no more than a disinterested glance. It was a plain and ordinary mom-and-pop motel, something less clean and attractive than the one run by Norman Bates, but it was heaven to me. I curled up in the tattered sheets, pulled the mothball-smelling blankets up to my chin, and slept eleven hours.

Back on the road by noon, I drove down across the Missouri border, skirted Kansas City, and angled down across the state heading for Arkansas. I stopped at my second third-rate motel just the other side of Springfield about nine o'clock at night.

"You sure that's you?" this motel clerk queried suspiciously, squinting at the driver's license picture, then at me. She was a bony young woman with a perpetual frown.

"The beard makes me look older," I improvised.

"Where's your hair?" she asked, looking at the top of my head.

"Radiation," I told her. "They tell me it'll grow back."

She looked at me, actually recoiling a bit. "You got cancer?"

"Not anymore," I assured her.

She regarded me with distaste. "Don't know that I ought to give you a bed," she mused aloud, then made a half-hearted moue of apology. "I don't guess it's catching?"

"I suspect you've had more communicable diseases in here than mine," I couldn't help saying.

That irritated her a bit, but she turned around and took a key from a pegboard behind her. "Cabin twelve," she said, placing the key on the counter. "Twenty-two dollars, up front."

I gave her a twenty and a ten.

"There's television, no cable, but it's got an antenna," she told me, handing back three one's and a five.

"That's fine," I responded. "Not much for watching anyway."

"There ain't no phone," she continued. "There's a pay phone across the road down by the Wal-Mart store."

"I don't need one," I told her. "Just passing through."

She looked at the picture in the billfold once again, then passed it back to me. "You sure look a lot different."

"That radiation will age a person."

She nodded. "Get your hair back, I think you'll be a sight prettier."

I thanked her and went out to find Cabin Twelve. It could've been a twin to the one the night before. It was a dump, to be honest, and I was beginning to feel that I deserved better. I figured I'd be ready for a Hilton at my next stop if my comfort ego wasn't restrained.

I took a shower, avoiding the water bugs and spiders that had been aroused, and then sat in a chair in my just-out-of-the-package underwear and watched television. As I'd been told, there was no cable accessibility, and all I could get was the local channels. I sat through a couple of insipid reality shows and waited for the ten o'clock news. When it came, I learned a little about the world and the nation and a lot about southern Missouri. I decided that I was old news since there wasn't a syllable uttered about me or my Mafia associate running loose on the lam. I turned off the set, pulled down the bedspread, turned back the covers, and found this bed almost as good as the one the night before.

⬛ ⬛ ⬛

My luck ran out the next day, a little after noon, deep into Arkansas. You can't believe how difficult it is to maintain a non-suspicious highway speed. Go slow and you attract attention. Go fast and you've got rapt attention. For four states, I'd hit about five miles an hour above the legal limit, sometimes fudging a bit when I was in a line of traffic going faster. I didn't want to stick out as someone purposely lagging back, so I kept up with the others. Perhaps obeying the state laws - or at least keeping close - made me forget about the little towns.

I passed a white post with a tiny white sign that gave the name of the town, and I even let off the gas just a mite as a caution. Seeing the back-side of another sign no more than a quarter of a mile up ahead, I started to accelerate. There couldn't have been more than five or six buildings in the "business district" that I passed, all of them only on one side of the road. I sure didn't know that one of them was a jail.

Just the other side of the little burg, I saw the black unmarked Chevy behind me with the dome light flashing. For a moment, I thought it'd be the other guy ahead of me that had gone through the town like a streak. Or maybe because the local cop figured my beat-up Saturn couldn't run away as fast. I wished I hadn't put Bobby's revolver in the trunk. However, I reflected,, I'd probably end up by shooting some wide-spot-in-the-road constable. Knowing that I had no other choice, I pulled off on the side of the road and waited while the policeman parked his car and came up to my window.

"Afternoon, officer," I greeted him pleasantly.

"Don't try being nicey-nice," he answered. He was a young fat fellow with bulges pooching out from his makeshift uniform. He wore a tan shirt, khaki trousers, and a mail-order hard billed cap. "See your license?"

I wondered about Bobby's, but I held off showing it. "What's the problem?"

"Didn't see the speed limit, did you?"

"No, officer," I said in my most cooperative manner. "I really didn't. What was it? Forty-five?"

He shook his head.

"Thirty-five?"

"Keep guessing"

"Lower than twenty-five?"

He nodded. "Guess you didn't see the sign."

There seemed to be no reason to continue this line of conversation, so I waited to see what he'd do next.

"I ain't seen that license," he reminded me.

"I'm getting to it," I reassured him, making a show of hunting for my billfold.

"Just turn your car around and head on back down towards town," he instructed, pointing back toward the little village. "You park there in front of the jail"

"Which building is that?" I asked.

"The one with bars on the windows," he told me. "It ain't hard to find."

I considered taking off at high speed, but decided against it. Or, rather, the Saturn made up my mind for me. Trying to decide what to do, I headed back toward the small gathering of buildings and parked in front of an ancient one with bars on the windows. The roly-poly cop parked his homemade patrol car beside mine, struggled out of the front seat, and waved me toward the front door.

We walked into an office littered with random and mis-matched furniture; an ancient desk, a rickety Naugahyde desk chair, a folding-chair for a visitor, plastic and thin-metal file cabinets, and an early-model computer - grimy with age - on a pressed-wood console. On one wall there were wanted post-ers, new and old. On another, a gun rack held two rifles and a pair of handcuffs. At one side of the room – honest - there was a makeshift holding cell that had been cobbled together out of two-by-fours and a solid-core door. The whole shebang was secured by a chain with a padlock.

The local cop walked around behind the desk and looked me up and down. "How much money you got on you?" he said.

"Not a hell of a lot," I answered, an idea forming in my head. "You saw what I'm driving . . . that look like I'm loaded."

He ignored my argument and snapped his fingers at me. "Gimme your billfold."

I took it out of my pocket and fingered the pair of twenties inside it.

"Gimme the whole damned thing," he barked, showing his authority. Without waiting, he snatched the billfold from my hand and helped himself to the two twenties as well as the five and three ones. "This all you got?"

I wasn't about to tell him about the money belt.

Not getting a response, he examined the billfold again, finally noticing Bobby Fowler's driver license. He looked at it closely, and then peered at me.

"This ain't you," he accused.

"Radiation treatment," I said, touching my bald head, hoping the same story might work twice.

"Bullshit!" he exploded. "This ain't never been you!" Hard suspicion came into his fat-folded eyes. He pulled a revolver from his holster and aimed it at my chest. "Who the hell are you, mister?"

I took a deep breath and decided I'd take my chance. "Mathias. Kevin Mathias."

He blinked, not recognizing the name.

"You read the papers?" I asked. "Watch TV? Listen to the radio?"

Still no recognition.

"Hear about the two guys who broke out of prison in Colorado?" I asked, prompting his memory.

Finally, I saw that he was seeing the light, albeit dimly.

"Oh, yeah," he began, a smile of delight coming to his face. "Them two guys that escaped outta prison?" He gave me his hardest, most official look. "You ain't saying you're one of them?"

"You must've read or heard about it," I encouraged him. "We're big time."

The porky officer didn't know whether to dance a jig or shoot me. "My God! I done captured public enemy number one!"

"Yeah," I agreed. "There'll be newspaper reporters, video cameras . . . you'll be on national TV."

"Yeah, I surely will!" he exclaimed, images forming behind his pasty forehead. Then, he frowned and waved his revolver toward the two-by-four cell. "You git in there." He fumbled in his pocket for a moment, then opened the desk drawer. He moved things around, finally coming up triumphantly with a key. He walked to the cell, unlocked the padlock, undid the chain, and then opened the door. "Git in there," he repeated.

"No, I won't," I said mildly, so affably that the tone caught him by surprise.

"Why not?"

"Because you're going to hand me back my billfold and tell me to be on my way," I told him matter-of-factly, reaching for the billfold.

The officer took a step backward, almost frightened. "Why would I do that?" he asked plaintively, and then tried to resume his authority. "You do what I said. Git in there!"

I crossed my arms. "You remember that there were two of us?"

His eyebrow lifted, puzzlement apparent.

"Vince Gianntana?"

He blinked.

I decided that he had a tic that came with a sluggish mental condition. "How do you think we got out?"

He shook his head.

One of the least bright and ill-informed acquaintances of my lifetime.

"My companion was Vince Gianntana," I explained. "You ever see any Mafia movies?"

At last, he made a connection.

"You arrest me, everybody in the country's going to know about it," I informed him, setting him up for the stinger. "Especially Gianntana's people."

The officer did a triple blink, a sure sign of fright. "Mafia?"

I kept my smile from coming. "They'll take it badly if you have anything to do with me being caught," I intoned gravely. "You'll be lucky if all they do is to kill you."

Officer Chubby tried a bit of unconvincing bravado. "Hell, they ain't going to do anything to a sworn officer of the law just doing his duty."

"The smart thing would be to let me go," I advised him.

"If I'd just go ahead and shoot you," he began, "they'd just figure it was over and done, wouldn't they?"

"Vince and I . . . we're close," I told him in my most somber voice. "You ever hear about hanging guys on meat hooks while they're still alive?"

The muscles of his face twitched as he pulled up a mental image of himself dangling from a sharp hook. He thought about it for several seconds and his manner suddenly changed.

"I just can't let you go!" he protested with a whine. "Hell, it's not the thing I should do."

"You got a wife?" I asked.

"No."

"Girl friend?"

"Sorta . . . well, maybe."

"Your mother alive?" I asked.

"What about her?" he asked, really tight about it.

"The old Mafia wouldn't have touched her," I said, pretending to deliberate the subject. "Don't know about the newer bunch."

We stood silently for at least a minute.

"Meat hooks," I reminded him. "You and your momma."

He made up his mind suddenly, handing me the billfold. "Here! Take it and get outta here! I ain't ever seen ya."

"Now you're using your head," I complimented him. "Bad as this would' be for me, it'd be worse for you and your old lady. Much worse."

I was half out the door when I stopped, turned, and gave him another sentence of advice. "If I get picked up down the road, I'll let Vince know it was you who made a call."

"I won't say nothing," he assured me. "I ain't never seen you."

Nonetheless, I worried about him even after I crossed the line into Louisiana; my concerns gradually replaced with a sense of relief and a chuckling realization.

I guess he'd seen more than one badass Mafia movie.

17

All I knew about Bruno Cady was that he was one hell of a flyer, that he hung out somewhere down near Baton Rouge, and that he was probably as crooked as they come.

My former cellmate seemed to have been his bosom buddy and, I thought, just maybe, he'd be the man to see about getting me out of the country. I had no passport, no valid identification of any kind, and I didn't have the foggiest idea of how to come by any get-out-of-jail-free documents. I did have a few thousand dollars still warming my stomach in the money belt; I hoped it would be enough to bribe daredevil Cady into flying me somewhere beyond the reach of this country's law.

When I reached Baton Rouge, it was late at night. It seemed a little too late to seek a motel, so I spent the night sleeping in the Saturn. I found a parking garage, pulled in, took a ticket from the automatic machine and moved up to the third level. I parked the car between a couple of big SUV's and curled up on the back seat of the car. Once, during the night, I heard someone walking in the facility, so I rolled down onto the floor. I hid under my coat just before a flashlight beam touched and illuminated the upper part of the car's interior, then swept on.

There were no more interruptions during the night, and I slept fairly well. In the morning, I paid my way out of the garage and, after some searching, found my way to the Baton Rouge Metropolitan Airport. I bypassed the main terminal and went to the private and corporate hangers to begin my search.

I started with a flying school organization.

"Pardon me," I asked an attractive young woman behind a counter. "I'm looking for a pilot that I understand hangs out in this part of the country. Bruno Cady?"

I got a blank look.

"Bruno Cady?" I repeated.

"Anybody here ever hear of a Brutus Catty?" she bellowed to the four men who were less than ten feet away from her.

"Bruno Cady," I said loudly, making sure that the name was correctly heard.

Four men shrugged.

I tried a half-dozen other places, but there seemed to be no knowledge of a Bruno Cady in the Baton Rouge area, nor were there any local pilots who'd ever heard of him. All I got were blank looks from those I questioned.

Then, I started to check out the airfields in nearby communities and, finally, ended my search in a little landing-strip facility about fifty miles east of the city.

It wasn't much to look at: a small-town facility that consisted of a rusted metal hanger large enough to house a couple of airplanes under repair. Adjacent to it, there was a tarmac strip that provided a small number of tie-down spots along the runway. Parked along it, most of the planes were old Pipers and Cessna's, and a few makes and models unknown to me. One plane, a sleek-looking, twin-engine job, looked out of place among the other forlorn aircraft.

Probably the property of a well-to-do local doctor or a rich-as-hell evangelical preacher, I surmised. *Hopefully, an aircraft owned by Bruno Cady.*

I walked through the partially opened hanger doors. On one side, I saw an engineless plane surrounded by scattered parts. On the other, I was a little surprised to see a spiffy, restored 55 Chevy convertible with the hood up. I couldn't see anybody, but there was a tiny hum of something electric near the automobile, so I walked toward it. A tall, stooped-shouldered man with a pot gut stepped out from behind the under-repair automobile, viewing my approach with something far less than hospitality.

"Can I help you with something?" he asked brusquely.

"Looking for a man named Cady. Bruno Cady?" I asked, watching for his reaction.

There was none. The man stood without comment, waiting for me to go on.

"Name mean anything to you?"

He took a step forward. "You want to take flying lessons, park a plane?" he asked. "If not, get the hell outta here, and let me get back to work."

His eyes, his glare almost made me take a step back.

"Nice to meet you, Mr. Cady," I said, surprised at my audacity. "Did Chris tell you to expect me?"

"The name's Bob Carter. I don't know any Chris, and I sure as hell don't know who you are!" he snapped. "You're wasting my time."

"B . . . C . . . same initials," I countered. "Rather a coincidence."

"So?" he responded, not denying it.

"I was thinking about a charter," I told him. "Hiring you to fly me somewhere."

He gave me a sneering face. "You don't look like you could afford much."

I glanced around, showing my own disdain for his operation. "You don't look like you could provide much." I tried again. "How about Chris Munoz?"

The stern-faced man continued to stare at me.

"Chris Munoz?" I prompted. "Supposed to be a pretty good friend."

He let that pass, and we continued in a standing stare-off.

"Where were you wanting to go?" he said finally. "Planes don't look like much, but they fly. I keep 'em going." He paused, but spoke again before I could answer. "Most times, it's cheaper to fly commercial."

"I was hoping Chris would've explained it to you."

He showed a violent sign of irritation; a chopping motion with his right hand signaling he wanted to cut this conversation. "I told you I don't know any Chris and, if we're going to do any business, I'd suggest you forget about Mister Chris, whoever he is."

"I've got four thousand dollars," I told him, hoping to keep a few dollars for the rest of my life.

"Where do you want to go?"

"An island in the Caribbean," I informed him. "Antigua."

"Antigua?" he bellowed. "For four thousand dollars? You're shitting me, ain't ya?!"

"I'm serious," I assured him.

"Well, get on a damned ship or catch a flight outta New Orleans," he sputtered, pissed as all get out. "I don't take no charters over open water for any damned four grand."

"I can't do that," I responded evenly. "If you're a friend of Chris, and if you know where he is, you'll know why I can't take chances on regular airplanes or ships."

He studied me for a few moments, a small smirk finally coming across his mouth.

"No papers, no passport . . . running from the law?" Suddenly, recognition arrived. "Lordy, you're one of them guys that busted out of that Colorado prison!"

"Maybe the four grand isn't enough, but Chris thought you might do it as a favor to him."

The man gave an odd chuckle. "Okay, I'm Cady, but I go by the name of Bob Carter around here." He hesitated for several moments, then went on, "You know, this old and dear friend of mine, this fella you call Chris . . . I don't know him from Adam. Maybe, he flew with me, caroused a bit with me down south, but he don't come to mind. Maybe, I'd know if I'd actually see him." He sighed. "Doing him a favor's ain't high on my list."

"It's no go, then?" I asked, feeling my soul drooping down.

"Not a chance," he told me curtly. "Sorry for you and your situation, but getting mixed up in it ain't worth it. Your four grand wouldn't do much more than cover costs, and I sure wouldn't see any profit."

"What should I do?" I asked, aware that I was pleading.

"Hell, you got this far" he said in reply. "Just keep on making up as you go. Get yourself down to the coast and try to hitch a ride somehow. Sign on with a freighter, maybe help out on a skippered sail . . . why did you want Antigua?"

"Read about it in prison," I told him. "No questions asked, phony passports available. Seemed like a good place to start getting lost in the world."

For a long time, we stood in silence.

"Nothing doing?" I asked, still hoping.

"Nope, not a chance," he said. He turned his back, dismissing me.

I spun around and walked out through the big sliding doors. I got back into my forlorn Chevrolet and drove away, full of despair, cursing myself as the blockhead I'd apparently become. While I was running, the flight to freedom with the wings of Bruno Cady had been a hope, a dream. Just reaching Cady had been a goal, some sort of an intermediate haven. I'd taken my cellmate's word that his friend would be my friend, an ally who'd have better ideas on how to avoid capture and escape from the country. Now, I knew better than the supposed honor among thieves.

Again, I was on my own.

I stopped at a cocky-locky motel where I figured to spend the night, hoping no cops would be checking out seedy spots for seedy occupants. I went out about seven in the evening for a supper at a nearby cafe, and then returned to the motel. I turned on the TV and tried to get interested in a movie, but my mind kept superimposing scenes of my inevitable capture and a return to a dreadful life imprisonment.

So it was understandable that I thought it was police pounding on my door.

Way things are going, it figures!

The portentous hammering came again before I could cross to the door, so I opened it with submissive caution, expecting uniformed men with grim expressions and lethal weapons.

Bob Carter - or rather Bruno Cady - stood there, a scowl on his face.

"Well, you gonna let me in or ain't you?" he muttered, not waiting for me to comply as he pushed into the room.

Unable to understand, I reacted slowly. "How'd you find me?"

"Ain't hard with that sorry looking car you're driving," he said bluntly. "I figured you'd hole up somewhere close around here." He paused. "How's Chris?"

"*Now,* you know him?"

"Sure," Cady acknowledged, sitting down on the edge of the bed. "Good kid, ought not to have ever been in jail. He just liked hanging out with people living on the edge." He shook his head. "Not a hateful bone in his body." He looked at me sharply. "That is, he wasn't when I last saw him." He paused, still giving me the once over. "That is 'til he starting being with people like you."

"Mass murderers, you mean?" I said in response.

"All I know is what I read about you in the newspapers," he told me, those hard eyes now fixed on mine. "Where's your buddy?"

"Gianntana?" I didn't want to tell this man too much at this time. "He went his way, I went mine."

"News people think you planned it together."

"Can't help what they think," I countered.

"Why didn't you have him help you out?" Cady asked, his eyes still steady and intimidating. "Looks like he'd be the right guy to touch."

"He gave me some money to get away," I told Cady. "It's helpful, but probably not going to be enough."

He started to speak, but I raised a hand to hold him off. "Why are you here?" I asked. "I thought you'd turned me down."

"Well, it ain't just because of your four thousand . . . although I'll sure take it anyway," he grumbled. "Truth is, I changed my mind. Got to thinking about young Chris and, I figured, if he told you to look me up, then maybe I'd better do a little something to help you on your way. Not for you so much, but kinda to pay young Chris for helping out back a few years."

"You're going to fly me out?" I asked, my face betraying my elation.

"It ain't just a favor, exactly," Cady admitted. "I gotta fly down to Mexico on a little job of my own, and I figure I could sort of accommodate you and do myself a good deal on the same flight."

"Just to Mexico?" I questioned, my elation suddenly deflated.

"Hell, it's outta the country, ain't that what you want?" he asked. "I'll getcha over near the Yucatan coast, and maybe help you get some phony papers that'll getcha to your island."

"The Mexicans big on catching fugitives and sending them back to the States?"

"Well, some are and some aren't," he told me. "You've gotta better chance there than down in New Orleans or over in Miami."

"What's your 'little job'?" I asked.

He smirked. "I'll tell you about it along the way." He turned and nodded at the door. "What about that crummy car out there? You steal it?"

I shook my head. "No, I bought the thing, but I don't have any papers on it. I just thought I'd ditch it someplace when I was through with it." I paused. "How soon?"

"Now's as a good time as any," he told me.

"Now?" I questioned, not able to believe it.

"Get your stuff together and let's go," he instructed, rising to leave.

There wasn't much to get together and, after a couple of minutes, we were out of the motel, loading my duffel bag onto the backseat of the restored Chevy.

"What about my car?" I asked, pointing to the Saturn.

"Leave it," he instructed, waving me to the passenger side of his car.

"They're going to get curious after a couple of days, aren't they?"

He grinned. "In a couple of days, what the hell does it matter?"

I took one last look at the scabby little Saturn as we drove away. Battered and bent as it was, it had served me well. I wished it a good owner, extensive bodywork, a good paint job, and many miles more.

18

Headed back to the airfield, Cady was sort of in a merry mood now, whistling and humming something that sounded out of the late 60's or early 70's. This was a different Cady than I'd met earlier, transformed by the prospect of whatever he or we were going to do.

"You can bunk in at the hanger," he said in a most cordial manner. "It's a cot and a blanket, but I 'spect you've slept worse."

I thought about the bitter cold nights and the spots on my body that still felt numb. "How soon do we go?" I asked.

He gave me a very big grin. "I don't believe in wasting time." He nodded his head. "I'll get you up a couple of hours before dawn."

"Tomorrow?" I expressed my surprise.

He grinned again. "If you'd have come tomorrow, you'd have missed me." His face sobered. "You want to give me the four grand?"

I hesitated, not wanting to ruin his good nature. "How about tomorrow morning?" I suggested, as pleasantly as possible. "Maybe like when we're in the air?"

He didn't grin, he laughed. "Don't blame you, kid," he chortled. "What's to keep me from taking the money, and taking you nowheres." He nodded, agreeing with his own logic and me. "Airborne, tomorrow morning, will be just fine." He gave me sidewise look of mock caution. "Best you keep it tucked in with you with a pistol under your pillow."

I laughed along with him, glad that I did have Bobby Fowler's revolver still in my possession.

At the hanger, he escorted me into a back room with a cot and an adjacent bathroom with a sink and a stool. He told me to turn out the lights and get some sleep, and then he bid me goodnight. I heard him close the big hanger doors and heard the car move away. I left the door open into the main hanger where an overhead nightlight gave a little substance to my surroundings and, lying there in the gloom, I wondered if I dared to be exhilarated.

Am I really safe now? Is this really deliverance?

I took the revolver out of my bag and put it under the pillow.

* * *

I felt his hand on my shoulder, shaking me roughly.

"Get up!" he commanded. "Time to get up."

I was groggy from a very deep sleep and wondered if it had been just a few minutes or a couple of hours since he'd left. "What time is it?"

"Three-thirty," he answered crisply. "Gotta get a move on." He walked out of the room and into the hanger, intent on getting his move on.

I was already dressed, but I took a few moments to tuck my revolver into my bag, to splash some water into my face, and to take a leak. I walked through the hanger and out the side door to where he was waiting by his car. I looked back at the parked airplanes, wondering why he wasn't near one of them.

"We taking one of them?" I asked.

"Nope," he said matter-of-factly, pointing to the restored Chevy. "Get in the car."

I got in, barely closing the door before he backed and then accelerated onto the road. "None of those planes yours?" I asked.

He shook his head. "Nothing back there is mine," he replied, giving a dismissive gesture with the back of his hand. "Rented the place, took care of it for the owner." He smiled at me. "We're leaving it all behind."

I didn't understand, but I didn't much want to ask. It turned out, I didn't need to.

"You know all that time running dope, taking chances, busting my tail, damned near getting killed," he began, "and I don't have a dime of my own to show for it." He gave a bitter laugh. "Oh, I had some pretty good money working for other people, but I pissed it off one way or another. Spent like I had it and always would have it." He took his eyes off the road, for what I considered too long a time, to fix me with his stare. "You know, I even had a couple of airplanes, but I ain't got one now." He finally returned his gaze to the road. "I'm dead broke, kid. That's the truth."

I felt the bottom drop out of my hope. "How are we going to fly to Mexico?"

"I'll have us an airplane," he said, cheerful now, almost gloating. "Matter-of-fact, I got her located. Twin engine Queen Air"

"You're going to steal one?" I guessed, showing some dismay.

He looked at me with surprise. "That bothers you?"

I shrugged.

"That don't seem likely," he mused. "You being a killer and all."

I thought it best not to argue about it.

"You got warm clothes?" he asked.

It seemed an unlikely question.

"Yeah, but . . . aren't we heading south?"

He pointed at the roof of his car. "You'll need warm clothes up there."

"In the airplane? Isn't there a heater?"

He smiled. "Not enough of one."

We drove for about forty-five minutes, moving along at a pretty good clip, and finally came to another little airfield in another small town. It still wasn't dawn, but the light from the night sky did a fair job of silhouetting another gaggle of weary airplanes lined in a row beside a darkened metal hanger. Cady parked the car, opened the trunk, and took out two pieces of luggage; a hard-case and a big, roly-poly soft-side. He handed me the hard-case to balance my duffle bag in my other hand.

"What about the car?" I asked, nodding back at it.

"Forget it," he said, a motion of his head beckoning me through a broken part of the field's wire fence.

"You're leaving your car where you're stealing a plane?" I asked in disbelief.

"Ain't my car," he answered, walking away and along the line of airplanes. "The guy that owns it will find it one of these days."

"You stole the car, too?"

He either didn't hear or didn't bother to answer.

I had a thought about it: *What the hell! I've busted out of jail, taken money that wasn't mine, stolen some old clothes, and played peeping tom on an Oriental lady! Now, I'm aiding and abetting a car and airplane thief, and probably getting ready to be a part of something even more sinister.*

Forget all the pretense of former innocence. What was the title of that old 1930's era movie? *They Made Me A Gangster?* I followed Cady to the last airplane, one larger than the others; a low-wing, two-engine job. I was considerably cheered at the sight of it; a sleek, powerful and substantial airplane.

Cady led me around to the other side of the plane.

"That's great," I groaned. "An open-air airplane. Where the hell's the door?"

"Beats me," Cady said with a cock of his head. "Damned fool used her for a jumpers' plane some of the time, and for hauling all sorts of crap some of the rest. I guess the door just got in his way."

"What kind of crap?"

"Fella ran a sort of delivery service, flying here and over to Texas," he answered. "Sometimes medical supplies, rush packages, sometimes some sort of tools that was needed somewheres." He paused. "Older fella . . . he's been sick lately."

"Why don't you steal something that's got two sides to it?" I grumbled. "We'll probably fall out of this one."

"We'll be okay," Cady assured me, tossing his soft-side bag through the opening. "Put your gear in there and climb in."

He vaulted into the plane and reached out a hand to take the hard-case, leaving me to get my own bag aboard. I crawled inside, feeling about gingerly in the gloom, not knowing what was where. In the darkness, I could hear him securing the other bags, opening a compartment or something.

"Pull a coat outta your bag," he instructed. "Gonna get cold as hell pretty soon."

Fumbling in the dark, I found the winter stuff I'd had in Colorado and Utah. I pulled out my coat and struggled into it after closing my bag.

While I was feeling my way into the co-pilot's seat, Cady was fiddling with the controls on the instrument panel. He flipped a switch and the lights on the panel came on, giving some illumination to the cockpit. Cady's hands were moving here and there; it was as though he'd spent his entire life in this particular cockpit.

I looked around at the interior of the plane. Perhaps, in earlier days, it had been an executive aircraft - a craft of beauty for its owners. Apparently, there had been a succession of owners, each contributing to the deterioration of the plane. There had once been seats, but they'd been taken out long before. The floor of the once luxurious aircraft was scuffed and scratched as were the simulated wood panels on the bulkheads. It was a spacious plane and, through a door ajar in the back, I could see a grimy toilet.

"Why are you stealing this plane?" I asked, turning to Cady with a new variation of my concern. "Does it have some special things about it that make it worth the risk of falling out of?"

"Damned good engine," he responded. He gestured to my lap. "Strap yourself in and you ain't likely to fall out."

For a moment, I thought I'd misheard.

"Did you say engine?"

He nodded.

"There's two, isn't that right?" I asked.

164

Again, he nodded. "Overhauled that engine myself. Did a damned fine job of it, too."

Again, only the reference to one.

At that moment, he touched another switch. The engine to my right coughed, began to stutter, and then settled into a roar. I craned my neck to look back toward the dark hanger, wondering if anyone was around to hear the noise. When I turned back, I noticed the other engine was turning almost lazily.

"Something wrong with that engine?" I asked, nodding to the sluggish engine.

"Nope," Cady responded. "That's the good one."

As if in response, the left engine revved up to full life, matching the roar of its twin. We started forward, Cady working the pedals to steer the airplane out across the hardpan, aiming it toward the semblance of a runway. As we came closer to it, even by starlight, I could see that it was asphalt of considerable age and wear. Once on it, we bounced and jounced severely, the wheels chunking in and out of numerous potholes. The jolting didn't seem to bother Bruno Cady; he gave both engines even greater power, and we began to gather speed. Hastily, I found a seat belt and strapped it around me just as I felt the wheels of the plane leave the ground. The jolting was now replaced by a less than reassuring sense of uneven bobbing, the aircraft rising and dipping, seeming for moments as if barely hanging in the air.

Finally, we were up, surging forward with a steady force, climbing into the night sky. The wind was rushing in the open side of the plane, already cold, and I knew it was mild now as to what it might be in just a few minutes at higher altitudes. I fished in my bag, found gloves, put them on and continued to rummage for anything else to keep me warm.

"Won't be so bad when the sun comes up," Cady commented, enjoying my discomfort. "You might want to stick that bag back there outta the way."

"I'll just leave it here," I told him. "You might decide to bank hard left while I was walking back there."

"You don't trust me?" he asked, merriment in his voice.

"Not anymore than I have to," I said matter-of-factly. I pointed to the right engine. "What's wrong with that one?"

"Needs an overhaul," he answered, looking out at the engine with look of serious contemplation. "Needs it pretty bad."

"How come you didn't overhaul it when you were doing the other one?" I asked.

"Bastard's too cheap," he replied. "Said he'd have to park it 'til he got more money."

"Park it?"

"Yeah," Cady answered. "It ain't really supposed to be in the air."

I took a few moments to digest this.

"Then . . . why are we flying in it?"

He took his time answering, then pointed out at the suspect engine. "Now, that power plant on the starboard side just might do fine this entire trip. Then, again, maybe she'll skip or fuss a bit, but I figured it was worth the chance." He glanced over at me, and I could see the smile on his face. "Then, too, it just might seize up and stop completely."

"What would happen then?"

Suddenly, the plane flipped sharply to its side with the wings nearly vertical, and my duffel bag began to slide toward the opening. I was hanging in my seat, held in only by the tight strap of my seat belt, but I managed to reach out and grab a strap of the bag before it soared out into space.

"Then we'd have to fly the rest of the way like this!" Cady exclaimed with glee. "Just that one engine holding us up."

Immediately, he whipped the airplane back to horizontal.

"You're a laugh-a-minute," I told him. I dragged my bag back toward me, securing it by tying it to the base of my seat.

"You ever fly a plane?" Cady asked.

I shook my head. "Ridden in a couple, that's about it."

"I'm good at it," Cady said cheerfully. "I can fly anything. Always could. Fly big planes, jets if I wanted, but I like piston planes. I like the way they feel, something more primitive yet honest about 'em." His face took on a shine of enthusiasm, warming to a subject that was both familiar and, probably, obsessive. "I can push 'em harder than the manufacturers say I can, and I can fly 'em so slow that any other pilot would stall and crash." He chuckled at his own prowess. "Why'd I pick this plane?" He shrugged. "It may not look like much, but she's got the range we need and the load capacity."

"And what would that load be?" I asked.

He shook his head. "Tell you when the time comes." He fixed me with a stare. "Best you give me that four grand now."

I glanced at my bag. "What if I told you it was in that bag of mine you almost dumped?"

"But it isn't, is it?" he countered.

Reluctantly, I undid my shirt and opened the pouch of the money belt. I counted out two thousand dollars, handed the bills to him, then closed the belt and buttoned my shirt.

"Where's the rest of it?" he said peevishly.

"You'll get it when and if I get clear," I answered. "I'll give you my word on that."

"Much good that is," he scoffed. "Okay, have it your way." He nodded to my bag. "You got your little handgun in there?

The one you kept under your pillow?" He reached into his shirt pocket and dug out a few bullets. "You sleep pretty hard."

For a moment, I was disconcerted, but I recovered without showing it. I took the revolver from the bag. "Good thing you didn't find my extra ammo while you were looking."

This time, Cady did look chagrined. He shrugged and handed over the bullets. "We're a pair, ain't we?"

"I don't think we'll have a lasting relationship," I told him, reloading the revolver. I tucked it inside my coat. "At least, let's hope not."

We flew on in silence for a while, watching dawn break. The sun rose, appearing in a crack between the horizon and a cloud cover. Shortly after, it disappeared inside a gray, thick haze.

"Which way we heading?" I asked after a while.

"In the general direction of Texas," he answered. "Just this side of the Gulf."

"Aren't they keeping an eye on airplanes along the border?" I asked anxiously. "AWAC planes or whatever they're using?"

He shrugged. "Lot's of traffic in the air. They might think we're suspicious and, then again, they'll likely not. Think we're just a family going home from New Orleans to Houston or maybe some business folks flying back to Galveston."

"When do we go into Mexico?"

He shrugged again. "Whenever I feel like it." He turned to catch my gaze. "It's instinct, nothing more. I just guess where's a good place to dip south, and that's when I go."

"Instinct? Meaning what?"

He gave me a grin. "A feeling that nobody will notice that we're changing course."

"What if they do?" I asked with some alarm.

"Well, it wouldn't be a good thing, would it?" he said in the form of a question, and then laughed.

I didn't think it was a laughing matter.

19

Early morning turned into daytime and we flew on. We were still over land, droning along, with wind whipping in through the open side of the plane. I thought I'd left the cold and winter behind, but I continued to search through my duffel bag, adding whatever warmth I could from the clothing inside. Cady seemed not to mind the cold at all, sitting behind the wheel, apparently calm and peaceful, doing what appeared to be his calling in life. He seemed so nonchalant, I was annoyed.

"You ever been caught?" I asked, my peevishness showing.

He heard the anger in my voice and it amused him. "Yeah," he acknowledged, nodding his head. "Couple of times. Nothing much ever came of it. Spent a couple of months in the hoosegow here, and another couple there. Usually was able to buy my way out . . . never ever caught much on me."

"But you're broke now?"

He smiled. "In a manner of speaking."

"What the hell are we doing, going to Mexico?" I asked. "I know it's something illegal, but what I don't know. You doing this for somebody else, for yourself . . . or what?"

"Need to know, buddy-boy," he muttered. "And you ain't got a need to know. Not yet anyway."

"Whatever I'm getting into, I got a need to know," I said in exasperation. "What is this? A drug run? Bringing back illegals? What?"

He didn't answer and, after a long while, I decided he wasn't going to.

"I guess it won't hurt to talk a bit," he said, unexpectedly. "Help us pass the time, and we ain't got a flight movie." He cocked his head toward Mexico. "Yeah, I gotta deal set up. There's folks waiting for me to set down in a little flat place where we pick us up a payload. One big enough to set me up for quite a spell, maybe retire."

"And?" I prompted.

"And that's why I brought you along," he responded. "I need a hand in making the transaction . . . and I figured you'd be willing to help out in exchange for getting you outta the country."

I would've asked another question, but the starboard engine made a hell of a noise and, as I glanced out at it, a belch of oily smoke appeared and instantly disappeared. Maybe it was my imagination, but I thought I saw the blades of the propeller falter for a moment and then return to a blur.

"Damn," Cady said mildly, not unduly alarmed.

"What was that?" I asked fearfully.

"Fucking engine," Cady said with little expression. "She'll probably give us some trouble before we're done." So saying, he banked the plane, and headed south.

"We going to put 'er down?" I asked, really apprehensive.

He looked at me in surprise. "Hell, no," he drawled. "We're going to Mexico."

"Over water?" I yelped.

"Shortest way," he explained. "We'll join the parade."

"What parade?"

He pointed up to his right.

I looked where he pointed and, tiny in the sky, I saw another airplane; a private plane of some sort, whether jet or prop I couldn't tell.

"We'll just fly along with the folks heading down to Cancun and Cozumel," he told me. "We're just one of a bunch."

"Don't they all have some sort of flight plans or something?" I asked. "Aren't you supposed to have something like that?"

"Yeah, if the pilot ain't too lazy, too contrary, or too damned stupid," he acknowledged. "Here we go."

I looked out and saw the land slide under a whole lot of water. I turned to watch the shore becoming distant behind us and, finally, disappear.

About that time, the good engine coughed, and I turned in panic.

Cady was watching me, his eyes alight with malevolent humor as the engine sputtered and faltered, then stopped altogether. We stared at each other for a few moments, then he touched something on the instrument panel and the engine fired into action once again, regaining its steady roar and steady performance.

"Pretty funny," I said.

"Just wanted to test your nerves," he said with smugness.

"My pants are still clean if that's what you're asking," I told him, angry as hell at this wild-assed baboon.

"I guess you're the right sort," he said, saying it so I knew it was sarcasm and not a compliment.

"Why don't you tell me about this big deal of yours," I suggested; anything to get him out of the deranged prankster mood.

He shook his head.

"What difference does it make?" I persisted. "It's not like you're likely to include me."

"You can count on that," he hooted. "All you're getting, buddy, is a ride outta the country."

"For which I'm paying," I reminded him.

"Look," he said, his words coming in an impatient manner. "When you came through that door, I wanted no part of you. This trip was already set before I set eyes on you, and you were lucky enough to be an afterthought. I'll take what little bit of money you're going to give me, but it occurred to me that I might need just a little help, someone to ride shotgun with me on this job."

"These are dangerous people?"

He nodded. "Not that I expect trouble . . . I've dealt with 'em before. We pick up the goods, pay for 'em—"

"I thought you said you were broke," I cut in. "Pay with what?"

"And then we'll be on our way," he resumed. "It just seemed to be wise to have more than one of us just in case someone decides that one is easier to subtract than two."

"On our way where?" I asked, sensing more danger than he'd indicated.

He gave me his sincere smile. "I'll drop you off, and that'll be the last you'll see of me."

I glanced at the open side of the plane.

He laughed aloud. "Not to worry. You've got that other two grand in your money belt, so I'll land you safe and sound to get that."

"That'd be pretty small potatoes."

"I covet every little bit," he responded merrily.

We droned on, the sun climbing higher, turning the end-less water beneath us into a dull silver sheen. On that now ominous ocean, I knew that ships of commerce and of plea-sure sailed with complacency and that, here and there, there were also drug smugglers and even pirates sailing among the innocent and carefree. I even supposed that we shared the air with other planes that were taking the risk of running cocaine, heroin, and God knows what else into the United States.

We didn't speak for quite a while. I gazed out at the sky-line, hoping to see some land, not at all comfortable with our passage over water. From time to time, Cady would start a nonchalant whistle, some golden oldie tune that I'd heard somewhere, but couldn't put words to. He seemed happy, apparently much at home in his element, guiding his stolen plane across the Gulf. If I didn't know better, I'd have taken him for a gentle soul, a man at one with the aesthetics of flight, content among the wispy clouds. With nothing much else to do, I studied the gauges on the panel, figuring out which one was air speed, which one was the altimeter, and the functions of a few other dials.

One gauge alarmed me.

"We got enough gas?" I asked.

"Aviation fuel," he corrected.

"Whatever," I said in irritation, pointing at the gauge. "Do we have an extra tank?"

He shook his head and smiled his insolent smile at me. "Plenty enough to get us where we're going."

"You have a filling station lined up? For flying back?"

"Don't need one," he told me. "I'll leave this bird in Mexico. If the old coot that owns her wants her back, he can come after it." Suddenly, the plane rocked violently, accompanied by a thun-der of sound as something whipped past us.

A rocket, a missile - God knows what!

"What was that?" I cried out, almost a shriek.

Cady gave me another of his grins, unperturbed. "F-15 Tomcat. One of the military boys giving us the once over," he commented. "Looking to see if we're druggies."

"How close did he come?" I asked indignantly.

"Oh, a wingspan or two," Cady speculated. "Think that's bad, wait 'til he comes back."

"What do you mean?"

Cady nodded toward the distant horizon. "If he thinks it's worthwhile, he'll come right back at us, playing chicken, seeing what we'll do."

"And what will we do?"

"Nothing much," Cady responded. "Most druggies head for the drink, to fly low and slow, hoping he'll go away."

"What are we going to do?"

"Well, we'll just stay right on course, and let him break off," Cady told me. "We might shake a fist at him as he goes by. Outraged private pilot, you know."

Minutes passed.

"I guess he doesn't think we're worth the effort," Cady said finally. "If we was heading back to the States, I 'spect he'd spend more time with us."

"I don't follow," I told him.

"Their job's to keep stuff from coming in," he informed me. "He could jolt me around a bit, call in a report on me . . . you never know." He chuckled. "Hate to disappoint him. Like I said, this baby won't be flying back."

"Where do we go after the—"

"You ain't got a need to know," he cut in. "Not 'til I say so."

For a half-hour, he went silent, not responding to any of my comments or questions. After a few attempts, I gave up and started staring at the landless sea. My thoughts flew back to the Colorado prison, thinking about what I'd be doing at about this time, about Chris and how he was making out. I imagined jail yard conversations which would be about me.

"Kev did it!" he'd be saying. *"He's out and gone!"*

"He's dead somewhere," someone would say in scorn. *"Out there somewhere frozen to death in some ditch, some clump of woods. Somebody, some day, will find his rotten body and that'll be the end of him."*

"Not Kev," Chris would retort. *"He's away clean"*

I wish!

20

I don't recall that I dozed. Perhaps I was always awake, but somewhat spaced out with the monotony of the flight. I was surprised to see that we were over land once again, much lower in altitude than before. Although I didn't have much sense of the distance to be covered or the speed involved, I doubted that we had crossed the Gulf to the Yucatan Peninsula. My guess was that we'd turned somewhere into the mainland of Mexico where we were speeding, lower and lower, across a brown, desolate landscape.

"Where are we?" I asked.

"Heading for the Promised Land," Cady cackled. "Everything's coming up roses."

"More like poppies, I'd guess," I responded.

He shrugged and nodded. "For a criminal, you don't have much of a bad ass attitude." He gave me a glance. "Now you're into dope dealing, so what's the problem?"

"Nothing, I guess," I answered.

We were skimming over the land now, dangerously near the rough, hilly, arid land.

"Is there a reason why we're five feet above the ground?"

He turned his head slightly to smile, but didn't take his eyes away from his line of flight. "No real reason," he replied. "Just for the fun of it."

We continued on for another ten or fifteen minutes when he pulled back on the wheel, nosed up, and flew at a slightly higher altitude. He nodded ahead, directing my view to a stretch of ground that looked almost level, almost clear of rocks and scrub brush. We made a pass over it, Cady banking the plane and looking down over his left shoulder. I craned to look past him and got a glimpse of a vehicle down below and a couple of men, one of them waving.

"Rendezvous as scheduled," Cady said with a note of triumph. "Flight attendants, please prepare for landing."

"You're not going to land there?" I asked.

"Yeah, if we're lucky," he responded.

We circled back as Cady brought the plane in fast, pulling back on the wheel, almost creating a stall. Then, he timed his recovery beautifully, the plane sinking down, the wheels bouncing, jolting us hard as we landed. We continued to bounce as we sped along the uneven, ground; the metal of the airplane screeching at the stress of our wild, wrenching ride.

"Nice landing," I commented as he cut back the power and the airplane skidded to a stop.

He gave me another of his roguish smiles, then gunned one engine and turned the plane around to face in the other direction. He throttled the engine back, letting both continue to run on idle. "Ready for takeoff," he informed me. He unbuckled his seat belt and moved to the back of the plane to drag the hard case out of a storage bin. He motioned for me to join him.

"Here's the way this thing is going to work," he said, gesturing to the case. "In here's the money we're paying these guys for the goods they're delivering."

At that moment, a black, mud-crusted SUV came to an abrupt stop nine or ten yards away from the plane. It turned its tailgate toward us and parked. Three Hispanic men got out of the SUV, two of them heavy, brutish thugs. Both of them moved to open the tailgate while the third, a slim, confident man that I estimated to be in his late thirties or early forties, took a couple of steps to approach the plane. All of them carried wicked looking weapons, the two thugs with assault-style rifles, and the slim man with a machine pistol in his right hand held at his side.

"C'mon," Cady instructed, leaping out of the plane and hauling the hard case with him. He turned to hail the slim man with an enthusiastic greeting. "Luis! So good to see you, again!"

Of the three, this Luis seemed the most sinister.

I stepped down out of the plane, feeling immediately the sultry heat. I needed to shed the heavy coat, but I didn't want to be without the revolver in its pocket.

The sinister man gave a slight nod to acknowledge the greeting, but his attention came immediately to me, his manner menacing. "Who's this man, Senor Cady?" He spoke English very well with just a touch of his native accent.

"Young friend of mine," he prefaced his introduction. "Kevin . . . ah—"

"Kevin will do," I cut in, not too eager to have my identity widely known, even in the center of nowhere in Mexico.

"I don't like this, Cady," the man, Luis, said after a moment of glacial regard, his voice severe. "Where's Anthony?"

Anthony? I hadn't heard that name before, and I wondered who?

"Unable to make the trip this time," Cady explained with an unperturbed air. He gestured to me. "Kevin's okay, you've got my word on that."

"It isn't like Anthony to miss this trip, not to represent the buyers," Luis persisted, his eyes upon me. "Not like him to trust the deal to others."

"He had no choice," Cady said with a heavy sigh. "He got cut up in a New Orleans bar, someplace he ought not to have been with a big deal going down."

Luis considered this. "Is he dead?"

Cady shook his head. "No, he's gonna be okay, but he's living on morphine for a few days." Cady hoisted the suitcase. "But we've got the money." To prove it, he laid the suitcase on the ground and knelt to open it. He opened the lid to display thick stacks of top denomination United States bills. He took one bundle of $100's and handed it to Luis for his examination. He waited for the nod of approval from Luis, then closed the suitcase and left it lying on the ground. He rose and spoke to Luis. "What about you? Got the stuff?"

Luis nodded and turned to speak to the other two in Spanish. They came forward, each carrying a large duffel bag. One, a burly hombre, set his bag beside the money suitcase and opened the drawstrings. He reached in for a plastic bag of white powder and showed it to Cady.

"Want to test it?" Luis asked.

Cady shook his head. "We've done enough business before, Luis," he said affably. "I know it's the good stuff."

"You should test it," Luis declared.

Again, Cady shook his head and turned to me. "You stick with Luis and help him count the money while we load the plane." With a nonchalant sort of salute to the drug dealer, he sauntered toward the plane, expecting the two men to follow with their bags.

Luis shrugged and waved his two men to take the bags to the plane. While we watched, Cady entered the plane and took each of the two bags as the two men hoisted them aboard.

Luis took a step toward the suitcase and motioned for me to join him as he knelt to raise the lid. He turned to me as he prepared to examine the contents. "How do you know Cady?"

I didn't answer. Conflicting thoughts raced through my head.

Perhaps it might look bad if I had little acquaintance with my pilot. Perhaps it might be worse if I knew him well.

"Are you his partner?" Luis asked, his eyes upon me, his tone demanding an answer.

"Not exactly," I replied.

He didn't like the answer, but he turned his attention to the suitcase of money, his hand reaching out to extract another stack of bills. He thumbed through the bundle, riffling the bills, and then suddenly stopped. Immediately, his stern expression turned to consternation.

"*Ay Carajo!*" he cried out, his hands ripping the band wrap from the money sheaf. He laid the top few hundred dollar bills aside and examined the underlying ones. My first reaction was puzzlement; the bills looked the same, but then I saw that they were not. Close, very close, but not quite the same. He tore apart two other stacks, examining bills masquerading as authentic money. He came up to me, fury in his face and voice. "What is this? What are you trying to pull?"

Before I had a chance to respond, we were both startled by the roar of the twin engines. As one, Luis and I turned to the sound, astonished by the sight of the Queen Air beginning to move, the two henchmen scrambling to get out of the way as the plane gained ground speed. For a few seconds, we were frozen in positions, not quite comprehending what was happening.

Suddenly, I knew and I was sick with self-reproach.

I should have known better!

Luis was only a second later in coming to the same conclusion: With a shout of angry command, Luis ran after the plane, firing his machine pistol at it. The two men hastily unslung the rifles from their shoulders and fired with scant attention for aiming. The plane was rolling fast now, the fusillade from the combined firearms seeming to have no effect as it increased its distance. Then, the Queen Air lifted off and climbed swiftly well out of range.

21

As the enraged hoodlums turned back toward me, I thought of the revolver in my coat pocket. Instantly, I realized that my four bullets and faulty aim would have no chance against the hail of fire that would surely come my way. Other than a nearby cactus, there was no place to hide.

I raised my hands above my head.

Luis walked back toward me with cold anger in his expression, fitting a clip into his machine pistol. "Do you have a gun?"

I nodded. "In my coat pocket," I answered, nodding to my right.

"Perhaps you should have used it," he said, coming close, raising the deadly weapon. He reached into my coat pocket, took out the revolver and tossed it away. "Now, there is no chance for you at all."

"Would you kill an innocent man?" I asked, my voice showing my fear.

He nodded. "I have, quite often."

"If I were a part of this, why would he leave me?" I argued, watching the muzzle of his pistol.

"A greedy man. More money for himself," Luis answered calmly, aiming the pistol. Loping toward us, the two burly hombres took their places beside him, scowling their frustration and anger. They were mean-looking, anxious for blood and barely able to restrain their rage, wanting to get at me themselves.

"Look," I said desperately. "I paid him to fly me out of the country. I knew nothing about the business you had with him."

"You made a poor decision," Luis said without emotion. "You must pay for our loss."

"I can get the money back," I shouted, grasping for the impossible. "And your dope, too!"

It brought a sad smile to Luis. "I don't blame you for trying," he said, almost sympathetically. He gestured to his companions. "They want me to kill you."

"Is killing me worth more than a couple of million dollars?" I persisted, guessing at the sum.

I saw the first sign of hesitation, the muzzle of the machine pistol lowered a quarter of an inch.

"We will find him and get our money," he told me, aiming again. "Even should he escape us, we have people in the States, and when he returns—"

"He's not heading back!" I broke in, speaking in a rush. "Maybe you'll find him here or somewhere else, but maybe it'll be long after the dope is gone, and long after the money is deposited in an offshore bank." I continued to chatter, hoping the end of each frenzied sentence wouldn't bring an explosion from his gun. "I can get your money and the dope back in a matter of hours. I *know* where he's going!"

Luis lowered the machine pistol, much to the irritation of his companions. "Tell me where," he commanded.

I shook my head. "I'll take you to him, but I won't tell you because you'll shoot me as soon as you know."

Luis considered this for a moment, and then turned to one of the men and spoke a command. This man, a broad-shouldered, big-bellied barbarian with a long, deep, whitish scar across the left side of his face, smiled broadly and revealed expensive gold inlays. He nodded, almost a motion of gratitude rather than servitude, and ran toward the SUV. He displayed an amazingly agile sprint for such a large and suet-laden figure. He opened a side door, stuck his head in for a couple of seconds, and then whipped around and held a gleaming machete high over his head. He slammed the car door and trotted towards us, twirling the wicked blade with great dexterity. It was a show of deadly skill that brought to me an even greater and sickening fear. He came up fast, moving past Luis, now within three feet of me. He paused and glanced at his leader for instructions.

"Manuel is an expert with the machete," Luis said with a trace of regret. "He can do many marvelous tricks with his blade." He made a little gesture to his underling, a sort of a signal. The desperado lashed his heavy blade out at me with such sudden speed that I scarcely saw it, only a flash as it fanned past my face.

I jumped back, far too late, frightened and amazed that he'd missed me.

Then, I felt the blood begin to stream from my forehead down into my eyes and felt the sting of the wound. I clapped my hand to my forehead and felt for the gash, fearing what I would find.

"No more than a scratch," Luis said in his gentle, almost apologetic manner. "Probably wouldn't even leave a scar." He waited for me to comprehend my situation. "Now will you tell me where we can find Cady?"

"If you kill me, you'll never know," I answered shakily.

"Manny will not kill you swiftly," the drug dealer told me. "At my command, he will cut you apart, piece by piece." He paused again, a touch of drama. "The fingers of your hand, the hand itself, a foot, an ear—"

"Oh, I will tell you," I interrupted. "I'll name a place, maybe the same one over and over, maybe a different one when the pain is intense. Maybe I'll tell you the right one, but I might just tell you lies." I pressed my hand harder on the forehead wound, trying to stanch the flow of blood. "I know you will not let me live. You may even kill me as horribly as you've described . . . but you'll never know for sure where Cady is heading, and where you can find him."

Luis regarded me for a long, long time.

An eternity.

"I don't think you're that strong, Mister . . ."

"Kevin," I reminded him of my name.

"But I admire your . . ." He paused, searching for a word.

"Audacity?"

He smiled, recognizing the word, and gave me a polite bow. "Indeed. You do appear to have some courage."

I shook my head. "I'm scared as hell."

His henchman, the machete expert, sensed the change in our conversation. He glared at his superior and, for a moment, I was anxious for the drug dealer as well as for myself. Luis returned the look with such evil intensity that the desperado stepped back, cowed by his leader.

Luis turned those cold eyes to me, yet a slight smile came to his lips. "I think you're bluffing, Mister Kevin, talking to keep yourself alive." He gave a shrug. "I will give you an opportunity to save yourself." He gestured to the car. "You will guide us to him."

"And will you let me go when I do?" I asked.

"I'll decide that if and when," he replied. "It is enough that I give you life for however long I choose."

While he herded me toward the SUV, the two underlings gathered up what they could find of the scattered money, both good and counterfeit, and I saw Manuel find my revolver. He stooped, picked it up, examined it, and then stuck it in the belt at his back.

You can never have enough guns, I suppose!

They loaded the suitcase and their weapons in the passenger side of the front seat. They put me in the cargo area of the vehicle, not even allowing me a seat. Luis sat on the bench seat in front of me with Manuel, while the other man got in behind the wheel. Manuel and Luis took turns looking back at me, holding their rapid-firing weapons ready should I try to fight or escape. I sat very still, my back against the tailgate. I considered whether I, should the situation present itself, could spring the handle and leap to freedom.

"It's locked," Luis said calmly, obviously reading my mind.

I shrugged. "Probably break my neck if I tried."

Luis chuckled.

We bounced along over the rough terrain for a number of miles, and then came to a slightly smoother lane called a road. The driver stopped the car and looked back questioningly to Luis.

"Which way?" Luis asked.

Now, of course, I hadn't the foggiest idea of which way Bruno Cady had taken his plane. I was pretty sure that Luis knew this as well. I had the feeling that he was toying with me, stringing out my life simply to enjoy my terror. Whatever the reason, to quote the old adage: *"Where there's life, there's hope."*

"Where are we?" I asked.

"Between Tampico and Vera Cruz," Luis answered.

I almost said Vera Cruz, but the name of the other city jogged my memory, reminding me, finally, of the words to that golden oldie tune that Cady had whistled from time to time, something about a city on the Gulf of Mexico.

"Tampico," I directed, hoping my voice showed a confidence.

"Where in Tampico?" Luis asked with a sinister smile.

"I tell you more as we go," I replied. "No specifics 'til we're closer."

Luis stared at me for a long few moments, then shrugged and gave instructions to the driver in Spanish. The driver nodded and turned the SUV left, tires spinning as he gunned it down the gravel road. We drove on, meeting other automobiles once in a while, passing several with scant concern for the safety of their occupants or ours.

"Would you like to know why you're still alive?" Luis asked unexpectedly.

It didn't seem the kind of question that called for a verbal response, so I merely nodded.

"I ran out of bullets," he told me. "Used them all shooting at your plane."

"Cady's plane," I corrected him. "I recall that you were reloading when you came up to me."

"Yes, but it gave just a little time for my anger to subside a bit." He laughed. "There was something else as well."

I lifted an eyebrow.

"You didn't run, you didn't cower . . . you took a deep breath," he told me. "You were ready to die."

"I didn't think I had much choice," I admitted.

"I was rather impressed," he continued. "As angry as I was, it seemed to be . . . to me, it was an act of bravery."

I wasn't about to tell him how mistaken he was.

"You didn't beg, you didn't whine," Luis said with a sort of respect. "I liked that in you."

"Thank you," I said modestly.

"Tell me about yourself, Mister Kevin," he said, a note of command coming into his voice. "Just why was Cady flying you out of the country? Are you a fugitive?"

I decided to be candid. "I escaped from prison. My cellmate told me about Bruno Cady and told me, if I ever got out, Cady would help me."

"What were you in prison for?" he asked.

Again, I decided to play the criminal. "Murder."

He cocked his head at that. "Really? A crime gone wrong? A crime of passion? What?"

"I shot two people," I told him, embellishing things a bit. "One on purpose, another who just happened to be there."

He didn't say anything for a few minutes.

"Did it bother you?" he asked. "Killing those people?"

I didn't know which way to go on this, but I decided to hedge my reply. "Some," I told him. "The second one, I guess."

He cocked his head again. "It never bothers me," he confided. "I have no feeling about killing. It's just something that, if it needs to be done, it needs to be done." He stared at me, seeking my gaze. "Do you find that disturbing?

I looked into his eyes, hoping I wouldn't look away.

"A person who has no feeling about others, what is he called?" he asked.

I shrugged.

"Come on," he said impatiently. "You know what he is called."

"Sociopath," I said uneasily.

"Psychopath" he responded matter-of-factly. "I've thought about that a lot."

"How do you mean?"

"Well," he began, warming to his subject, "when you kill someone, and you have no feelings about it . . . no regrets, no guilt, you have to wonder about yourself."

I nodded.

"You know, you read about such people and you think, *I'm* one," he admitted. "But, then, I don't particularly enjoy it either."

"That's good," I said lamely.

"I think it is," he went on seriously. "It would make me some sort of a monster if I really liked doing it. Do you think I'm a monster?" He paused, waiting for my response.

"It's just business," I said hopefully.

He nodded. "What I'm saying is that I feel nothing." He paused again, reconsidering. "Of course if I'm angry, if the person has really done something to make me mad, I *do* get a certain satisfaction."

"I'd suppose so," I said, just to be saying something.

"Yes," he nodded, agreeing with his own assessment. Then, he remembered to question me. "Did you kill out of anger or, perhaps, like me?"

I didn't like where this was going, so I changed the subject. "When we get to Tampico, you said you'd be appreciative if I got your money and . . . and, ah . . . your materials back."

He nodded again. "I don't think you have any idea of where to find Bruno Cady, but if you do, I might let you off." He nodded to his henchmen. "If you don't, it would make me look bad if I didn't kill you."

"I'll find him," I said, desperately hoping for some miracle.

"I just wanted you to know that I won't enjoy killing you," he said.

"But it won't bother you either," I finished.

"Exactly," he agreed. "As you said yourself, it would only be business." He smiled at me. "As a matter of fact, I rather like you."

22

We drove for a couple of hours over back roads, moving across a couple of major highways that these drug runners apparently liked to avoid. The day was wearing down, the shadows of desert cacti lengthening across the arid landscape. Of course, I thought and thought, trying to think of some way of getting away, but there seemed to be no possibility. Locked in the rear of the vehicle with Luis, Manuel, and the driver; with all wickedly armed and dangerous, the situation seemed hopeless.

There had been no further discussion about the business of cold-blooded killing, Luis apparently having had his say on the subject. The trio spoke in Spanish, a few words here and there that I suspected concerned me, but I couldn't be sure. If Luis had taken a liking to me, as he had said, it was apparent that his companions had not. I caught numerous malevolent stares from Manuel, and I could see the driver darting equally malicious glances back in his rear view mirror. I had the feeling Manuel was suggesting my instant demise, but Luis was, so far and for whatever reason, resisting such action. I was nervous and, despite Luis' claim of detachment, I felt that he was rather enjoying my discomfort.

"What really happened to Anthony?" he asked at one time. "Did Cady tell anything near the truth?"

"I don't even know who Anthony is," I replied; my bewilderment obvious.

"He represents the people whose money you stole," Luis informed me. "They will be very angry."

"The money Cady stole," I insisted on reminding him. "Along with mine."

Luis shrugged.

Had I suggested the piss stop, I'm sure it would have instantly put them on the alert. They'd have suspected some sort of a trick for me to get away and, if they'd permitted it at all, they'd have watched me with even greater scrutiny. However, it was the driver who first called for relief in his native tongue. Manuel joined in the plea, and even Luis seemed to consider it a good idea. Gratefully heeding a permissive command, the driver pulled over by the side of the road and leaped out, obviously most anxious to relieve himself.

Luis gave me a questioning look.

"It would be a relief," I admitted.

Luis considered this, and then turned to his hefty companion. "Watch him closely, Manny!"

Manuel seemed greatly distressed, more for his bladder than for the duty of watching me.

"Big guy speaks English?" I asked.

"He's bilingual," Luis answered smugly. "What about you?"

I shook my head, admitting one of my shortcomings.

We all got out and stood beside the road. The driver and I were the first to irrigate the desert, Manuel standing uncomfortably watchful behind me. The driver finished first, and he began an earnest Spanish dialogue with Luis. After I zipped, I stepped to one side.

And Manuel did an unbelievably foolish thing. He stepped forward anxiously, fumbled to open his fly, then took aim at a barrel cactus three feet away and tried to bore a hole in it.

The opportunity was there in an instant and, instantly, I knew it.

To my left, Luis and the driver were facing each other, intent on their conversation. Manuel was totally engrossed in his stream of consciousness, completely unconcerned with me. He was totally forgetful of my revolver - or should I say Bobby Fowler's former handgun - tucked in his belt at the back of his trousers.

Let me tell you about what happens when a man is in the middle of a strong pee. Scarcely anything will make him cut it off, not even the sensation of feeling that revolver being pulled right out of his pants. Believe it or not, he *did* turn his head in alarm, but it didn't quite diminish his flow.

"Hey!" he said, not even a shout, but an exclamation of dismay.

You can understand a man really doesn't want to wet his pants even if an enemy has just taken one of his guns away.

I ignored Manuel for a moment, knowing Luis was my first concern. He was turning, curious about the strange utterance from his underling, his arm raising the machine pistol.

Without hesitation, I shot him in the right foot.

Luis went down with a howl of pain, dropping his machine pistol, both hands clutching his right brogan. I picked up the machine pistol while he was writhing in pain, glanced at the driver who, unarmed, was staring at me in absolute shock. I glanced back at Manuel who, at last, had choked off his water-works and was turning to me.

I shot him in the left foot.

With two of them on the ground, crying and swearing both in Spanish and English, clutching their injured tootsies in some sort of one-legged lotus positions, I turned back to the driver.

"No, Senor!" he begged me. "No, no, Senor!"

"Sorry," I said, hoping he understood English, then shot him exactly as I had the others.

Now, this may have seemed cruel and despicable of me, but you must remember that these people were not really nice. Luis had admitted a psychopathic killer tendency; Manuel had demonstrated a lethal proficiency with the machete; and, well, the driver was hanging around with bad company. If I'd lived up to my criminal reputation, I would have killed the lot of them, but it seemed the humane thing to keep them off their feet, so to speak. As they rolled around on the ground, moaning and carrying on, I had a fleeting, callous thought: They might be limping for the rest of their lives.

"*Adios, amigos!*" I said, flaunting my bilingual capability as I hurried toward their SUV.

"You'll die for this!" Luis shouted after me. "I will find you! You will not die easily!"

The driver had, in his hurry, left the keys in the ignition.

"Way to go, amigos," I said aloud to myself.

I got in, started the auto, and took a last look at the fear-some threesome thrashing about, trying to take shoes from their injured feet. I gunned the SUV away, spraying a little gravel in their direction as a final spurt of indignity.

Make no mistake; I was not taking Luis' threat lightly. I had injured a very bad man, and I had no doubt that he would likely be another of my concerns in the near future. It was certain that he intended to kill me; it would not matter to him that what I had done was to save my own life. By unbelievable good fortune, I had defeated him - no pun intended - and shamed him in front of his subordinates. Luis would not forget me.

After a few miles - kilometers I suppose - I pulled off the highway onto a dirt road, parked the SUV and looked around inside, taking stock of what I'd confiscated along with the auto. The rifles were in the passenger's side of the front seat, along with the suitcase with the pseudo-fortune. I opened it and did a quick tally of the money. I was surprised to discover, while not a fortune, there was nearly ten thousand in authentic bills inside. Bruno Cady had run a successful if risky scam: He had a couple of stacks of real money, one of which he'd handed to Luis. For all the others, he'd placed two, sometimes three genuine hundred-dollar bills on the top and bottom of each stack, filling the middle of each bundle with counterfeit bills. Now, it became clear the role Cady had always planned for me: I was to be the Judas goat tethered to the counterfeit money, a body to be sacrificed when the drug runners learned of his trickery. I thought of the man that Luis had mentioned, Anthony. Luis had expected to see this man, apparently someone who had played a regular part in their previous dealings. I wondered if that person might be found, someday, in a shallow grave somewhere in Louisiana. I had no doubt that, for Cady to have given up even these thousands of dollars, it meant the drug money was probably two or three million or more. Undoubtedly, the actual money was packed in that soft-side bag that Cady had guarded so intently.

I sorted out the authentic bills and put them in my money belt. I was undecided whether to keep the counterfeit stacks or not. Although Luis had not been fooled, these were not bad replications of the real thing. Probably quite foolishly, I thought that they could possibly be of use to me somewhere along in my flight. Or, perhaps, I wanted to confront Cady with this evidence of duplicity whenever I caught him. Whatever, I decided to keep the phony bills along with the real McCoy.

After that, I checked my revolver and discovered the next to last bullet had gone into the driver's foot. I didn't think a one-bullet gun would be a good choice when I had so many other options, so I chucked the revolver along with the rifles in the scrub brush. Then, I placed the machine pistol - something I discovered to be a mini-Uzi - and several clips of ammunition into the suitcase along with the bogus money. I continued my search of the automobile and found a loaded Glock automatic in the glove compartment. Although I'd never had much use for guns in my life, suffering bad fortune with the one in Denver, I nevertheless felt better about my growing arsenal of deadly weapons. I stuck the Glock under my belt in the back, to carry much in the same manner as Manuel, hoping I wouldn't blow my ass off.

Through the gathering darkness, I drove without much knowledge of where I was going. Finally, I came upon a well-paved highway and turned toward what might be the correct direction for Tampico. There were quite a number of automobiles moving along; a pretty good indication there was something ahead worth driving to. After a few minutes, I saw a road sign giving me the distance in kilometers to Tampico, and I felt a surge of satisfaction. I drove at a constant speed, trying once again to flow with the traffic, neither speedster nor slowpoke.

It was late in the evening when I drove into the city, not at all certain of which way to go or what to do. It was not exactly a resort city from the looks of it - more of an industrial metropolis. It was a port city and the signs of the oil industry it served were evident. Oil storage tanks were everywhere, Pemex trucks and signs wherever I looked, and much of what I saw of the city had a sort of a grungy look. It was almost as though the oil had permeated the streets, the buildings, even the trees and shrubs. I drove aimlessly, turning this street to the left, another to the right, more or less just exploring the city.

I *was* aimless. I didn't have much idea of what I intended to do, but finding Bruno Cady seemed to be a goal. What I'd do if I found him, I didn't know, but I suspected the Glock at the small of my back might have a purpose after all. I was mad, angry as hell at what he'd done to me. Except for exceptional good luck, I'd have been dead, either by Manuel's machete slices or by bullets from Luis. Human sacrifices, I understand, were quite common in this part of Mexico many years ago, and Cady had callously tried to add another corpse to the total - mine.

My thoughts of Luis and his band of lame desperadoes worried me. I don't know how much clout the drug runner had in these parts, but I doubted he would be out of action for a long time. Even now, the word might be out to look for a gringo in a black SUV heading into Tampico.

I ditched the auto, parking it on a side street not far from the docks. I took the suitcase, repositioned the Glock inside my shirt, and set out down one of the waterfront streets.

Let me tell you, this place looked tough. There were dozens of little bars, none of which looked safe to enter. As I passed by the open doors of each one, sounds blared forth of loud Mexican music, shouts and cackles of laughter, drunken exclamations, and occasional barks of unmistakable anger. Even with a gun in the suitcase and another in my shirt, slinking along the dark streets, I was wary as a mouse in an alley of hungry cats.

I came to a bar that looked a little less dingy and dangerous, a bright place on an otherwise dimly lit street.

As good as any, I guess.

I turned through the entryway and almost faltered in my step. It was not nearly as bright on the inside as the vivid lighting outside. Here was a large room, shadows everywhere, the bar showing the best illumination. Heads turned as I walked further into this iniquity den. There were sailors of different nationalities, Mexican men of many different sizes and shapes, and a few immodest Mexican women scattered among the patrons. Most eyes looked at me first, and then to the suitcase I carried.

With grim resolve, I screwed up my courage and headed straight for the bar and found an empty stool. A bartender turned to me with a quizzical look.

"I speak only English," I told him matter-of-factly, not apologetically.

The bartender regarded me for a few moments more. "I speak seven languages," he told me with a nod of his head to his customers. "We have an international clientele." He was a heavy Hispanic man, in his late forties or early fifties, I guessed. There was nothing pleasant about his expression, but I thought I detected some basic good humor.

"I spend only United States money," I also told him. "That is, if you'll take it."

"Dollars or pesos, whatever," he said. "What'll you have?"

"Just a beer, I guess," I replied, putting a five-dollar bill on the counter.

He served me with a bottle and a glass. "Don't worry about Montezuma," he said, gesturing to the glass. "Not in my place."

I nodded my thanks, poured the beer down the side of the glass, building only a thin cap of foam.

"You a tourist?" he asked.

"Not in the usual sense," I told him.

"Tampico has some areas that you'd find a little more comfortable," he informed me, his eyes sweeping the tavern. "I could call you a taxicab if you'd like."

I shook my head. "Actually, this is the area I was looking for."

He raised his eyebrows. "Here? At night?"

"Maybe tomorrow would be better," I conceded. "Perhaps you could recommend a place to stay? Something afford-able?"

"You expect clean?" he asked.

"Hopefully."

He took a long look at me, and something like tired dis-may touched his features. "Do you have any idea of where you are? Not a place for naive young men." He sighed. "You don't know me yet you ask for recommendations?" He sighed again. "Of course, three blocks up the street, there's an afford-able hotel. Clean enough. However, when you're asleep, three men will enter your room, cut your throat, and take everything you have."

"How do you know?" I asked, assuming this was humor.

"Because I will point you out to them, and we will split what you have four ways."

"It wouldn't be much," I lied. I was sure many had been killed for much less than what I had in my money belt or even for the contents of the suitcase. "Are you such a scoundrel?"

"Scoundrel?" the bartender repeated the word with something like delight. "Why not a knave or a blackguard? A man of obvious learning in my poor place. What a change!"

"You read a lot yourself, I take it?" I guessed aloud.

"In several different languages," he responded. "Drink your beer."

He moved to another area behind the bar to help two belligerent customers who were beginning to show their resentment of the time he was spending with me. I didn't lack for company for more than a few moments.

"*Americano*?" the girl slid onto the stool beside me, bending forward to give me a glimpse of her breasts in her loose, low-cut blouse. "Can I do something for you? Something nice, you like?"

I gave her a nice, friendly smile. "I'm sure I would, but I'm damned near broke."

"You have enough, I betcha," she said, not backing off at all. She was small in stature, a pretty Hispanic woman showing a little tendency to fleshiness. If not careful, she'd be fat while still young. Right now, she was damned attractive. "My name is Juanita. You can't afford much, I give you special rate."

"Another time," I told her.

After a few seconds, I realized I'd made a bad mistake. Her face turned angry, and she turned to speak rapidly and harshly in Spanish to a nearby table of rough looking men. I didn't like the looks on their faces.

"Juanita!" The bartender spoke sharply. With an outburst Spanish, as grating and severe as hers, he laid into the girl and her circle of friends. The girl flashed something back, a retort that made everyone nearby laugh, but she sashayed away to a distant end of the tavern.

"I knew you were trouble when you walked in," he said to me.

"I just came in for a beer," I responded. "I wasn't looking for trouble."

"That's why you got it," he said, by way of explanation. "They think you'll be easy."

"They'd be unpleasantly surprised," I told him, feigning toughness.

"Finish your beer and go," he advised me. "Try the hotel, three blocks. I was not really serious about night intruders, but you should assume that I was. Sleep with as they say . . . with one eye open."

I inclined my head toward the table of toughs behind me. "Will they follow?"

"I'll try to give you a head start," he said with a smile. "Walk quickly."

I nodded my thanks, drank down half of my beer, and rose from my stool. I picked up my suitcase and headed for the door. Behind me, I heard chairs scrape on the floor, and then heard the bartender's voice in a jovial tone, addressing the group with a spirit of bonhomie.

Once outside, I sprinted toward a distant sign, hoping it was the hotel. I'd neglected to ask my bartender advisor which three blocks he meant. After I'd covered a couple, I looked back and saw a few men coming out of the bar, but I couldn't tell if they were looking for me or merely leaving to seek other pleasures in other saloons.

In its prime, the hotel must have been a modest, reputable lodge in the heart of the portside industrial district. An old building, perhaps it had been a comfortable abode for merchants and seamen who did business or sailed into this busy anchorage. Now, it was rundown and forlorn, a seedy-looking place I'd have rather not entered, but for the advice of my newfound bartender advisor. Of course, he might've been simply steering me into a real den of thieves, but it seemed the only close-at-hand refuge from whoever might be following from the bar.

I went into the shabby lobby, and spoke briefly to an aptly shabby desk clerk who, thankfully, did do English in a somewhat manner of speaking. Between my limited Spanish and his splintered English, we managed to find a suitable amount of money for a night's stay. I got a room key numbered 205 and walked up the worn carpeted stairway to the second floor hall. I found my room, turned the key to open the door. In the dark, I searched for and found a light switch on the wall by the door.

From the illumination of a bedside lamp, I found a surprisingly clean if austere room. There was a double bed, a small table with two chairs near the single window, a sink and a metal clothes rack topped with a shelf. I turned back the covers on the bed and determined that the sheets were relatively clean although I suspected they had not been changed since the previous occupant had slept there. Dead tired, I didn't much care. I turned the lock on the door, and found there was also a sliding bolt to deter any night visitors. Somewhat reassured by this discovery, I wasn't at all sure it would hold back anyone with even an ounce of determination. I took one of the chairs, tilted it, and wedged it under the door knob. I stepped away, satisfied it might give me a few moments to defend myself should the portal be stormed.

I considered sleeping with the Glock under my pillow, changed my mind and placed it on floor within easy reach. I took an additional cautionary step of adding the machine pistol to my arsenal. I turned out the light and climbed under the covers, each weapon with the muzzle carefully pointed away from me. With my expertise in firearms, I envisioned that, somehow, I'd manage to shoot myself during my sleep.

I lay awake a while, thinking of what next I must do. To seek Bruno Cady now seemed to be a foolish venture - I didn't know what I'd had in mind. Certainly, I was angry about his treachery, but what of it?

I was out of the States, in a foreign country, which was all I'd really bargained for. True, Cady had taken a couple of thousand of my money, but, as fate turned out, I'd realized a gain of many thousand in return. True, he'd put me in harm's way with Luis's cutthroat band, but I'd survived.

I really began to think that Cady had inadvertently helped me more than he'd hurt me. While not a fortune in my money belt, I decided I had more than enough to buy me a chance of freedom. I didn't know exactly how I'd go about it, but having a sizable amount of money was better than trying to continue my escape as a penniless foreigner. With a sigh of satisfaction, I closed my eyes, vowing to sleep lightly just in case.

Did I sleep at all? I wasn't sure. I know my night was filled with racing thoughts, my mind filled with speculative plans for the morrow, examining my options. I reflected upon sleep itself, thinking I hadn't had what you'd consider a fear free slumber since before my arrest and trial. In the hostile world of prison, I had never quite ever wanted a deep slumber, a complete oblivion. Most times, you wanted to stay at the edge of consciousness, just in case, just in case.

23

When daylight came, apprehension came with it. I know despair and fear are usually associated with the dark, but for me, night had been a time of optimism; my plans workable and plausible. Sunlight brought reality. Here I am, a fugitive in a foreign country: I don't speak the language, I'm carrying deadly weapons and counterfeit money, and I have no identifying documents other than another person's driver's license.

I stayed in the room until about nine o'clock in the morning, and then took to the streets carrying my suitcase. Still wearing my winter clothes, I felt extremely conspicuous. I moved around the waterfront area until I found a catchall store that carried many varied items. In it, I purchased some sun country clothing; casual shirts, walking shorts, and underwear. I found a large backpack that I thought would be a hands-free means of carrying my clothing and toiletry items. For whatever illogical reason, I also decided it was large enough to hold all those counterfeit bills. I also found a tote bag that was appropriate for carrying and concealing my weapons.

I paid for my purchases, and found a cramped dressing room where I changed into a new short-sleeved shirt and casual trousers. I transferred the automatic pistol and the Glock to the tote bag, and then stuffed my belongings and the bogus bills into the backpack. I stuck the hard-side suitcase into another corner and returned to the streets.

I roamed the waterfront, not knowing what I should say:

Excuse me! Do you speak English? I'm afraid I've lost my passport, but I need to get to Antigua . . . any suggestions?

The first person I talked to would probably turn me over to the police:

Excuse me! I have quite a bit of cash. Could you tell me where I could get a counterfeit passport? I'll pay!

Of course, I'll probably be speaking to the local chief of police!

Tampico appeared a major seaport; great tankers being filled with oil, freighters of different sizes being loaded with crates and grains. Some smaller vessels, tug boats, fishing trawlers, and utility ships, were busy in the water around them. I walked for a long time, not really knowing what to say or what to do. There were great risks involved if I tried to find a passage, even greater ones should I linger too long in this foreign city. I didn't want to think of where Luis might now be or what he was planning to do should he find me. I was sure that I was, now, his most sought after target. My escape had not only insulted his megalomania, but added injury as well. For what I'd done to him, revenge was likely much more on his mind than finding Bruno and the money.

Getting out of Tampico was going to be not just a problem, but it appeared to be an improbability. I tried conversations with a number of seamen, most who didn't speak my language, nor I theirs. When I did make a rare contact with a speaker of English, my words were usually lame; awkwardly trying to hint that I needed passage out of Mexico with no questions asked. Of course, those who did show the slightest interest seemed more suspicious than sympathetic.

"You trying to buy passage on our ship?" one sailor asked gruffly.

"I have some money," I responded.

"Funny place for a guy like you to be," he told me. "You got papers, a passport?"

"I lost mine," I said lamely.

He looked me over carefully. "You might talk to the captain," he said, shaking his head as he spoke. "I don't think it will do any good."

"Where are you heading?" I asked.

"Texas," he replied.

"Thanks, just the same."

I wandered around the waterfront, visiting seedy looking bars that afternoon, trying to find a way out of Mexico. I even hinted at a sizable bribe from time to time, but all I got were blank looks. On a couple of occasions, I saw suspicion in the eyes of the people to whom I posed my shady request, so I hightailed it away, hoping my abrupt departure would not set up a call to the Mexican authorities. As evening came, I knew I had little chance of leaving this country without some sort of identification papers. I had money enough, I supposed, to buy forgeries, but I had no idea of where to look or whom to ask.

When darkness came, I returned to the bars of the waterfront, looking at various rough customers, wondering if they'd help if I approached them.

Eventually, rather desperate in my failures, I headed back to the saloon where the night before, the bartender had shown some affability. He might be as wary as the rest, but he must've had some sort of an idea of my predicament by my aberrant tourist behavior. Perhaps for a price, he'd be willing to give a name where I'd get help.

The saloon was as loud and raucous as ever; a dreadful din mixing music and drunken conviviality shouted in a half-dozen different languages. My night-before counselor, behind the bar; noticed me immediately. This time, there was no smile, almost an expression of dismay. I walked over to the bar and stood for a few minutes while he waited on customers. Finally, during a lull, he walked over to me. "Back again?"

I nodded. "I wonder if I could ask you for some help?"

He said nothing. This evening, he seemed quite different than before, a sort of tension in his manner that fluttered a concern in me. Nonetheless, I pressed on, hoping he'd help."I need a passport," I told him. "Papers."

He regarded me for a few moments more. "You're in trouble?"

I nodded. "For something I didn't do."

"Why should I believe you?" he asked, beginning to wash and rinse glasses in the sink behind the bar. "Why would I want to get involved?"

"No reason at all," I conceded. "I just don't know where to turn."

"You'd be amazed at how many people come in here looking for your kind of help," he told me with a heavy sigh. He put the glasses on a shelf behind the bar, and then turned to face me with an aggrieved expression.

We stood, staring at each other.

"Forget it," I said, preparing to leave.

"Wait a minute," he said suddenly. He turned and spoke in Spanish to another bartender who nodded. Then, he motioned for me to follow. I walked to the far end of the bar where he stepped out and drew me toward a door. "Maybe I can help you out . . . if you have some money."

"I've got some," I told him. "Would it cost a lot?"

He nodded. "A couple of thousand U. S. dollars."

"That's okay," I told him.

"You got it with you?"

I nodded.

"I mean . . . with you, right now?"

"Yes," I assured him. "Is this something that can be done right away?"

He gestured to the door. "Come with me. I can introduce you to someone who might be able to help you." He gave me a congenial smile that seemed just a little too much. "Of course, for my part in this, I'd want to be paid as well."

"How much?" I countered.

"Another thousand," he told me. He opened the door into a shadowy, dimly lit corridor. "Do you have that much as well?"

I hesitated, and then nodded. "I can handle that."

"Good!" he said, the feigned smile returning. "Come with me."

He entered the gloomy corridor, waited until I entered, and closed the door behind us. We both stood still for a moment, each expecting the other to move forward first. My benefactor shrugged and moved ahead.

It was a long corridor in a building that was larger than I had expected. The cafe in front masked the extensive back interior sections of a mostly vacant two-story structure. Along this lower hallway, there were doors on either side; a couple that opened into dark, empty spaces. At the end of the hall, a stairway led to the upper floor. The bartender gave me a gesture to precede him up the stairs. Instead, I signaled for him to go before me. Again, he seemed to hang back, and then moved up the steps.

Perhaps it was the dingy appearance of the hall, a somewhat sinister setting or perhaps it was the manner of my so-called benefactor. As I climbed the steps behind him, I reached down to quietly unzip the top of my tote bag. I slipped my hand down and found the grip of the Uzi.

At the landing at the top of the stairs, the bartender opened the door into a harshly-lit storeroom. In comparison to the gloom of the stairway, from what I could see, it was illuminated by a high wattage bulb hanging from the center of the ceiling. I could see no one in the room, but I caught an alarming glimpse of a pair of crutches leaning against the far wall. Just then, my accommodating guide took my arm and, with sudden force, thrust me through the door.

Half-expecting such a deceit, I whirled away from the bartender, dropped the tote bag, and the Uzi came out smoothly. I set myself to cover everyone including my duplicitous escort. In the center of the large central space, Luis, with a heavily bandaged foot, was seated in one of two straight-backed chairs. Across from him in the second chair, a bound and bloodied man sat with two Hispanic thugs hovering over him. These two were new faces to me; undoubtedly replacements for those I'd hobbled. For their part in letting me get away, I wondered if Manuel and the no-name driver had suffered worse injuries from their psychopathic leader.

Luis looked at me in astonishment, and then gave a scowl to the bartender who had suddenly found a sheepish expression for his face.

"Come in and close the door," I said to the bartender, waving the barrel of the machine pistol as a gesturing threat.

He did as he was told, giving me an apologetic lift of his right hand. "Sorry, Senor," he said to me. "You should never have come back." He nodded to Luis. "I had no choice. They came here looking for you and I had to tell them. They said if you come back . . ." He didn't finish, looking with fear at Luis.

"Great," I muttered. "Just great . . . of all the gin joints in the world . . ." I waved the pistol once again, gesturing for him to move to join the others. I did a quick look at my surroundings, noting a number of free-standing, box-laden metal shelves against a wall. At the far end of the room, there was a trio of tall windows, each with a tattered pull-down shade.

From the frozen-action scene in front of me, it appeared that the two standing toughs had been methodically beating the man in the chair while Luis had watched.

"Luis," I spoke to my former captor. "We meet again."

Luis was not in a good mood. He struggled to rise and took a lame half-step toward me. "You sonofabitch! I should have killed you. I shouldn't have let you live."

"I don't believe you really intended to let me live," I responded. "How's the foot?"

"You sonofabitch!" he exclaimed again.

"No argument," I told him, thinking of my mother. "What do we have here?" I waved the men aside, which gave me a better view of the battered man in their midst. "Is that Cady?"

"It ought to be you," Luis said, his eyes darting, sizing me up, wondering how he was going to take me.

I lifted the machine pistol. "Don't even think of it," I said, sounding ridiculously like an action-movie derring-doer.

Luis's two new henchmen looked anxiously at their limping leader.

"Have you killed him?" I asked, pointing the barrel at the slumped, bound figure.

"Damn near," came a mush-mouthed voice, Cady's head beginning to rise. His face was badly bruised, his eyes nearly swollen shut, a lip split and puffy. "Who the hell you are, get me outta here."

With the battering around his face, I was surprised he could speak as well as he did.

"Sure," I responded. "Like I owe you that favor."

"We will kill the both of you!" Luis said with sudden bravado. "There are . . ." He glanced at the bartender. ". . . four of us!"

"There seems to be a lot of bullets in this thing, ought to be enough," I countered, waving the Uzi. "I think they come out very fast." I raised the machine pistol up to a firing position. "Why doesn't everyone just lie down with your hands behind your heads?"

No one moved.

"Then, I'll shoot anyone who's standing after I count to three . . . one, two—"

Four of them went to the floor with hands behind their heads.

I moved over to the bartender and nudged him with my foot. "You can crawl over there and take away their guns."

He didn't move.

"Or I can shoot you and let the next guy do it."

The bartender got up to a kneeling position and crawled to the first gunsel. He searched the man's pockets and found something.

"Take it out very slowly."

The bartender took a flat-shaped automatic from the pocket and laid it carefully on the floor.

"Slide it over to me."

He did as he was told.

"Now, the next."

The bartender repeated his careful crawl and search, disarming the second man and Luis. From the gang leader, he came up with a revolver, a closed switchblade knife, and a small gun in an ankle holster on his good leg..

"Luis, you are a menace, aren't you," I said, sweeping with my foot all the weaponry up against the wall, far from the stretched out banditos. I motioned for the bartender to rise. "Untie the unfortunate gentleman in the chair," I instructed.

The bartender fumbled for a few minutes, unable to untie the knots.

"Never mind," I said with a sigh, waving him back down on the floor. "I'll take care of it." I unsnapped the blade of the razor-edged knife, wincing a bit at the sight of it, and cut Cady's bonds. I stepped back away to keep everyone covered including Cady.

"You okay?" I asked him.

"Not as bad as it looks," he muttered, his swollen mouth slightly blurring his words. He sat for a few more moments, moving his arms slowly, touching his face gingerly, and then glared at the men sprawled around him.

"Just sit there for a while," I told him. "I've got to figure out what to do."

"I'll kill you," Luis said into the floorboards. "Cady, too!"

"I take it they were trying to get information from you," I said to Cady. "Like what you did with the money and the dope."

"It belongs to us!" Luis said, lifting his head to stare his defiance.

"See what you've gotten us into, Cady?" I asked. "All this trouble because you got greedy."

Cady peered at me through the slits in his puffy face. "Mathias?"

"The same."

The injured man shook his damaged head slowly. "Get me out of this, kid."

"I'm more interested in getting myself out," I responded.

"You are both dead men!" Luis proclaimed from the floor. "I will take great delight in killing the two of you."

"You know, Luis, you're in a hell of a position to keep making these threats," I told him. "If you'll just throttle back your temper, maybe we can work out a deal."

"What deal?" the drug dealer said in a tone of scathing disbelief.

"Well, look," I began. "The original deal was that Cady was going to bring you a lot of money for the dope. I don't see why we can't go back to that original premise." I paused, expecting protests. Getting no response, I continued, speaking to Cady: "What say we take Luis here . . . not his companions . . . to wherever you've put the drugs and the money, and we'll make the exchange just as it should have been before."

Silence.

"Luis gets the money, and Bruno gets the dope."

Silence.

"Come on, guys," I pleaded. "Let bygones be bygones!"

"No deal!" Luis shouted. "I've been dishonored. It *all* belongs to me!"

"Bullshit, kid," Cady chimed in. "This is my last chance, and I'm taking the whole kit and caboodle." He rose from his chair slowly, carefully, testing his capability to stand. He turned to me. "Get me outta here, and I'll make it worth your while."

"You're all dirty, greedy men," I said tiredly.

Cady began to walk, unsteady, but he made it only three feet away from the chair, heading in my direction, when I pointed the Uzi directly at him.

"What?" Cady asked as he stopped.

"Stay away from the guns," I warned. "Or I just may let them keep you."

"I can get you outta the country, kid," he offered. "Ain't that what you want?"

I didn't answer.

"I'll make you a good split . . . ten percent of the money, and ten percent of whatever we get for selling the dope."

"I'm more interested in what to do with these people," I said.

"Kill 'em," Cady suggested. "Easiest way, won't have to worry about 'em any more."

I pointed to the shelves against the wall. "See if you can find something over there to tie them up."

Cady remained in place.

"Can't you move?" I asked, sounding sarcastic, but I was really asking for a physical report.

"Yeah, I guess," Cady grumbled, his fingers touching his bloody mouth. "Gonna need some dental work, maybe."

Muttering under his breath, he shuffled across the room and began rummaging through the items on the shelves. "Got some picture wire and a couple of rolls of duct tape," he said loudly. "Outta do."

"Bring the tape," I instructed. "Start with Luis." I stepped over and nudged the bartender with the toe of my shoe. "You can help him."

Luis swore in furious Spanish, while Cady and the bartender bound his arms behind him with the duct tape. They wrapped his legs and, finally, shut him up with a generous swatch of silver tape across his mouth. Before turning to the others, Cady gave him a surprisingly agile kick in the ribs.

"No kicking a man while he's down," I admonished.

They tied the other two in similar fashion, and stepped back to let me inspect their work. "Looks good," I commented as I gestured to the bartender. "Now, him."

"Let me hold the gun, and you do him," Cady said, talking slowly to be better understood.

"Don't be ridiculous," I countered.

"I'm hurting, kid," he whined. "I won't shoot nobody."

"Why don't I believe you?" I said, waving the Uzi at him.

Cady shrugged and began to tie the bartender's hands. It took a few minutes to finish up; all four of them were now trussed securely.

"This ain't much good," Cady complained. "Somebody'll come find 'em, and they'll be after us again."

"I got news for you, Bruno," I said in exasperation. "I'm not any good at killing, and I'm tired of hearing you suggest it."

"You was doing time—"

"For something I didn't do," I cut in. "Now, are you serious about getting me out of the country?"

"Sure," Cady agreed with a bloody smile. "You're calling the shots."

Belatedly, I got the notion that my confession of innocence might've been a mistake. The way Cady looked at me, I wondered if Ii hadn't lost a little of his respect. I lifted the machine pistol. "I may not like it, but I *will* hurt you if I have to."

I don't know if he was impressed.

"Suppose any of these guys have a car?" I asked.

Cady pointed to one of the thugs. "I think he's got keys to an old Chevy. That's what they brought me here in."

I knelt down beside the man, ignoring his malevolent stare and muffled angry grunts. I searched through his pockets and came out with a ring of keys. I found a key that was appropriate for an old Chevy, and patted the miscreant on the rear as my way of saying thanks.

"Let's go," I said, rising.

Cady looked at the pile of weapons.

"Good thinking," I told him. I took the handguns and placed them in my tote bag, zipped it shut, and motioned Cady toward the door. "Let's go."

Cady started slowly for the door.

"You going to be able to make it?" I asked.

"They worked me over pretty good," he said, not increasing his speed.

"Was it worth it?" I asked, opening the door for Cady to shuffle out onto the stair landing. I closed the door behind me and motioned for Cady to continue down the steps.

"Way it turned out, I guess so," Cady said, picking his way down painfully. "I guess I'd have told 'em what they wanted to know in another few minutes or so."

We reached the bottom of the stairs.

"Is there a back way?" I asked.

Cady nodded. "Brought me in that way," he responded, nodding toward a door. He opened it and we walked out into an alley.

"There's the car," he said, pointing to an old Chevy parked near the building. "It got me here . . . I guess it'll get us somewhere else."

"Let's give it a try," I said. "Think you can drive?"

He looked at me in disbelief.

And I knew, for once, he wasn't faking.

With a sigh, I ushered him to the passenger side door, opened it, and watched as he painfully seated himself inside.

I exchanged the machine pistol for the easier-to-handle Glock, then pitched my backpack and tote bag onto the back seat floor, out of Cady's reach.

Holding the Glock in my left hand, I showed it to him. "Now, this is a little awkward to use while I'm driving. If you try anything stupid, I might accidentally kill you . . . so be good. Tell me where to go."

"Go to hell," he said softly, distinctly.

"Thank you, Kev, for saving my life," I said lightly. I inserted the key and started the engine. "Now, tell me where to drive. Or would you like me to let you off right here?"

"Outta the alley," he directed, pointing. "Take a right and I'll tell you as we go."

I took a moment to orient myself with the dashboard. I turned on the headlights, moved the shift lever into *Drive*, and steered the Chevy away from the curb. Fortunately, the old car was an automatic, so I didn't have to worry about shifting gears. I really wasn't too worried about a tussle with Cady; he looked pretty damned bad. He seemed content to lie back against the seat, trying to recover from the hammering he'd suffered, and let me drive him away from his most immediate danger. In all probability, he was figuring to put some distance between himself and the banditos. I would bet he was now worrying what to do about me later.

I followed his directions, driving along the streets of the waterfront and, after a while, I drove along an ocean drive to a small marina some few miles along the bay.

"Stop here," he said in a rasping voice.

"Where?" I asked. "At the marina?"

He nodded.

I pulled over to the side of the road, parked, cut the engine, and turned off the lights. "Now what?"

"We wait," he said tiredly.

24

"How much longer . . . and why?" I asked. We'd been parked for over thirty minutes, and I was beginning to think this was another of Cady's tricks.

"'Til midnight," he responded, pointing out to sea. "That's when we'll rendezvous."

"Rendezvous with whom?"

"Our way outta here, kid," he said with a sigh. "Damn, I ought to be in a hospital.

"Who are we meeting?" I asked, now worried about confederates.

"Relax, kid," he said in his weary voice. "You pulled me outta a bad situation, and I owe you." He paused. "I'm sorry about leaving you with them bastards."

"Why do I doubt your sincerity?"

"You got a right to be sore," he admitted. "Thinking of myself, I didn't give a damn about you."

In the soft moon light, I could see his features, even the wounds and bruises.

"This was my big chance, the last chance I'd probably get to make a really big score," he continued. "I was planning on doing all this on my own when you showed up, and I figured you'd do just fine as a distraction." He paused. "You smoke?"

"Nope."

"Well, shit," he grumbled. "Don't smoke any more myself, but a smoke would be really good right now."

"Sorry."

"Meaning to ask," Cady began a question. "How the hell did you get away?"

"Luck," I responded, not wanting to tell him more. "Nothing, but pure luck."

"Like to hear about that."

"As you're fond of saying, 'you ain't got a need to know'."

He sat for a few more minutes in silence, gazing out at the moonlit sea, and then started again: "Figured you was a badass, some sort of killer outta the pen. Figured it'd serve you right to end up with them drug dealers." He paused. "You really never ever killed anybody?"

I decided to be honest. "Never."

"Even if you had, it wasn't the right thing for me to do," he said. "I apologize, and that's the best I can do. Like I said, I'll cut you in for a part of the deal."

"I was never interested in the money, and I'm sure not interested in being a dope dealer," I told him, somewhat sanctimoniously.

"You turning the deal down?" he asked, incredulous.

"I'll keep what's mine," I told him, not telling him about the money I'd taken from Luis. "That's all I want . . . and your word that you'll get me to somewhere safe."

He didn't say anything for a few moments. "You sound too good to be true," he said finally. "Think you can trust me?"

"No, but I don't believe I have any other choice. How many people are we meeting?"

"Just one," he replied, gesturing out to sea. "She'll be bringing the ship in at midnight."

"She?"

"My daughter."

This was a surprise. "You've got your daughter involved in this?"

"It's a family affair," he said, an almost whimsical manner.

"Jukes and Kallikaks," I said under my breath, thinking of the famous genetically-inclined crime families.

"What?" Cady asked.

"Nothing, really," I said, changing to a new subject. "How did you get caught by Luis and his merry men?"

"My own damned fault," Cady growled. He gave an apologetic gesture. "After I dumped you, I landed in a field where Minnie was waiting—"

"Minnie? Minnie's the daughter?"

"Minerva," Cady supplied the full name. "She hates it . . . doesn't like to be called Minnie much better."

"Who gave it to her?"

"Her mother," he explained. "I wanted something like Katie."

"Katie Cady?"

"Yeah," he said. "Something catchy, don'cha think?"

"Poor kid," I said under my breath.

"What?"

"Nothing, go ahead."

"Well, I put the bird down, and we loaded the stuff into a van. We drove here to this dock where we had the ship, loaded it, and we were set to leave." He gave a shrug, something like body language chagrin. "We had a fight about it, but I was trying to cut a deal for a local guy to buy the plane."

"The plane you stole?"

He nodded. "She got really pissed. Told me I'd likely get myself killed."

"You damned near did," I reminded him.

"Well, she was right, and so are you," he went on. "She didn't want to hang around the dock with a big load of cocaine and all that money, so I told her to take it out to sea. Told her to come back and pick me up at six in the evening. If I didn't show, then she was to try one more time at midnight. I told her if I didn't make it that next time, she was to shove off and keep the whole kit and caboodle."

"And Luis and his gang found you?"

"'Fraid so," he acknowledged. "I never even got to see the prospective buyer . . . and the rest you can guess up 'til you came in."

"Think she'll come back at midnight?"

"She might," he replied, not sounding particularly sure of it.

"How close are the two of you?"

"So, so," he said. "I wasn't what you'd call a real good father, but we got along all right. Never beat her or anything. I use to bring her things from overseas whenever I thought of it."

"A thoughtful dad," I mused.

"Yeah, I guess so," he went on, either not recognizing sarcasm or ignoring it. "Lived with her mother most of the time, but I'd come see her when I could."

"Where's the rest of the family?" I asked.

"The old lady? I don't know. Off somewhere doing whatever she does to get by. We weren't married very long."

"Divorced?"

"I'm not sure. Can't remember if I signed any papers or whatever it takes."

"Something I don't understand," I said, changing the subject again. "You're a pilot and you've got a plane, stolen as it might be. How come you didn't just fly on back into the States without all this rigmarole with the daughter and the boat?"

There was a long period of silence, and I wasn't sure he was going to answer.

"Look," he said finally. "As far as I was concerned, I never figured on taking it back into the States.

I let that pass for the moment. "What about this fellow, Anthony?"

He looked at me with those penetrating eyes. "Just like I told Luis. He got himself cut up in a New Orleans bar."

"You do the cutting?" I asked.

He grinned. "Nope, not that I wouldn't have if I'd needed to." He shook his head. "I'd just planned on running out on him, same as did to you, but he got himself into his own kind of trouble, so I figured it was just his dumb luck."

It was his story, but I couldn't accept such a coincidence. "He trusted you with the money?"

"Oh, yeah," Cady said easily. "Never had a problem with Tony."

"What about flying the dope back into the States," I asked, returning to that part of my inquiry.

He shook his head once more. "I'm through trying to get it in, too many DEA guys and other agencies really watching what comes in." He sighed, drawing a deep breath. "Ya gotta see that I'm getting on . . . I'm now in my late sixties . . . and I'm still doing nothing other than getting paid as a go-between for the guys that are making the real dough. Sure, they pay me pretty good, but not good enough. So, when my contacts in the States told me to make this run, I knew it had to be my last chance to score. I been taking risks all my life, so I figured why not take one more . . . a big one."

He paused, and I didn't know whether he was going to go any further. He still hadn't satisfied my queries.

After a while, he began again: "They've been screwing me, so why not me doing them?" He gave a snort of laughter. "Look, here's the way I set it up. Some people in the States give Tony and me the money to make the buy in Mexico. I knew I might get my balls shot off making the switch, but I'd done business with Luis and his bunch before, and I figured he just might not catch on 'til it was too late." He shrugged in his apologetic way again. "That's where I used you . . . and I'm sorry, but it worked like a charm. He didn't think I'd fly off leaving you there."

"Which damned near got *me* killed."

"Right," he said gruffly, a spasm of coughing catching him. "I think I'd better have a doc look at my insides when we get clear," he said after he recovered. "Anyway, I based my plan on that I *would* get away. A couple of weeks ago, I made some other contacts, and gave 'em a chance to buy the stuff at a bargain rate."

"Such as?"

"They're paying a little over a million," he told me. "The deal is that I deliver the load to a freighter out on the open sea. We make the rendezvous, they get the dope, and the problem of getting it into the States is theirs. I walk away with something like three big ones." There was a pause, then he added, "'Course I'll cut you in for a good share . . . seeing as how I did you dirt, and you saved my life."

Of course, I didn't believe him.

"Say," he said suddenly. "Why did you come to help me?"

"Don't flatter yourself," I told him. "They were an inch away from capturing me just as they did you. I walked into a trap and got out of it, again through sheer luck." I lifted the Glock. "And having a weapon didn't hurt either."

"Well, whatever," Cady said philosophically. "I'm mighty grateful just the same."

"After you make the exchange," I asked. "Where do you go from there?"

"We'll talk about that when the time comes," he said.

"No, let's talk about it now," I told him. "Understand this, Cady. If I stay in Tampico, I'm dead meat as soon as Luis gets loose and finds me. If I had the time, I'd find some other way out of Mexico, but I haven't got that time. Like it or not, I'm stuck with you, and you're stuck with me."

"Of course," Cady said in what was sounding like a patronizing assurance. "You can—"

"You try to double-cross me again, and I'll shoot your balls off . . . and whatever's appropriate for your daughter, too!"

In the darkness, Cady chuckled.

25

A little before midnight, I put on my backpack, and we moved from the car onto the pier to stare out at the moonlit sea. Most of the anchored motorboats and sailing craft were dark, only a few showing lights to indicate people aboard who were still awake. Far out at sea, we could see the lights of a distant freighter slowly moving north. It was a quiet, serene scene and, for me, there was a sense that all the violence of the earlier hours had been in some sort of a different world. It was almost as though those events had not really happened. Standing there, I had the feeling I was a different me; all my dreadful experiences of the past few years belonging to another person.

Then, I looked at my battered companion, and I was back in my hellish world of danger and desperation.

Nearly on the hour, I saw a dark shape on the water approaching, no running lights showing.

"Is that her?" I asked.

"Probably," Cady answered.

As the craft came nearer, I was somewhat surprised and somewhat elated at the sight of it. When Cady had said *ship*, I'd assumed he meant *boat*. It appeared to be more than an offshore fishing outfit: It was a gleaming white craft of substantial size, quite capable of seagoing in my opinion.

It turned as it approached, showing a handsome profile. It was a steel-hulled vessel, with a flybridge atop a sleek, fiberglass deckhouse that included a substantial canopy overhanging the short aft deck. Completing the turn, it began backing slowly toward the pier

"Nice ride," I said to Cady.

"Technically, it's a yacht. Fifty-footer," he said.

"Steal it?"

"Rented it," he answered gruffly.

I had my doubts about that, but I didn't voice them. Instead, I said, "Couldn't have been cheap."

He tried to grin. "Your four grand might help a little."

"Renting to these two, the owner must've been out of his mind," I said under my breath.

"She'll be suspicious of you," Cady told me, gesturing toward the incoming yacht. "Let me do all the talking."

"Long as you say the right things."

In a few minutes, the yacht slowed and stopped about twenty feet from the end of the pier.

"Who's with you?" came a woman's voice from the craft.

Under the flybridge cover, I could see her silhouette against the sky.

"It's okay, Minnie," Cady called out. "He's a fella we're taking along."

"I don't think so, Bruno," came back her retort. "Tell him to leave or I'm not coming any further."

"Dammit, Minnie, I tell you it's okay," Cady snapped. "I'm hurt, and I'd be dead if it wasn't for this fella."

There was a long period of silence.

A very long period of silence.

"Who are you, mister? And what do you have to do with my dad?"

"He got me into this mess!" I called back. "He's going to get me out of it!"

"What mess?" she asked.

"We'll explain it later!" Cady bellowed. "This isn't the time and place to be shouting out our business!"

"You didn't say who you are!"

"Bring the damned thing in, Minnie!" Cady exclaimed in exasperation.

A couple of more minutes went by and, finally, the yacht began slowly backing toward the pier. Whatever else her capabilities, this lady knew how to maneuver a sizable yacht. She brought it to the pier with a series of short, precise moves, then cut the engine. Seconds later she scrambled down to the aft deck and threw a line to Cady.

Moving stiffly, he fastened the line to the pier.

"What's wrong with you?" she asked.

"Beat up a bit," he answered, then turned to me. "Let's get on and get out of here."

Wearing my backpack and carrying my tote bag, I stepped through the rail opening onto the aft deck where, with the help of his daughter, we assisted Bruno to board the yacht.

After she finished inspecting him, she turned to me in anger. "You do this?"

I shook my head. "The guys he cheated outta their money *and* their dope."

I don't know what I'd expected from a girl named Minnie, but she stacked up much better than any expectations. I guessed her age in the middle-to-late twenties. Wearing the briefest of shorts and a Cozumel tee shirt, she was tanned, slender, and attractive with a pretty face in spite of it being very angry.

"I don't like this, Bruno," she said to her father, not taking her eyes off of me. She raised a pistol in her hand that I hadn't seen before.

In mine, I raised the Glock that she hadn't seen before.

"Mexican standoff?" I suggested.

"Don't shoot him, Minnie," Cady groaned. "We could use another hand on board when we make the trade."

"We can handle it by ourselves," she countered, aiming the pistol.

I followed suit by aiming the Glock.

"Both of you stop," Cady groaned again. "Darling, get me below and get me patched up. I ain't got the strength to break up this damned fight."

The girl seemed uncertain.

"Let's put our guns away and help your father," I said in my most reasonable tone of voice. I lowered mine and stuck it under my belt.

For a moment, I thought she was going to fire. Then, she lowered the pistol with nowhere to put it. "Who are you? You never answered my question."

"Kevin Mathias," I answered. "Somebody you never heard of."

She didn't speak for a few moments, and then a look of realization came into her eyes. "I've heard of you all right! You're damned famous! You're that killer who escaped from prison up in the States!" She raised her pistol again, turned her head toward her dad, but she didn't take her eyes off of me. "Fine, Bruno! You bring a mass-murderer aboard!"

"He says he never killed anybody," Cady responded.

"Sure," she said sarcastically. "That's what they all say."

229

"Well, he didn't kill some people when he had the chance," Cady told her. "And these were people that needed killing."

"Would you put that thing away?" I asked her. "What your dad is telling you is the truth. I don't know why you'd believe me . . . no one else has . . . but I really am innocent."

"What are the chances?" she said scornfully.

"One in a thousand, I don't know," I said tiredly. "Go ahead and shoot if that's what you have to do. I'd rather be dead than back in jail for something I didn't do."

She thought about it for a few moments.

"Give me your gun," she said finally.

Without a protest, I handed over the Glock.

"Go inside with Bruno, and see if you can fix him up," she said. "I'll cast off and we'll discuss this later."

She kept her pistol pointed at me while I went to assist her father. I laid my tote bag on a deck seat, got his left arm over my neck, my right one about him and under his armpit, and helped him walk under the canopy into the deckhouse.

This facility was the electronic center of the yacht with a ship-to-shore radio, depth measuring instruments, radar units, etc. In addition, a teak wheel in the center of an instrument console provided a duplicate control facility to its companion up on the flybridge. A high-pedestal leather chair provided seating for the yacht's driver, and a matching leather bench on one side of the enclosure afforded comfort for others.

Over at the other side, four carpeted steps led to a lower level. Cady labored his own way down to the yacht's salon, and then lurched over to an L-shaped white settee. As he sat heavily upon it, I took off my backpack and looked around.

The salon was stunning; teak wood furniture, cabinetry and panels with brass fittings throughout. Opposite from Cady's settee, there was another L-shaped upholstered seat, this one fronted by a rectangular teak work and dining table. Looking forward, on my left was a compact galley with a stainless steel sink, a small refrigerator and a range-oven.

With a groan, Cady stretched out on the settee, and then groaned again.

"Try not to bleed too much," I told him. "Shame to ruin the decor."

I went to the galley sink and found some tea towels. I wet them and began to wash off the dried blood on his face. I unbuttoned his shirt, gently prodding around the bruises on his chest and ribs.

"Anything broken?" he asked.

"I don't think so," I ventured. "You spitting up any blood?"

"Nothing except outta my mouth," he told me, exploring the inside of his cheeks with a tentative finger. "Loosened a couple of teeth, but they might firm up if I give 'em a chance."

"All in all, I'd say you came out pretty lucky," I ventured. "Give yourself some rest and you ought to be okay."

"You a doctor?" he asked, sarcasm returning.

"No, but you seem to be getting your vile nature back," I countered. "That ought to be a good sign."

I felt the surge of the yacht as it began to pull away from the dock. Wherever we were going, we were on our way.

"You feel okay if I leave you alone?" I asked, watching him as he gave a tortuous sigh. "Want me to get you into a bed?"

"I'll be okay right here for a while," he answered, squirming a bit on the settee, trying to find comfort for his bruised body. "I'll just rest here for a while."

I stepped away and, in only that short span of time, his eyes closed and he seemed to fall asleep or to give a pretense of it. I went back up to the aft deck, where I watched the lights of Tampico diminishing as we motored away. Noting that

Minnie's full attention was focused on piloting the yacht out to sea, I retrieved my tote bag from the deck. I returned to the salon where Cady was now sleeping soundly. I waited beside him for a few minutes, to make sure of his slumber, and then did a quick check of the below-deck quarters.

At the stern, there was a large master stateroom with a queen-sized bed that looked terribly comfortable. The amenities were considerable; the stateroom nicely furnished with another settee, a cushioned chair, a writing table, and, of course, a private head for the skipper and whomever.

Closing the door to that stateroom, I picked up my backpack and tote bag and walked forward through a companionway, past the galley and the head, toward the bow of the yacht. In the fore section of the ship, I passed two doors on either side of the aisle and hurried to another one at the far end. I opened it and peered inside, then closed it after seeing that it was a dark storage space for a varied quantity of equipment and supplies. I returned to the facing doors on opposite sides of the central aisle, opened the port side door and took a step inside.

I found the light switch and flipped it. Here was another luxurious cabin, a smaller replica of the master suite, but as elegant in its appointments and furnishings. On the double bed, and scattered about the room, there were items and clothing of the woman. I wondered, briefly, why Minnie hadn't occupied the master suite instead. Perhaps Bruno had said dibs on it.

I crossed to the other door and went in. The same size as its match across the way, this was a bit of a downgrade by comparison. The standard wall-attached facilities of the cabin were exactly the same; a large closet, chest-high tiers of sliding drawers, a desk, a television console and a settee.

Instead of a large bed, however, a pair of twin bunks had been substituted. Perhaps it was configured to separate children and youths from their parents or, just as likely, quarters for a navigating crew.

Looking around, I was a bit surprised to find the drug suppliers' duffle bags with their vinyl sacks of cocaine. I also found the soft-side bag of real money Cady had stolen. I would have thought these ill-gotten gains would've been kept under watchful eyes in either Bruno's cabin or in Minnie's. However, I guessed neither of them had expected a third passenger aboard.

I continued to explore, really startled to find a weapons cache hidden under the left-side bunk. There were four rifles, two automatic pistols, a Uzi, a huge revolver, and enough varied ammunition to sustain a half-hour battle. It looked like Cady and company had not only planned a drug smuggling enterprise, but stocked an awesome arsenal to defend it.

I wondered if Minnie, with my Glock in her possession, had forgotten this stockpile of guns below deck. Then, too, there was the Uzi in my tote bag. I wondered if I should take it out as a show of defiance to my lady skipper, then decided against it. I tucked the tote bag under the bunk with the rest of the weaponry, pondered at my foolishness for doing so, and then re-entered the salon. I checked Bruno once again, decided that he was out for the rest of the night, and moved out onto the aft deck.

I went up the ladder to the flybridge and joined Minnie Cady at the wheel. I stood for a while beside her as the yacht cut through the gentle swells of the moonlit sea. She switched on the running lights, then gave me an askance look.

"He's okay," I told her. "Battered up a bit, but nothing really serious."

"What happened to him?"

"Seems he got caught by the people he swiped the dope from," I answered. "He said something about them catching him while he was trying to sell that stolen airplane."

"He was a damned fool for going back into town," she said curtly. "We'd have been long gone." She paused. "Without you."

"I've promised not to be a bother," I told her.

"You already are."

"Make the best of it," I shot back. "I don't know what brought the three of us together or what the hell's going to happen because of it, but I'm going to ride it out and see where we all end up."

"Probably dead!" she snapped at me.

"Well, so be it!" I snapped back. "At least, you and your dad went into this on your own accord . . . I'm just reacting to wherever and whatever the damn circumstances drive me."

"Sure," she said sarcastically. "Driven to horn in on our deal. Expecting a cut of what we've set up."

"I paid your father to fly me out of the country," I began wearily. "I didn't know anything about any drug deal 'til he put me down in a Mexican field with three cutthroat drug dealers, then stole their dope, their money and what little of mine, and flew off leaving me there to be murdered."

"No big loss to mankind," she said scathingly. "I'm not buying that 'innocent' crap."

"No reason you should," I acknowledged. "I'm tired of trying to make people believe me."

"How'd you get away?" she asked, her voice full of skepticism.

"Luck, nothing more," I told her, a familiar choice of words.

"If that's true," she said with obvious disbelief, "how and why did you get him out of trouble?"

"I'll let him tell you after he wakes up."

"Is he really all right?" she asked.

I shrugged. "Doesn't appear to be anything broken, no signs of internal injuries . . . at least as far as I can tell. He's not vomiting or spitting up blood." I shrugged again. "My old man is a doctor."

"You learn anything from him?" she asked.

"As little as possible," I answered. "Still, I guess I learned some things. Maybe that'll make you feel easier about him."

"I really don't give a damn about him," she said firmly.

I was surprised. "Well, you keep asking—"

"Because I need him alive and well when we transfer the goods," she cut in. "A beat up old guy and a girl . . . I don't want those drug guys to get the idea that we're easy pickings."

"As your dad said, maybe that's a good reason to bring me along," I suggested.

She gave me a scornful look. "I don't think you'd be much good in a fight."

"A while ago, you had me pegged as a cold-blooded murderer," I reminded her.

"Doesn't mean you'll be of much help if these guys get greedy."

"You think they will?"

She hesitated. "I don't know these people. My father made the deal. Things might go just as smooth as he says they will, but with those kind, you never know." She gave me a sideways look. "You get yourself a new gun?"

"You mean from the forward armory?" I said lightly.

She gave me a chagrined smile. "I forgot about 'em."

"They're still down there," I told her.

"You might as well have this back," she said, handing the Glock to me. "You could've wiped us all out by now."

"When did you remember them?" I asked, curious, putting the Glock at the back of my pants.

"About the time you'd have discovered them," she admitted. "I figured I'd get you while you were shooting Dad."

"All heart," I commented.

"No love lost here," she returned the sarcastic tone. "Don't give me any crap about blood being thicker than water."

"I wouldn't dare," I responded.

We continued to chug along through the glittering sea, the yacht moving at what I considered a pretty good speed. Tampico's lights had long since vanished, and we seemed to have the ocean much to ourselves. Once in a while, the wind would blow Minnie's hair across her face, and she'd brush it back with an almost angry motion.

"You dislike him that much?" I asked.

She gave me a cross look. "What business is it of yours?"

"None, I suppose," I responded. "It just seems a little strange that you'd throw in with him . . . feeling the way you do about him."

For a few moments, I thought she wasn't going to respond. Then, as though making a grave decision, she began to talk: "Man's near seventy, never made a really big score in his entire life, never saved a dime, spent everything he ever earned . . . and I'm talking about thousands . . . on cheap women, gambling, booze and dope."

I didn't know what to say.

"I was born to an easy Miami trick," she continued. "Bruno wouldn't have even known about me if my mother hadn't used me to try to blackmail him out of some money. The only thing she got was a few bucks for rutting with him again."

"He said he sent you things from time to time."

She gave a bitter laugh. "Once! Once! He sent me a fucking Jamaican doll he picked up from a grass hut vendor at Dunn's Falls."

We let the Caribbean breeze cool us while we stood on the flybridge, Minnie turning the wheel every so often to adjust her course.

"When's the big deal take place?" I asked. "We're meeting a freighter?"

"Told you about the whole thing, did he?"

"He told . . . I didn't ask."

"Same time he promised to cut you in, is that it?" she asked, more of a challenge than a question.

"Something like that, but I don't expect anything," I answered.

"Sure," she said in disbelief. "Why wouldn't you?"

"The dope thing, I guess," I replied.

She cocked her head and looked at me with a skeptical smile. "Of course not," she said in a cynical manner. "Kill people, but won't deal drugs."

"Look," I said to her. "Even assuming that I had killed those people . . . and, damn it, I didn't . . . that could have been a crime of passion . . . angry over whatever. Believe what you will, but that's a lot different than becoming a deliberate criminal. You and your dad are running dope . . . and that's a crime that you people decided to do."

"But you'll take the money," she shot back. "When the time comes, you won't be any better than we are."

I shrugged.

"Let me tell you something about dope," she went on, obviously angered at my accusation. "There's a market for it in the States, more than any other place in the world. People want it, and they'll pay for it. They'll pay anything for it."

"And ruin their lives."

"Whose fault is that?" she responded in scorn. "Americans are dumb. They pick their poison, and if they ruin their lives, then whose fault is it? Their own!"

"Maybe they don't know what they're getting into," I countered.

"Then, they're stupid!" she said vehemently. "Whatever happens to them, it's okay. It's more than okay . . . it's what they deserve!"

"What about kids born to crack mothers?" I asked. "What about ten and eleven-year-olds who get hooked on their first experience?"

"Too damned bad," she said with finality. "I'm in it for the money, and so are you."

I decided it was time to leave the flybridge and go below. With her at the wheel, and Bruno sleeping off his injuries, I decided it was a good time to try to get a little rest. I didn't trust either of them.

I went down the ladder and entered the main salon where Cady was sleeping soundly. I went into the forward stateroom and picked one of the lower bunks to catch a little shuteye, stashing my backpack beneath it. Feeling a bit foolish with such a glut of arms close at hand I, nevertheless, took out my Uzi and laid it beside me and placed the Glock under my pillow. As I've stated before, I've learned to sleep lightly, but I took the precaution of locking the door, and piling a couple of the rifles on the deck just inside the door. If Minnie or her dad changed their minds about having me aboard, something to stumble over might give me a couple of seconds to come fully awake and ready for whatever. I turned out the lights and scarcely needed any effort to get to sleep. The motion of the yacht, the steady drone of the diesels, and the sound of the bow cutting through the waves, created a soothing atmosphere, giving me pleasant and, finally, untroubled dreams.

■ ■ ■

I slept for about three hours, feeling renewed and refreshed upon awakening. I went down the companionway and took a quick shower in the head, redressed in shorts and a lightweight shirt. I placed my Uzi in the tote bag, deciding not to show it, wondering if I was being appallingly stupid. With my light clothing, I knew it was impossible for me to wear the money belt, so I examined the stateroom, opening drawers, realizing that anyone actually doing a search would be sure to find it in any one of them. I examined nooks and crannies, and then had a bright idea.

I had noticed that the bottoms of the lower drawers sat a bit high off the deck of the stateroom. I pulled open one of the large drawers, reached my hand inside and felt over the back panel. Unable to move my hand any further to gauge the depth underneath the drawer, I withdrew it, stood and looked around the stateroom. In a small writing desk, I found a supply of short pencils and a yellow legal pad, the latter giving me an idea.

I returned to the open large drawer and, inserting the flexible pad, I bent it over the back panel and pushed it down. From this improvised measuring gauge, I guessed there seemed to be a depth below the drawer of at least three inches, perhaps even a bit more. I believed there was adequate room to hide my money belt, so I fed it in over the back panel and jiggled it down into the space below, using the pad to tamp it down flat.

When I finished, I ran the drawer in and out. It tracked smoothly, not catching on the belt. Although it wouldn't be easy to fish out when I needed it, I would feel no qualms about busting the drawer if necessary. Damage to the yacht would be the responsibility of the Cady family, not mine.

Before I left, I tucked the Glock into my belt. For a man who wasn't at all fond of guns, I was beginning to like mine, a little more comfortable with than without it

I opened the door into the salon. Cady was still sleeping soundly where I'd left him, apparently too bruised and tired to have moved to the aft stateroom where he'd have been more comfortable. I moved out onto the deck in the darkness, realizing that dawn was still many minutes away. I climbed the ladder to the flybridge where Minnie, at the wheel, was staring ahead into the foam-capped black sea.

"You must be getting tired," I said to her.

She nodded. "How's the old man?"

"Looks okay," I told her. "Want me to take over for a while?"

"You know how to run this rig?"

"Not exactly, but I'm a quick study," I replied. "Show me the basics and give me the heading. I'll let you take a break."

There wasn't much to learn and, five minutes later, I was at the wheel getting the feel of the craft, Minnie watching to see that I was doing it right. The twin diesel engines drove the yacht at a good clip through the ocean, responsive to the slightest touch. I didn't have any idea of how it would respond in heavy seas, but it was a splendid ride in the calm Gulf waters. I paid close attention to the instruments, staying on the heading that Minnie had given me, and the joy of piloting this magnificent craft helped me to distance myself from the troubles now behind me.

"I'll check on Bruno and make a little breakfast," she told me, preparing to climb down to the deck.

"Nothing poisonous," I said flippantly.

For the first time ever, I saw her grin as she descended.

26

I stayed at the helm of the cruiser as dawn came and splen-dored into a rosy morning. The scattered clouds were rimmed with reds, purples, and golds; every shade and hue shifting and evolving into a beautiful tropical day. I switched off the run-ning lights and watched the rising sun turn the sea into shim-mering brass and, finally, into a blue-green color. After an hour, the sun grew hot, but the warmth felt good as I guided the yacht through the gentle waves. On occasion, I spotted other ships, large vessels appearing tiny on the distant horizon.

Tampico was long behind us, and there was no sight of land in any direction. Somewhere, in front of me, there were likely more dangers and uncertainties, but the long stretch of injustice, imprisonment, and humiliation seemed to be wash-ing away in the churning wake of our yacht. If and when I ever found a safe sanctuary, I hoped bitter memories might fade and leave me thankful for a new and untroubled life.

Minnie's head appeared. "Breakfast is ready. Cut the engines and come on down."

I switched off the diesels, descended the ladder, and joined the others in the salon. Bruno was sitting up, bleary eyed, rubbing himself to assuage his aches and pains. He labored to stand and, in a crablike walk, made his way aft to the master stateroom and closed the door behind him.

Minnie was dividing her attention between the eggs and bacon frying on the galley stove while also keeping watch on the ocean through the portholes. "We'll drift a while and save some gas," she said to me. She gestured to the pot on the stove. "Help yourself to coffee. Hope you like it strong."

"Any way is fine," I told her. I took two cups from a galley locker, poured coffee for me and for her as well. "You're in a better mood."

She flashed me a look. "Don't count on it."

"I won't," I responded.

I sat at the table while she finished the eggs and bacon. She ladled them onto plastic plates, one of which she handed to me, keeping the other for herself as she sat down at the end of the settee.

"I'll fix some for Bruno if he wants any," she said, taking a sip of her coffee. "He'll probably make do with a drink."

I nodded, looking around at the interior of the salon, admiring it once again. "How much would something like this outfit cost?" I wondered aloud.

"If you've got to ask . . ."

I laughed. "How many days did you charter?"

"Enough," she said, plainly intending not to tell me more.

"When do we meet your clients?"

No answer.

We sat and ate in silence.

"More coffee?" she asked finally.

"As long as you're at it," I said, handing her my cup.

"You ask a lot of questions," she accused.

I shrugged; a mannerism I was getting good at. "Just trying to find my way."

"Then, hang on for the ride," she told me crossly. "We'll tell you when and where to jump off."

"Just as long as it's on land," I said as a mild retort.

She handed me a second cup of coffee, poured a cup for herself, and we sat in silence while we drank.

Then, she took a sudden interest in the top of my head. "I guess you're not naturally bald."

I touched my incoming hair, wishing it either shorter or longer. "I must look pretty strange."

"Strange, not pretty," she said.

Bruno came out of the aft cabin, looking a little more presentable than we'd seen him before. His puffy face was washed, and he was wearing a different shirt over his blood-specked jeans. He came to the table to join us as Minnie rose to get him a cup of coffee.

"You look better," I told him.

He gave me a wry expression.

"Want anything to eat?" Minnie asked him.

He shook his head. "Where are we?"

"A lot of nautical miles out of Tampico," she replied. "We're tuned to the right frequency and ready for our coordinates."

"Ought to be sometime early tomorrow," he said gruffly. "I hope I'm feeling better by then."

"What did you promise him?" she said, jerking her head toward me.

"I don't remember," he said wearily. "I was punch drunk at the time."

"What did he promise you?" she said, turning to me.

I gave her a hard look, feeling my patience coming very close to the end. "Look," I said with heavy emphasis. "Give me a safe ride to somewhere out of the jurisdiction of the United States, and I'll call that square."

"Too little," she protested. "Doesn't sound right."

"We'll give him a share, Min, it's all right," Bruno said with a dismissive wave of his hand. "The kid's okay, so leave him alone." Then, his face changed, curiosity claiming him. "Back there in the field . . . how *did* you get away from Luis and his thugs?"

"Luck," I said, not wanting to get into details.

"That doesn't tell me much," Cady persisted.

I sighed. "One of them got careless with a gun, and I got the drop on them," I explained, sounding like a western gun-slinger.

"The hell you did!" Cady exclaimed, shaking his head. "I can't see that with Luis."

"Whether you can or not, that's what happened," I told him.

"So what did you do then?" he asked.

"Well, lacking the killer instinct that you two want to accuse me of, I shot each one of them in the foot, took the car and ran for it," I told him. "I was in that bar, looking to buy a phony passport, when the barkeep brought me up to where they were holding you."

Cady smiled. "Wondered what happened to Luis' foot." Then, a new thought came to him. "What happened to the suitcase with the counterfeit bills?"

I could see he had the sixteen thousand seed money in mind. I shrugged, figuring I had more than earned it. "I guess Luis still has it."

"Shit," he grumbled, apparently believing me. "Coulda used that money."

"Didn't you get enough, Bruno?" Minnie said, vexed at her father's manner. "You got a couple of million." Then, with undisguised suspicion, she looked at me. "Sure you didn't get it?"

"Wish I had," I lied, glad I'd hidden the money belt. Now, however, I was thinking about the unhidden counterfeit in my back pack.

Why I'd hung onto the phony stuff, I couldn't begin to say. If it hadn't fooled Luis, why would I think it would be useful to me?

I vowed to dump it overboard at the first opportunity, and to do so without being seen.

The discussion ended, and I did some on deck exploring. At the bow, I leaned precariously over the side to see the name of the yacht - *Bonny Sue*.

Figuring my current streak of good luck had just about run its course, I would've expected something more like the *Pequod*, the *Bounty* or some other harbinger name of impending disaster.

I sat on the aft deck to bask in the sun while, in the deck-house, the two of them poured over charts and muttered their plans. After a while, Minnie moved to the nearby controls, fired up the diesels, and we were chugging along again.

Despite what seemed to have evolved into a somewhat easier relationship with the pair, I still was not comfortable with this larcenous father and daughter. Certainly, I thought Bruno was capable of murder, and very possibly experienced at it.

Minnie?

I thought I detected something in her that was more bluster than wickedness. She was no angel, probably as devious as they come, but she didn't quite fit the hard-boiled image she tried so hard to project. When I'd foolishly surrendered my gun at the dock, she could've ended things right then and there. She could've shot me, dumped me at sea, and gone on about the drug-dealing without a third party to worry about.

Even *so,* that possibility might yet be their plan.

However, there was nothing I could do except keep a wary eye on my shipmates, and worry about getting a nasty sunburn out here on deck.. Despite those anxieties, it was impossible not to enjoy the pleasure of a magnificent tropical day at sea. I sat in comfort, my eyes on the serene beauty of the undulating, white-crested waves, and the cloudless blue sky above.

It was my backward glance across our foaming wake that I picked up a moving speck on the horizon behind us. I watched it, trying to recognize whatever it was. Finally, I realized it was not on the water, but skimming above it. As near as I could tell, some sort of an aircraft was making wide sweeps back and forth across the sea. As it came nearer, I could see it was at a higher altitude than I'd first thought, high enough to provide its occupants with a commanding view of the ocean below. I stood up to get a better look and, with a feeling of foreboding, I retreated into the shadow of the deckhouse cover.

"Guys!" I said over the drone of the diesels. "You'd better take a look at this!"

They looked back at me in some annoyance. Minnie slowed the engines and joined me on deck, her gaze following mine as Cady stepped up behind us. "I don't see anything," he said, his voice showing complaint.

"Right there, Bruno," Minnie said to him, pointing at the still-distant object. "Plane or a helicopter."

"So what?" Cady said, ready to turn back to the deck-house.

"Coming from Tampico," I offered my opinion.

This roused Cady's interest. "Doesn't mean it's them."

"Doesn't mean it isn't!" Minnie interjected.

"How would they know that we left by sea?" I asked.

"Most logical way out," Cady mused. "Or maybe, someone at the marina saw us pull out and told Luis."

"It may not be his bunch at all, but let's take no chances,"
Minnie said, a note of command in her voice. "You two better
stay out of sight."

A few moments later, she was up the ladder and behind
the controls under the flybridge canopy.

"Come back down!" I called to her. "You'd be a sitting duck
up there!"

"Better they see me!" she shouted. "They'll be looking for
two men, not a woman!"

"Don't bet your life on it!" I shouted back, and turned to
Cady. "Just in case, maybe it'd be a good idea to break out
the firearms."

He nodded his agreement, and we hurried down to the
forward cabin. Cady knelt and reached beneath the bunk to
pull out, one or two at a time, the entire array of weapons. He
considered them for a few seconds, and then handed me one
of the rifles. Next, he lay flat on his stomach and reached far
beneath the bunk, bringing out a large plastic case I hadn't
seen before. He opened it to reveal a lethal looking assault
rifle. He took it out with a practiced ease, unfolded the stock,
attached a double magazine, mounted a scope, and then
began to ready it for firing.

While I handled my rifle with a great deal of clumsiness,
Cady's actions were swift and assured. He checked the mechanism and the scope with nimble-fingered rapidity, glancing
repeatedly at my awkward efforts with unconcealed contempt.
Even though I had shown a bumbling initial ineptitude, I did
manage to finally find such important parts as the trigger
and the cocking mechanism. Assuring myself that there was
ammunition in the rifle, I nodded my readiness.

Cady gestured to the other weapons. "Bring along a couple more. We might be needing 'em."

With three rifles in my arms, I struggled out of the stateroom, following Cady as he moved to the deckhouse, where he stretched out prone on the deck inside the shadow of the canopy overhead.

"What are you doing?" I asked.

"You'll see," he said, nodding to the deck for me to join him.

I put the rifles within reach and knelt beside him.

Cady patted the assault rifle. "We may have a surprise for our friend, if it's who we think it is."

"Quite a weapon," I said, not sure whether in appreciation or dismay.

"Swiss," he told me. "Troops use 'em."

"How'd you get one?"

He gave me a smile and no answer.

From my kneeling position, looking back, I could now see that the moving object was, indeed, a helicopter coming directly toward us.

Belatedly, I saw the wisdom of Cady's firing position. We were well enough inside the *Bonnie Sue* deckhouse that we could not be readily seen. If it really was a threat, the helicopter would have to be at about a thirty degree angle or lower for an observer to get a line of sight into the yacht. And, with the contrast between daylight and the deckhouse cover's deep shadow, seeing and recognizing us wouldn't be easy. Of course, the downside of our defensive position was we would have a very limited field of fire. We couldn't get a very good shot at the helicopter without coming out from what little cover our yacht provided. I didn't like the odds of a gunfight between a helicopter and our cumbersome water craft.

"Listen, you guys!" Minnie shouted from the flybridge. "Don't do anything foolish! Stay outta sight, and maybe they'll go away!"

The way Cady fondled the assault rifle, I wasn't at all sure he would heed his daughter's excellent advice.

I could see the helicopter was one of those larger commercial types, sort of a sleek-shaped fuselage with a wide-door opening on the right side. From my vantage point, I could see a couple of men leaning out, peering intently down at us. Seated behind them, I thought I could see a couple of others. As the helicopter came closer, I could see a rifle in the hands of one of the occupants, and I had no doubt as to lethal purpose of these low flying intruders. It was a small squad of armed men looking for a specific target.

Us!

Obviously not designed as an attack helicopter, it was still a great advantage for its heavily armed occupants. It had height, speed and mobility against our slow moving vessel. As it approached us from our stern, no more than twenty feet above the sea surface, I felt very vulnerable, very exposed, very afraid.

The noise of the oncoming helicopter added to the sound of our diesels, creating a din that was becoming unnerving. The overhead rotor blades were beating and beating, the surface of the sea saucering under its powerful down-draft.

"It's Luis," Cady shouted. "Sitting in the seat by the pilot."

It was, indeed.

For just a moment, in the bright sunlight, I could see him clearly, some sort of a high-tech lethal weapon in his hands. Then, the helicopter flashed past us, and I could only catch glimpses of it through the deckhouse front windows as it circled about us.

"I'm waving at them!" Minnie shouted. "Being real friendly!"

I listened to the helicopter engine's receding drone, tracing its path as it circled ahead of us, and heard the thundering roar as it came around behind us once again. Now, it hovered directly behind us, only a dozen feet above the ocean, the occupants obviously trying to see inside the deckhouse. Dangerously close, the down-draft from the helicopter's whirling blades added a rocking motion to our yacht as we cut through the sea, Minnie driving the yacht at full speed.

"Think they can see us?" I asked, words almost unheard in the racket of engines, thumping overhead blades, and waves beating against the yacht.

"No, but I can see them," Cady said, raising the assault rifle into position. He steadied himself, his finger on the trigger, putting his right eye to the sight. "Hold it still, Minnie, darling."

He was an instant away from shooting, when the helicopter moved up and to the right.

"Damn!" Cady swore, relaxing his trigger finger, but remaining fixed in his position. "Almost had him."

"Think they saw us?" I repeated. Given the sudden change of the helicopter's position, I was pretty sure they had.

"I don't think so," he answered. "We're almost invisible in here."

"Maybe they're using special goggles or something," I ventured.

Cady took his eye from the sight to give me a scornful look. "You really don't know a lot about certain things, do you?"

I might've said that killing skills were not high on my needs list, but I thought that this was not the time for such a discussion.

"He's not sure of us," Cady gave his opinion. "Not sure we're the ones he's looking for."

Suddenly, from the helicopter, a bullhorn voice cut in over the racket, "You! Stop the ship! Everyone aboard, come out on the deck! Show yourselves!"

Luis' voice!

Of course, we didn't slow down or show ourselves.

There was a rattle of gunfire, but nothing hit the ship.

"That was a warning! I *order* you to stop!" the amplified voice insisted. "Stop and show yourselves!"

"Hard right, Minnie!" Cady shouted. "Hard right under him!"

Minnie's quick action, changing direction, was probably more a matter of her instinct rather than a response to Cady's command. The move must have surprised our airborne antagonists as well, since the stutter of gunfire came several seconds later and only a couple struck the yacht.

Minnie dropped to the deck from the flybridge and, at first, I thought she'd been hit, but she was unscathed, seeking what little shelter the deckhouse offered. She flew to the inside wheel, her eyes wide, a look of confusion as well as fear on her face.

"They can't get a good shot firing head on!" Cady shouted. "Their best shots are from the back and side angles!"

Sure enough, the helicopter came again to our port side, flying twenty feet above the ocean, giving the shooters a clear field of fire.

"Tell me where!" Minnie shouted.

"Left!" Cady shouted. "Left! Under them!"

She turned the wheel hard to move the yacht directly beneath the helicopter, then turned the ship again to match their direction. She gunned the *Bonnie Sue* to speed ahead, giving us, momentarily, the up angle to fire our weapons directly into the nose of the pursuing helicopter.

Cady got off one short burst before the helicopter veered away, and we were vulnerable again. Immediately, the airborne guns stuttered, bullets striking the yacht.

"Hard right!" I shouted.

Minnie wheeled the yacht to the starboard, and the hail of bullets abruptly ended.

"We can't keep this up!" Minnie shouted. "They'll get us next time for sure!"

"I'm afraid you're right, daughter!" Cady shouted back. "Let her run and let 'em come!"

He rose and hurried out onto the deck, the assault rifle stock firm against his shoulder. "Back me up!" he shouted.

I followed, with my rifle settled against my shoulder, and watched the helicopter angling toward us. As soon as we stepped into the sunlight, the automatic gunfire began once more. I heard the passage of bullets in the air and felt their impacts on the ship. Bullets were slamming into the ship, tearing rips in the flying bridge's fabric canopy, punching holes into the deckhouse and breaking glass.

Cady began firing as the helicopter came nearer, his weapon on full automatic. I followed suit with my rifle, aiming as best I could. I fired shot after shot, as fast as my weapon could feed the ammunition. Close beside me, another rifle began to bark; Minnie was standing with us, aiming at the oncoming helicopter.

It would've been an awesome sight for an onlooker - three people standing in a rain of bullets on an unpiloted, wildly racing yacht, firing their own barrage back at the hovering helicopter. The pilot was trying to maintain a like speed with the yacht while maintaining an advantageous firing position. With no one at the helm of our craft, we were all over the ocean, changing directions erratically. If it was hard for the airborne shooters to get a bead on our ship, it was almost impossible for us to keep a sight on the helicopter, the aircraft zooming, rising and dipping, the ship bouncing crazily through the waves.

Suddenly, Cady dashed inside the deckhouse and, a moment later, the diesel engines ceased their steady snarl. Both Minnie and I staggered, nearly falling, as the yacht abruptly went from high speed to a wallow. I bounced against the rail, felt a sharp blow to my right thigh, and nearly catapulted over the side.

"Damn it, Bruno!" Minnie shouted. "What the hell are you doing?"

The helicopter had overshot us, zooming ahead. Now, it was circling, coming back, its occupants undoubtedly relishing the thought of blowing the sitting duck out of the water.

Cady came out of the cabin, replacing the magazine in the assault rifle, and then raised it back to his shoulder. "Now, maybe I can get a shot." He moved quickly to the rail and crouched down, settling into position, positioning his eye at the sight.

The helicopter was approaching fast, canted at an angle, positioning to fire down at us. It was coming in for the kill, the men aboard sure they had wounded our vessel and, now, they would come in for the *coup de grace*!

I limped to the rail, thinking of crouching, and then decided against it. The rail offered no protection, so I thought it best to do my shooting standing straight up. Apparently, Cady came to the same solution and rose to stand beside me. Minnie joined us, raising her rifle to the sky.

We started firing in unison, a fusillade of shots aimed at the oncoming whirlybird. Immediately, the airborne gunmen returned fire, a barrage answering our salvo. I felt the tug of one bullet as it caught the loose fabric of my shirt, another skimming just past my ear, a third knocking the rifle from my hands. I ducked to retrieve it from where it had fallen on the deck and saw that the wooden stock was splintered, nearly destroyed. Nonetheless, I brought it up and held it as well as possible, firing at the helicopter until the bullets ran out.

I started to limp into the cabin for another weapon when the helicopter made a sudden erratic maneuver: It abruptly nosed up, the rotor blades whirling madly, churning a wildly impossible ascent into the sky. Amazingly, the rotor blades came to a near vertical position, as the helicopter continued to climb a hundred, two hundred feet. Then, it rolled over backward and began a fluttering, wounded fall. Suddenly, a man's body arced out and flailed all the way into the ocean waves. Moments later, the helicopter flipped right side up, and crashed into the sea with a tremendous splash. For a few seconds, the fuselage remained half submerged while the rotor blades spun and created a whirlpool of the water. It was an awesome spectacle; a giant mixer blending its breaking parts and broken bodies into a lather of destruction. Then, the helicopter sank from view, the rotor blades still beating above the water surface, whipping the craft down into the ocean depths.

A minute later, the sea returned to gentle waves, only a few scattered pieces of the wreckage bobbing up and down.

27

"Anybody hurt?" Cady asked, turning to see.

"I'm okay," Minnie replied. "God knows how!"

Then, they both turned to stare at me.

"What's wrong?" I asked, surprised at their curiosity.

"You're hit," Minnie said. "You've been hit."

"Nonsense," I told her. "Close call, but nothing—"

I looked down and saw the wound a few inches above my right knee and, all at once, I felt a wave of pain and nausea. My leg was suddenly on fire and it collapsed under me. I fell to the deck, grabbing for my thigh, and felt blood welling from the wound into my hands. The surge of agony became constant, and I cried out, including some fancy swearing.

Cady merely stood and looked down on me. I had this notion that he might be considering putting me out of my misery. In my anguish, I really might not have cared. Minnie was the first to move to me, kneeling down, looking at the leg.

"There's a first aid kit in the locker by the stove," she said to Cady. "Get it . . . some towels, anything you can find to stop the bleeding."

Cady was in no hurry to comply. He took a satisfied look at the empty sky where the helicopter had been, then slowly shuffled into the deckhouse on his way to the salon. In what seemed to be a very long time, he returned with a large medical kit which he handed to her along with several towels and washcloths. She bent close to examine the wound, studied it, and then put a clean towel on it. She looked up to Cady. "Hold this, Bruno," she instructed. "Put some pressure on it."

Bruno regarded her, making no move to comply.

I reached down and put my hands on the towel. "I'll do it," I said, my anger at Cady's indifference overcoming my own pain and nausea. "Do what you need to do."

With a darting look of fury at her father, she rose and walked away, going forward on the deck toward the bow. A few moments later, she came back with a bucket of water.

"Sea water," she told me. "Ought to be clean enough." She knelt beside me once again and took the bloody towel away. With a cloth, she began to sponge off the blood, occasionally pouring water directly on my leg to expose the deep, dark wound.

"Looks like it went clean through, no bone damage from what I can see," she told me. "I think it looks worse than it is. How bad does it hurt?"

"Like hell," I moaned.

She nodded, then looked inside the medicine kit and rummaged around.

"Anything for the pain?" I asked.

"We got a lot of cocaine in the cabin," she said cheerfully.

I didn't know if she was being serious.

Her hand came out of the medicine kit with a packet of syringes, each of them filled with a liquid. "You allergic to morphine?"

"I don't know," I answered.

She made no comment as she plunged the needle into my skin.

She fussed over me for a few minutes, continuing to bathe the wound with sea water, then with an antiseptic. She dressed the wound with bandages while Cady stood over her, watching. I could almost hear his thoughts, reckoning I'd be of little help if we had more trouble with the dealers on the freighter.

"We're lucky to be alive," he said unexpectedly. "Got off damn lucky as far as I can see."

"Glad you feel that way," I muttered, still angry.

"Well," he ventured with a wry smile. "It was you who could've put 'em away when you had the chance."

Of course, he was right.

"You may be okay, but you could have some trouble with that leg if you don't see a doctor pretty soon," Minnie told me, lecturing to my thigh. "I've done what I can with what's aboard, but sooner or later, you'll need some real doctoring." She looked up at me, straight in the face. "Bruno's right. We are damned lucky."

I nodded.

"I must've got the pilot," Cady said, wandering back over to the rail, looking out at the sea at the scene of his conquest. "I thought for a minute, he was going to pull some fancy-dan maneuver, but he was just plain dying at the stick."

"You sure you got him?" Minnie said sarcastically. "Kev and I were shooting, too."

Cady, with his back to us, shook his head. "Naw, it was my automatic fire, you can bet. You was just plinking at him."

"Give me a hand, and let's get Kev into the cabin," Minnie said, reaching to help me rise. "Think you can walk?"

"Maybe hobble," I said, coming up to stand on one foot. I was suddenly very dizzy, and Minnie slipped her shoulder under my arm.

"Come on, Bruno!" she said sharply. "He's your pal."

Cady gave no answer, and we both looked at him. I was ready to curse him into my assistance, but I could see that his attention was riveted on something out in the ocean.

"What is it?" Minnie asked.

"Something . . . somebody out there," Cady replied. "I think I see a head."

Minnie helped me to the rail beside Cady, and we all gazed out into the swelling sea. After a few moments, I spotted the head and shoulders of someone bobbing on the waves. Whoever it was began to wave.

"I'll be damned," Cady said. "One of 'em survived."

"He wants us to pick him up," I said.

"Fat chance," Cady responded.

"Well, he's swimming towards us," Minnie observed, her voice turning sarcastic. "What's our next move, Captain?"

Cady chuckled at his nautical promotion. "Start up the engines and see if he can catch up with us."

"That's pretty cold, Cady," I said, gritting my teeth against the pain. "I hope you were kidding."

Cady gave me a very strange look. "A few minutes ago, whoever he is, he was trying his best to kill you." He nodded at my leg. "Probably the very guy who put that hole in you."

The swimmer was coming closer, and I could see something beneath the surface of the sea. Sure enough, something white on the end of one of his feet.

"It's Luis!" Cady said, a throaty laugh following his announcement. "Trust the devil to take care of his own."

"Hey!" shouted the swimmer. "You gotta pick me up! You can't leave me out here! It's the law!"

"Law?" Cady yelled. "What law did you ever know, Luis?"

"The law of the sea!" Luis called out. "You have to help people in the sea!"

"Keep coming, Luis!" Cady shouted. "Maybe we'll save you if you can get here!"

"You sonofabitch!" Luis yelled. "There may be sharks out here!"

"They'll not hurt you, Luis!"

"Professional courtesy," I said almost under my breath.

Cady scowled at me for ruining his revised lawyer joke.

"Bring him aboard," I said to Cady, looking to Minnie for support. "We'll tie him up and keep him locked down 'til we can find someplace to put him ashore."

Minnie didn't return the look.

"Damned dangerous man," Cady said, watching Luis paddling toward us. "You think we'd be safe with him aboard?"

"Well, he's not too mobile," I responded. "I shot him in the foot, and that ought to slow him down."

Cady gestured to my leg. "Maybe he's the one who did you a favor in return."

Luis was twenty feet away, flailing his arms to stay afloat, watching us anxiously, waiting for one of us to say or do something. "Take me aboard, Cady!" he pleaded. "I know I don't deserve it, but I'm begging you!"

"You didn't listen when I begged you to stop beating me!" Cady retorted. "Serve you right if the sharks do come and eat you . . . piece by piece!"

Luis shifted his attention to me and to Minnie. "Lord in heaven! Young man! Young lady! Don't let him leave me to die!"

"Bring him aboard, damn it!" I said. "No matter whatever he's done—"

Cady's assault rifle gave a short burst, then another - and Luis disappeared in a spray of bloody froth.

"Damn you, Cady!" I shouted. "You murdering sonofabitch!"

Cady gave me a smile and turned the rifle slightly in my direction. "I don't care what you call me, sonny, but *that* sonofabitch would've killed one or all of us once he set his sore foot on this deck."

Words welled up in my throat, but I didn't say them. There was no point. What Cady had said was undoubtedly a distinct possibility. Luis, himself, had admitted to the pleasures of homicide, so it was no loss at all to the rest of the world. Had we managed to get him to shore, even to whatever police that shore might provide, he would have undoubtedly found a future way to slay his fellow human beings. He'd survived the helicopter crash, and cheated death by only a few minutes. Perhaps, unlike the others, he'd had some sort of a chance to beg mercy from his Creator.

Most likely not.

"I think I'd better lie down," I said to Minnie, nodding to Cady and his rifle. "If you can persuade him not to shoot me."

"I'm in debt to you for pulling me out back there in Tampico, Mathias," Cady said to me. "But, the way you've been lipping off, I figure just getting you out of Mexico more than pays that debt."

"What are you going to do, Bruno?" Minnie asked, misgiving in her voice.

"I'll drop him off in the Caymans," Cady replied. "After we make our deal."

"What about the cut you promised him?" she asked.

Cady shrugged. "I ain't necessarily a man of my word."

Minnie looked at me, expecting anger.

"It was all his talk in the first place," I told her. "If you can spare it, I need just enough money to buy me a passport and transportation to somewhere in South America."

"Let's get you inside," she said, slipping her shoulder under my arm once again. Once we were moving, she paused to turn to her father. "You really are a murdering sonofabitch!"

He gave her the finger, a nice sort of fatherly gesture.

She assisted me all the way to the forward cabin, and steadied me as I hopped to my bunk. Almost tenderly, she helped me prop up my injured leg, supporting it with a rolled blanket.

"Pain shot working yet?" she asked.

"Some," I answered. "Took a bit of the edge off of it."

"We'll meet the freighter sometime tomorrow," she told me. "We'll make the trade, and then head on to the Grand Cayman."

She sat down on the opposite bunk and regarded me, her face set solemnly. "Truth was . . . truth is . . . I didn't want to split anything with you."

"Doesn't matter," I said, thinking of the money I'd hidden under the drawer.

"I know, but it does seem like you don't deserve this shit," she said. She pointed to my backpack under the bunk. "How much do you have in there?"

"Not much at all. Take a look for yourself," I told her with a sigh, hoping that she wouldn't, wondering how I'd explain the counterfeit bills. I was beginning to feel dopey enough not to really care. I settled back in the bunk. "I think that shot's taking effect . . . or maybe it's shock."

"You rest," she said. "I'll see that Bruno leaves you alone."

"I wouldn't count too much on his fatherly love," I cautioned her. "The mood he's in, he'd probably toss you overboard, too."

She laughed. "I might do the same to him." She paused and, once again, became serious. "I'm a hard person, Kev.

Harder, than you have any idea of. Don't trust me any further than my old man."

"Well, you seem to have some softness in your nature," I countered. "I don't think you liked what happened any more than I did."

"He did what had to be done," she said. "I'll give him that."

"I couldn't have done it," I said to her. "I wouldn't have, and I don't think you would've either."

She rose without responding to that. "I'm going to get us going again. You take it easy, and see if you can't sleep away some of that hurt." She paused at the companionway door. "I've got some pretty strong pain pills, and we can go again on the morphine if you need it."

"Thanks," I said, but she'd already left, closing the door behind her.

28

It was late morning when I awoke, the earlier sharp, stabbing pain now replaced with a steadier kind of hurt. I peeked under the bandages to examine the wound and, as ugly as it appeared, it didn't seem to show signs of worsening. As yet, there did not appear to be a telltale appearance of infection, and I could move the leg if I had to. I had some fuzzy recollections of the night - Minnie coming in to take a look at me.

Had she gone through my backpack and my tote bag?

I couldn't be sure, but I believed she was there only to see how I was doing. I could recall her cool hand on my forehead, checking for fever. I laid my right hand palm on my forehead, and then wondered if a fevered hand could detect a fevered brow. I decided I felt okay, not great, but okay.

I swung carefully out of the bunk, wondering at my inborn stupidity for doing so. I stood for a couple of minutes, to see if I was going to get dizzy and pass out. If I did, I wanted to pass out on a comfortable bunk, rather than up on the deck and, maybe, keel over the rail.

Satisfied that I was stable, I hopped to the steps and, sorely, climbed them into the deckhouse. No one was there so, favoring the injured leg, I limped my way out onto the aft deck. Cady and his daughter were up on the flying bridge driving the yacht. I stepped back inside, spotted the medicine kit on the table and moved to it, thinking of giving myself another injection of morphine. I rummaged around in it for a moment or two, and then decided that I'd try to get by with a couple of the strong painkiller pills. I took them with a drink of water, then hobbled over to one of the settees and sat down.

Minnie came down a couple of minutes later. "You're up?" she questioned in a manner of disapproval.

"For the moment," I replied. "I took a couple of pain pills."

She nodded. "How do you feel?"

"Like I've been shot in the leg."

"You want me to look at it?"

I shook my head. "Took a look at it myself," I told her. "You did a pretty damn good job."

"We'll see," she said solemnly. She undid the bandage on my leg, ripping off the adhesive tape with an almost professional manner, and removed the gauze pad over the wound. With greater concern than my own, she examined both the entrance and exit areas of the injury. She made a soft clucking sound that could have meant either satisfaction or the lack of it.

"It looks okay, don't you think?" I asked.

She shrugged. "Not bad. No sign of infection . . . that's good."

"You were in a couple of times last night," I said. "You get any sleep?"

"Some," she responded.

"Bruno took the master stateroom?"

She nodded without comment and began to treat the wound. She cleaned it carefully, and redressed it with fresh gauze and adhesive strips. As she attended to me, her head bowed and intent upon her nursing ministration, I'll admit I was beginning to be strongly attracted to her. In spite of her tough-as-nails manner, and an undoubtedly incorrigible past, she was capable of showing some tenderness and compassion.

She caught me looking at her, flashed an embarrassed smile, and then turned peevish. "There!" she exclaimed brusquely, rising quickly. "That's the best I can do. If you don't have any infection set in, you'll be okay."

"You don't have to be angry for showing some concern," I told her, sorry to see the hard-edged side of her emerge. "You didn't like what he did any more than I did."

Her lips tightened, annoyance showing. "What I think or do is none of your business."

I found myself becoming angry with her as well. "Is there anything here that I could use as a crutch?" I asked, almost a demand.

She shook her head. "Not the sort of item you'd figure on carrying," she said crisply. She gestured to my leg. "Best thing is for you to stay off of it."

"I've never been shot before," I responded peevishly. "It serves me right for ever boarding this ship. I should've found some other way."

"Meaning?"

"Whatever you and your father are up to," I said tiredly. "The two of you are a puzzle, and I don't know what to expect when you meet up with this tanker or freighter or whatever."

We faced each other in silence for a few moments. I regretted my anger, and I hoped she felt the same.

"You needn't be involved," she said finally, her vexation no longer evident. "As far as trusting us . . ." She didn't finish.

"Why set this up at sea?" I asked. "It seems like kind of an awkward arrangement."

"That's between them and Bruno," she replied. "He got in touch with me, told me to charter the yacht, and told me that he was bringing goods that would set the both of us up for life. Sounded good to me, so I did what I was told."

"Wouldn't it have been easier somewhere on land?"

"Probably, but that wasn't what the clients wanted," she responded.

"When does the rendezvous take place?"

"A couple of hours," she replied. "I'm getting ready to contact them now."

"And what happens when we meet?"

She hesitated, as if considering whether or not to tell me. Then, she said, "We meet in mid-ocean, make the trade, then we go our separate ways."

"I mean . . . how will the swap take place?" I said, thinking of my first exchange disaster.

"They launch a boat from the freighter, bring us the money, load the goods, and I hope that's the end of it."

"You *hope* that's all of it," I suggested. "This seems to be a rather dangerous profession."

"No reason it shouldn't go down as planned," she said.

I couldn't help voicing my suspicions. "If there's any double-dealing, we're into another war."

"I don't think that'll happen," she said, although not too convincingly. "They're happy to get this amount of cocaine without paying top price, and that ought to make them happy."

"People in this business tend to be greedy," I countered.

"That's why we brought the guns," she admitted.

"Speaking of guns," I said. "How are we on ammunition after our last battle?"

"Enough," she assured me. "More than enough."

"I wish I could be sure."

"If you can make it," she said, nodding again to my leg, "It would be good if you could be on deck when we meet . . . and fully armed."

"I can do that," I said, not at all sure of my capability.

"Good!" she exclaimed. "Just stay down and off of it 'til it's time."

With a nod of dismissal, she walked over to the communications center and flipped a switch on a radio. She went through dialing procedures and found a channel that, first, crackled, and then became quite clear.

"Joyride, here," she said into the mike. "Come in, if you copy."

"Good morning, Joyride," a man's voice said cheerfully in response to her sign-on. "We've been waiting to hear from you."

"We're close," Minnie responded. "Probably less than two hours."

"How is everything?"

"Everything's fine," Minnie assured him, matching cheer for cheer. "Looking forward to seeing you."

"We'll talk then," the man continued cordially. "Thanks for checking with us."

After she turned off the radio, she came back out to me.

"These are Americans?" I asked.

She nodded. "As far as I know. I don't really care."

"Assuming all goes well, we're off to . . . where did you say? Cayman Islands?"

"That's the plan," she agreed.

"Is that where you picked up this yacht?" I asked.

She didn't answer.

"There's bound to be some questions about all the bullet holes," I ventured.

"Not if we're not around to answer them."

I thought this over, and then asked: "Are we going to be any place close to civilization?" I touched my leg. "I'm not going to be able to walk very far."

"We'll see to it that you get to a doctor," she assured me. "Count on it."

"I'll almost have to," I remarked.

"You feel up to steering the ship for a few minutes?" she asked.

"I think so," I responded. "Even if I pass out, I'm not likely to run into anything."

She stepped to one side, as I limped to the wheel console.

"Stay on this course," she said, pointing to the instrument panel. She went out on the aft deck, and called up to her father: "Bruno! Kev's going to run the ship! Time to bring out the goods!"

I settled into the deckhouse console seat and took control of the yacht while Cady came down to join Minnie. They worked for about twenty minutes, bringing the duffle bags out onto the aft deck. They unloaded all the clear sacks of cocaine into sort of a display and covered them with a tarp.

"We'll show 'em the whole lot," Cady called to me. "Let 'em test any bag."

"I'll take over now," Minnie told me, coming to my side. "You take a bit more rest."

I nodded, vacated the seat, and limped over to the leather bench where I tried to make myself comfortable.

"Want a beer?" Cady asked, suddenly affable, his murderous mood seemingly past.

"Sure, why not?" I answered. "I'm full of morphine and Percoset. Beer might be just the thing."

Cady went down the steps and, a couple of minutes later, returned with a couple of bottles of Mexican beer. He handed me one, then sat down beside me with the other. Minnie gave us a roll-of-the-eyes expression, a look Cady didn't miss. "You want one, doll?"

She shook her head and turned her gaze through the bullet crazed and shattered glass of the deckhouse windshield.

"Gonna make it okay, son?" Cady turned to me, his tone of concern likely feigned.

"Made it this far," I answered. "Shame not to make it, now."

"Good boy," he said jovially, tipping his bottle, and taking half of it in three sustained gulps. "Ah, that's good. A fair sail, bags of money, merchandise to sell and a beautiful Gulf day! Ain't life grand?"

I took a sip of the ice cold beer. "Nothing's perfect," I said caustically. "What? No lime?"

"Not today, partner," he said. "But when we hit shore, we'll be able to buy us a whole grove of 'em." He paused. "They grow in groves?"

I nodded, taking another sip. "On trees."

Evidently having exhausted his reservoir of affability, he raised his bottle in sort of a salute, then rose and sauntered out onto the aft deck. I took my time finishing my beer, watching Minnie guide the yacht. I found myself feeling drowsy and, after a few minutes, I drifted off to sleep. Between the Percoset and some sapping effect from my injury, I was lulled into that weird narcotic slumber that so often becomes the source of nightmares. My torpor was fraught with dangers, and even a few fleeting erotic fantasies that may have included Minnie. In between these eerie sleepscapes, I occasionally roused to the reality of the yacht moving through the ocean, the engines droning, Minnie practically motionless as she sat behind the wheel.

"Ship's in sight!" she called out, breaking me free from one of my narcotic reveries. "Off the starboard bow!"

Cady came in from the aft deck, his skin showing early sunburn. "Yeah, I saw her," he said. "Run with her 'til she stops, and we make the trade."

"How much distance between us?" Minnie wanted to know.

"Something comfortable for both of us," Cady replied. "We'll keep well out of rifle range."

Beyond Minnie, through the damaged forward windows, I could see the freighter, tiny in the distance, thinking it would be a half-hour or more before she came to us. Despite Minnie's assurance of a probable easy transaction, there seemed to be a lot of nervous tension in the deckhouse: Cady and his daughter watched the oncoming ship intently.

It was moving faster than I had expected, a big cargo freighter cutting through the seas with ease. It was not an unsightly or outmoded vessel, but what appeared to be a relatively modern and trim ship. Perhaps I'd seen too many old movies, but I half-expected something scabby and rusted, with a gang of ruthless cutthroats hanging over the rails ready to commit unspeakable deeds.

Instead, the ship was sailing smoothly; the only people on deck appeared to be ordinary sailors, going about their work. When it crossed directly in front of us, it seemed to be gathering speed. Actually, it was moving at a steady pace and, for a few moments, I wondered if our smaller craft could keep up. Minnie put more power to the diesels, and turned the yacht to drive parallel to the big ship. After a couple of minutes, we were moving side-by-side, keeping about two hundred yards of distance between us. On board the ship, two men, in tee shirts and shorts, gave us waves of welcome. They looked much more like happy-go-lucky tourists than cocaine dealers; seemingly pleasant fellows taking a freighter cruise.

271

Then, the big ship began to slow, and we could see deck-
hands working to lower a lifeboat from the deck, three men
aboard. Minnie throttled back and brought our craft to a bare
crawl, then to a full stop with engines idling. We watched
the smugglers' lifeboat settle into the sea, and we heard the
sound of an outboard starting. The small boat veered away
from the freighter and headed our way.

"Show time!" Cady said, not concealing his delight.
"Another day, another million!"

"Stay back here in the deckhouse," Minnie told me, leaving
the wheel console and striding out onto the aft deck. "Cover
them when they come aboard."

I nodded, then hobbled down the steps, through the salon,
and into the forward stateroom. I retrieved my Uzi, and limped
back up to my station inside the deckhouse. Minnie and Bruno
were standing at the aft rail, the girl with a pistol tucked into
the top of her shorts. Bruno was not armed, but I could see
the assault rifle on the deck at the stern, only a stride away if
it was needed.

"Hi, folks!" came a friendly, southern-accented voice.
"Beautiful day! Great day to do a little shopping, wouldn't you
say?"

"Bring your shopping money?" Cady sang out.

"Permission to bring it aboard, sir!" the happy voice
responded.

I felt the bump as the boat touched our yacht, and then I
saw the heads and shoulders of two of the three men standing
at the bow, their boat lower than our vessel. These two were
both Caucasians, the same men we'd seen waving at us from
the freighter. To me, they still looked more like tourists rather
than felons. One, with short-cropped blond hair was wearing
a white tee shirt with blue sharks chasing a frightened green

grouper. The other, with a white tam over his dark shaggy hair, wore a dirty tee shirt that proclaimed that *Cancun Sucks.* Also, he had a ring in his ear and another in his nose.

The pair dipped down out of sight for a few moments, and then came up with an Anvil case between them. Together, they lifted it up to Bruno who took it from them and put it down on the deck. He reached out a helping hand to assist the first man aboard, and then his ear-ringed, nose-ringed companion who was carrying a small kit bag.

"Thank you, partner," the blond-haired man said, his eyes darting around, looking appreciatively at Minnie, then spying me with the Uzi back in the shadows. "Looks like you all ain't too trusting, are ya?"

The second man gave a nod of greeting, but didn't speak.

The blond-haired man took a speculative look at the yacht, surveying the damage from the helicopter attack, and gave a low whistle. "What the hell happened?"

"Pirates," Cady replied with a sly smile, and said nothing more.

The blond-haired man waited, then gave a shrug. ""Don't know what you all have been through, but I guess ya got a right to be on your guard." The drug buyer gave a slight shake of his head. "Folks, me and my buddy here, we ain't carrying." He gestured back to the lifeboat. "Mario out there has something if things get nasty, but this here's just a friendly little transaction, and that's the way we want it. I'm sure you feel just the same way." He nodded at the tarp. "I 'spect that's what you got to sell. Maybe we ought to take a look."

Cady nodded, stepped over to the tarp and pulled it back, revealing the pile of clear plastic sacks. "What we got is five hundred kilos of pure powder cocaine, street value over nine million bucks. Test it if you like."

The other man stooped to pick up one of the bags, poked a hole through the plastic, then opened his kit and took out his testing apparatus. There were vials of different liquids, and he took a pinch of the white powder and dropped it into one of the vials, shaking it as it turned color.

While he was studying the results, Bruno and the amiable smuggler opened the Anvil case and revealed it full of money. I had a strange feeling about the case itself, not so much about the money. It seemed an extraordinary carry case, heavy to lift and handle, especially out over the open sea. Bruno, however, was entranced with the sight of the money. He gave me a quick and knowing grin as he reached beneath the surface bills to extract a packet of hundred-dollar bills. He thumbed through the sheaf, nodded, then reached deep for another and repeated the process.

"One million dollars as agreed," the jovial one declared. "Hundreds, fifties, just as you asked."

"Better be," Cady said bluntly, continuing to examine, continuing to count.

The man testing the cocaine turned to his companion, smiling. "Not exactly top stuff, but close enough."

"Well!" crowed the loquacious one. "Let's load up and be on our way." He turned to Cady. "Satisfied?"

"Looks great!" Cady exclaimed enthusiastically.

"Mind helping us load the goods?"

"Not at all," Cady agreed.

The blond-haired man closed the money case, snapping the locks shut, and turned to the sacks of cocaine. He and Cady stuffed the plastic sacks back into the duffle bags, sharing smiles and light-hearted banter. The ear-ringed, nose-ringed smuggler swung over the rail and stepped back onto the lifeboat. With the help of Mario, who I could now see, he accepted the duffle bags as Cady and the other man handed them over the side.

Minnie took a step inside the deckhouse, and I moved close to her. "Something doesn't seem quite right," I told her in a low voice. "Maybe it's me, but . . ." I left my thoughts unsaid.

She nodded. "Me, too." She moved toward the deck, just under the canopy, her hand near the automatic pistol in her waistband.

The transfer was finished quickly, and the crew from the lifeboat seemed ready to depart.

"Been a pleasure," the blond-haired man said, extending his hand to Cady, nodding his head both to Minnie and myself as a gesture of appreciation. "Nice doing business with you. Hope we can do it again."

Cady responded in kind and waved, as the blond man stepped down into his boat and we heard the outboard rev up.

In that same instant, I saw the small object arcing up and toward our yacht, and I knew immediately what it was.

A grenade!

Minnie saw it, too, and she reacted immediately. She leaped up, landing one foot on the side rails she attempted to bat the grenade away. Instead, she tipped it and, as she went down, it began to fall toward the deck. In one frenetic motion, I threw the Uzi away and, with a push off my one good leg, I dove for it. Falling hard on my bad leg, with my hands cupped below - as if trying to prevent a volleyball from touching down - I caught it on my fingertips and thrust up with all my might, flinging the grenade toward the open water behind the yacht.

Perhaps if Cady had ducked to the deck, perhaps if he hadn't tried to spike it into the ocean, he would have been saved, but he took the explosion fully, his large body shielding us. The blast gave us an instant view of a bloody horror before it blew him over the side and into the ocean. Fragments from the grenade peppered the aft deck of the yacht, some whistling dangerously near. Minnie gave a muffled outcry and I thought she had been hit, but it must've been concern for her father. She half-rose to rush to the rail, but I grabbed her by the arm and threw her back into the deckhouse. "Get us out of here!" I shouted. "Now!"

She jumped for the console and hit the engines full, the yacht surging forward just as we saw another grenade lobbed toward us. We were fifteen feet away when the second grenade fell into our wake and exploded.

"We've got to go back for Bruno!" Minnie shouted.

"Forget it!" I commanded. "He was dead before he hit the water! He's gone!"

She turned the wheel hard, the yacht heeling in a sharp turn.

"Don't do it, Minnie!" I told her, scrambling up, trying to limp toward her as the yacht rocked and slammed across the waves.

"The dirty sons-of-bitches!" she exclaimed, peering through the crazed and broken windshield glass, aiming the yacht directly at the lifeboat which was now attempting to flee to the ship. The man, Mario, was trying to get more speed out of the little motor. One of the men, the talkative one, was trying to shoot past Mario with an automatic weapon, but only a couple of bullets hit our yacht. I had a fleeting thought that someone aboard the freighter might be aiming at us, but I remembered we were too far out of range. I was dreadfully aware that Minnie had our craft at full throttle, bearing down on the lifeboat with grim determination. I didn't like the idea of an impact, even if our yacht would come out the biggest bruiser.

Ahead of us, the man at the helm of the small boat realized that we were almost on them. Frantically, he turned the boat sharply, hoping to steer out of our way.

Precisely what Minnie wanted him to do.

She pulled the wheel hard, turning right, sending our heavy craft skidding across the waves, piling a wall of water over the lifeboat, swamping it, and tumbling the occupants out into the sea.

Minnie pulled back the power and let the engines idle as she walked out onto the aft deck to survey what she had done. I limped out to join her.

Three heads were bobbing out in the ocean, no sign of the lifeboat or its precious cargo to be seen. I thought of the five hundred kilos of nearly pure cocaine settling to the ocean floor. I couldn't help but picture the giddy fish that would be doing strange and unusual things to other denizens of the deep for days to come.

The three men were now trying to swim toward the freighter and we could see that they were looking toward us, wondering what we would do next.

"Sons-of-bitches," Minnie repeated softly. She returned to the console and revved the engines to drive us away.

I stood on the aft deck and watched the bobbing heads become mere specks, and then they were finally lost to view. "Ship's leaving," I said to Minnie. "Not picking them up."

Minnie didn't turn her head.

Not once.

29

Before dark, we set the sea anchor, and turned on the yacht lights. Earlier, despite the pain in my leg - aggravated by my hard dive for the grenade - I washed the aft deck to remove Bruno's blood. The grenade had done some further superficial damage to the yacht, but apparently nothing functional. Nonetheless, I couldn't help but empathize with the feelings of the owner whenever he or she eventually retrieved their precious yacht. Repairable, I suppose, but it was a banged-up, shot-up, sorry-looking vessel when compared to its original appearance.

I emptied the Anvil case out onto the floor of the salon where Minnie and I combined its contents with the money from Bruno's soft-side bag. She was sitting cross-legged on the carpeted deck and, with me on the settee, we counted up a total of a little more than three million.

"That's a lot of money," she exulted. She threw a quick glance at me. "Don't worry, you'll get your fair share."

"Good," I acknowledged. I rose and dragged the empty Anvil case up the steps and out onto the aft deck. Not quite sure whether to keep it or dump it overboard, I left it there for future consideration. I limped back to the salon to take my seat on the settee, looking down at Minnie who was smiling at her stacks of money.

"You don't believe me, do you?" she asked petulantly.

"Yeah, of course," I replied, not believing.

"You've earned it," she said with conviction. "We'll split it when we get ashore."

We stuffed it all back into the soft-side bag, leaving it in the salon as a sort of symbol of triumph, celebrating our adventures and misadventures. As night came on, we sat on the aft deck at a small table, and made an evening meal from frozen dinners cooked in the microwave and a bottle of white wine. We ate the meals, more for sustenance than taste, and set about finishing the contents of the bottle. Taking a bit of a safety risk under a cloudless sky, Minnie turned off the yacht lights, and we raised our eyes to the heavens. Above us, the expanse of space was impossibly alive with the half-moon and crystalline stars, undiminished in their magnificence. The sea around us was dark, calm with gentle swells of occasional phosphorescence. The sea, the sky, and the cooling whispers of a Caribbean breeze had a calming effect upon Minnie and, in the serenity of the night, she was thoughtful and reflective

"I can't imagine why, but I feel bad about Bruno," she said, sipping her wine, moonlight giving faint luminosity to her face and trim body.

"He was, after all, your father," I said, not a particularly sage comment.

"He wasn't a good man," she continued. "Not that I'm much either."

I didn't have anything to say in return.

"Still it was brave of him to do what he did," she went on.

I was puzzled.

"I mean, shielding us like he did from the grenade," she said in all seriousness. "That was very brave."

Frankly, I thought Bruno had badly miscalculated the fuse time and paid for it in the worst possible way. Nonetheless, a little charity seemed appropriate. "Yes," I muttered. "He did save us."

She looked at the Anvil case that I'd left on the deck, then at me. "What made you suspicious of them?"

I looked at the case and nodded. "I wondered why it was such a heavy, stout thing to carry their money in. They didn't want the cash blown up in the blast."

"They expected to come aboard and take it back," she said, stating the obvious. "What if the blast hadn't killed us?"

"They'd have finished the job," I told her.

She sat and mused for a while, then said, "Think of how much more we could've had if we hadn't lost the powder."

I didn't comment.

She stared at me, a smile that could've been either tolerance or scorn. "You didn't mind that at all, did you?"

"Glad to see it at the bottom of the sea," I admitted. "Three million ought to be enough for anybody."

She continued to stare. "You *are* a bit of a Boy Scout, aren't you?" She paused, thoughts turning. "You really never have killed anybody, have you?"

I thought about that. "Maybe not until today."

"You mean the helicopter?"

I nodded.

"I don't think you hit anybody or anything," she told me. "Me, neither. It was like Bruno said, he was the guy."

"Nice to have someone to lay it off on," I said rather sarcastically.

"No, really," she persisted. "He had the automatic rifle. He was pouring all those bullets into that outfit." She nodded, agreeing with herself. "You and me . . . all we were doing was just blowing holes in the air. I didn't feel like I put one shot where it counted."

My gut feeling agreed. Even at the time, amidst the frantic warfare, I hadn't had the sense that I'd put any shot anywhere near the helicopter, but I couldn't be sure. I've always said I was no killer, but lately, who knows?

"And you're thinking about the guys from the ship?" she spoke with some heat.

I shrugged. "I didn't interfere."

"Scumbags!" she exclaimed. "It was us or them, and you know that."

"I suppose so," I conceded.

She drank the last of her wine, then rose and moved down the steps into the salon. A minute later, she returned with a second bottle. "Might as well celebrate," she said, pouring my glass full, then her own. "We're rich!"

I touched her glass with mine, a toast to our somewhat tainted windfall, and watched as she drank deeply.

"How'd you get so screwed up?" she asked suddenly. "I mean about those murders you were supposed to have committed?"

"What difference does it make?" I said.

"I might believe it this time," she said.

So I told my story yet again and, this time, I think I'd found a believer. At least, she nodded during my narrative, either in acceptance or to encourage me to continue when my recitation wearied me.

"Where do you go from here?" she asked after I'd finished.

"I don't have much of an idea," I admitted. "My original intent was to get to Antigua where I could build myself a new identify. Problem is, I've got to have some sort of identity even to get there."

"We can take care of that in the Caymans," she assured me. "And get you a doctor." She nodded at my leg. "How's it feeling?"

"Doing okay," I told her, more to reassure myself than her. "What will you do?"

She gave me a wide-eyed look, almost startled at my inquiry. "I'll go my way, you'll go yours," she said, bringing that hard-boiled dame back to the surface. "I'll have enough money to find a good life, and do to others what they've always done to me."

"Sounds a bit bitter," I ventured, wondering if I should've made the comment.

"And I've a right," she shot back. "Do you know how I grew up? Do you have any idea?"

I shook my head.

"We lived all over Florida when I was a kid," she began. "Tampa, St. Pete, Key West. I don't know what Mom was like before she married Bruno, but I know what she was like after. She told me she married him because he was a pilot. She thought he'd work for some airline, and she'd be rich. Or, at least, closer to rich than she'd ever been before." She paused, searching her memory. "I can remember him a little bit when I was very young . . . maybe three or four. He'd come to our house, and he'd be there for just a little while. Then, he'd be gone, and I'd forget about him."

She stopped abruptly.

"Go on," I urged.

"It's a corny story," she said brusquely. "Nothing different than thousands of others."

"I'd like to hear it anyway," I told her.

She paused as though she wasn't going to say anymore, and then continued, "When I was in school . . . fifth and sixth grades . . . I never went two grades at the same school except in Ft. Lauderdale . . . I actually had a couple of friends!"

She paused again, showing some reluctance to continue. "Mom wasn't really bad, but she was a weak person. She'd work as a waitress, work in a bar, work in a hash house, it didn't really matter. She'd take up with anyone who'd ask her and, sometimes, she'd make money on her back and—" She broke off and stared at me defiantly. "You have a mother like that?"

"Was there love between you?" I asked, surprising her.

She blinked several times rapidly. "I don't know," she answered. "I think so . . . in her own way."

"Where is she now?"

She shook her head. "I haven't seen her in eight or nine years. She wouldn't be old yet . . . late forties."

"Maybe you ought to look her up," I suggested, thinking of the money. "Maybe make it up between the two of you."

Her laugh was scornful.

We talked on: Minnie, mellowing with still another glass of wine, telling me about her teen years, how she'd taken off before finishing high school, learning to live on the street.

"I shuffled around a bit," she admitted. "Spent a lot of time in and around Miami, ran with some people I shouldn't have, did some island hopping in the Caribbean."

"Drugs?" I asked.

"Taking or dealing?" she asked flippantly.

"Whichever."

"Not that it's any of your business, but I wasn't exactly Miss Prim and Proper," she told me, an edge in her voice. "One thing was important. Whatever I did, I knew what I was doing and why I was doing it. Wherever I went, I knew where to find the back door. I never got arrested. And I never got slammed by the people I worked with or by the cops."

She told me, with some pride, that she'd never followed her mother's example of selling herself for money. She had, eventually, gone back to high school in the Virgin Islands to get a diploma, and had supported herself in a variety of jobs. She'd worked as a clerk at a grocery store, as a receptionist for a doctor and, her last employment, as a part-time hostess and blackjack dealer at a casino in the the Virgins.

"How did you and Bruno get back together?" I asked.

She laughed again. "I don't know how he found me, but after coming home after work, there he was, waiting for me just outside my apartment building. He made like the long, lost father who was delighted to see his little girl," she reflected, her words now slightly slurring. "I told him to get his ass outta my sight and never come back."

I waited for her to continue.

"Well, he told me that he was sorry for everything he'd never done for me, and told me that he had the chance to make it up to me. He said he had a plan to make us both rich."

"I'm surprised you believed him," I said.

She gave me a look. "I never said that I thought Bruno was dumb. Neglectful, indifferent to my mom and myself, but I knew he'd been involved in some big money deals. When he said he could put together the deal of a lifetime, you bet I believed him." This time, she gestured to the salon steps. "Down there's the proof of it."

"Having lots of money is important to you?"

Her lip curled just a little. "It's important to anybody, Kevin. You can never have enough."

"How much of the deal did he tell you," I asked.

"Enough to get me interested and keep me interested," she replied. "He had enough money to front everything. He told me to charter the yacht, and where to meet him."

"I mean the particulars of the deal," I persisted.

"Some of it," she said with a nod of her head. "He told me that he was making a run and, if he pulled it off, he'd be at Tampico with a couple of million in cash . . . and enough cocaine to make a lot more."

"Did he tell you about the dangers that might be involved?" I asked.

"No, not really," she replied. "Oh, I knew that he'd be running some risks, that goes with that sort of a job. I didn't know it was going to be the shooting war that it's turned out to be."

"I don't suppose he thought so himself," I said charitably.

She shook her head. "I'm sorry it didn't work out for Bruno, but that won't keep me from enjoying his share as well as mine."

We gazed out at the moonlit ocean for several minutes, neither of us saying a word. For me, I was trying to let the beauty of the night replace the calamity of the day. Minnie, too, seemed far away, her face showing nothing of her thoughts.

Then, without a look or a word to me, she rose, unbuttoned and dropped her blouse, unfastened her bra, pulled down and stepped out of her shorts and panties. She appeared blithely unconcerned by her nudity or my intent notice of it. With a lithe walk to the stern, she stepped down to the diving platform and dove into the sea. Aroused and entranced, I moved to the rail and watched as she broke to the surface. She swam to the bow of the yacht, then turned onto her back and swam lazily toward the stern, revealing herself to me.

If it hadn't been for the leg, I'd have joined her.

She continued to swim, a nymph delighting in her water world, playfully seductive, teasing me to come to her, knowing full well that I could not. It was an erotic, sensual performance in the gentle swells of the dark sea. There were long moments when she disappeared from view, and fear for her seized me. In those prolonged periods, I wondered if some dreadful creature from the ocean depths had taken her, or the sea itself had drowned her. Then, she'd reappear, her slim, voluptuous body gliding, her arms lifting and stroking, lovely and lewdly frolicsome.

After a while, as though bathed clean of the events of the day, she came to the climbing ladder, reaching up for my hand to draw her up, wet and shivering, into my arms. "You could've gone off and left me," she chided, pressing her body against me. "Taken the ship, the money, and left me to drown."

I touched the damp nylon pouch, hung by a cord around her neck between her breasts. "I imagine that the key to the ignition just might be in here."

She laughed gleefully, then kissed me, her hand moving down inside my shorts, her passion strong and insistent. Locked together, I was totally unaware of any hurt in my injured leg as we shuffled down to the salon. We moved into the large stateroom, her hands helping me to undress just before I laid her beneath me upon the bed.

■ ■ ■

Afterwards, my leg hurt like hell.

Some time after midnight, she rose and left the stateroom. A few minutes later, I dressed and limped into the salon where I found her with clothing retrieved and back in place. I also found the loving Minnie had been replaced by the cool and controlled one who asked, "You want to stay at anchor or push on through the night?"

Wherever the blithe spirit had gone, I did not know. I realized that it was back to business as usual; a shady business at best.

"Let's keep going, Minnie," I responded, knowing that was what she wanted me to say. "I'll be happy to be on land again."

She nodded, picked up the large moneybag, and entered the master stateroom. When she came out, she started for the steps, and then paused to speak to me: "By the way, that's the first time you've called me Minnie. My old man called me that and I let him. From now on, it's either Min or 'Hey, you,' but never Minnie again."

I nodded.

She took the first stint at the flybridge console, preferring the clarity of open air rather than trying to see her way through the crazed and splintered glass below. I stayed in the salon and leafed through a number of the magazines that had come with the *Bonnie Sue*, most of them old copies concerning sailing, yachting, and money management. I took a particular interest in the latter, struck with the thought that I could possibly end up with some of the loot from these adventures.

My leg felt very sore, and it seemed more a bother now than before. I worried that my fall, plus the sexual frenzy, might've caused further injury. I tried to convince myself that it was nothing much more than some additional bruising. I consoled myself that the amorous exertions and labors of love were well worth the upsurge of pain.

Knowing that I'd have to relieve Minnie - sorry, but I couldn't get used to the shorter version - at the wheel sometime in the early morning, I took to my bunk again and, after staring into the darkness for a while, I drifted off to sleep.

30

She shook me awake, disturbing a slumber that I gave up grudgingly.

"You're running a fever," she declared, a cool hand on my face.

"I feel kinda dopey," I admitted. "I'll be okay."

She shook her head. "Let me look at the leg."

She took off the bandages and examined my leg, clucking at the sight of redness around wound. "Damn, looks like it's getting infected." She allowed herself a small smile. "I expect you're going to blame this on me."

"You were very athletic," I reminded her, bringing another grin.

She retrieved the medicine kit, redressed the wound, searched through the kit for a few moments more, and then pushed it aside with a sigh. "Nothing much here to be of great help. Pain killers and the usual stuff, but we need something for the infection."

"I'll be okay . . . really," I told her. "I'll take over. You need some sleep."

"We'll stop a while," she suggested. "You and I should both get some rest, and we'll go on first thing in the morning."

"If it's all the same, I'd just as soon push on and get somewhere for some medical help," I countered. "This leg's not going to give me much rest anyway."

She shrugged and started for the master stateroom. "Call me if you need me."

Painfully, I moved to the seat behind the deckhouse console steering wheel, peered through the crazed and shattered windshield, and guided the battered *Bonnie Sue* through the dark hours of early morning. I stood up from my position every once in a while to move around, ignoring the discomfort, although concerned at the stiffness of my leg. I didn't look under the bandage, but above and below it, I was seeing a faint flush that seemed to be spreading. Being the son of a doctor, for whatever little professional knowledge he'd passed on to me, I knew that the right medication had to be administered fairly soon, or I'd be in deep trouble.

When the sun was at mid-morning, Minnie came up the steps rubbing her eyes. "How do you feel?"

"Don't ask."

"Let me see," she said, bending to look at my leg. She took off the bandage and shook her head. "We ought to make it to the Cayman Islands by nightfall tomorrow." She looked up at me anxiously. "Think you'll be okay?"

"How are you at amputating legs?" I asked.

"Well, I know what to do with one if I have to," she responded with macabre humor, nodding to the sea. "Try to stay off of it." She turned and headed for the ladder, then climbed up to the flybridge console.

I felt like hell, but I fought the deep desire to sleep and stayed awake for an hour or more. I ate a little something for breakfast before I finally gave in and headed for my bunk.

The rest of that day was sort of a fevered stupefaction, wide awake lucidity at times and a fuzzy doze at others. I lay in my bunk, full of sweats and chills, knowing I was sicker than I'd hoped to be. I thought Minnie would do what she could, but I had no illusions about her either. She seemed to have a tender side to her, showing concern for my well being, but I didn't know just how much I could depend on her should I become too big of a burden.

I slept, I dreamed:

I was on the ocean, hovering over the dark, turbulent waves, and there were heads bobbing – three - no, maybe four! Yes, there were four! I couldn't make out the other three, but I could see the one floating nearer. And, suddenly, Chris was there beside me, laughing and pointing at_the head which was Cady's, eyes open, mouth moving, but I couldn't hear the words. Then, the head winked at me and rolled over, and there was no body beneath it as it vanished beneath the waves. Then, Chris was gone, and Minnie was diving into the ocean right at the spot where Bruno's head had disappeared. She came up from the depths to the surface floundering, looking around in all directions, panic on her face, looking at me in anger and shouting, "Help me find him! Help me find him!"

I woke with a start, wringing wet with sweat, somewhere between delirium and sanity, and Minnie was there, her arms helping me to sit up, and then helping me to stand.

"You look like hell," she told me.

"I suppose," I acknowledged. "I'm having some hellacious dreams . . . and, boy, you were playing an interesting part in them."

She was in no mood for any hallucinatory revelations. As opposed to her earlier nursing care, I couldn't tell whether her concern was more for me or for what a burden I had become. I tried to lighten her mood. "If I get too bad, just chuck me over the side."

"I hope to make it by dark," she said brusquely. "I *am* worried about you. I don't have a lot of experience in this sort of thing, but you could lose that leg if anything goes wrong."

"Such as?" I managed to ask.

She sighed. "Anything could happen. This ship may have more damage than we know, the engine could stop running or we might hit a storm . . ." She threw up her hands in dismay. "Who knows? What else could go wrong on this damnable trip?" She rummaged through the medicine kit once more. "Here," she said, handing me a couple of pills. "Take these. They won't help the infection, but maybe they'll keep you a little more comfortable." She handed me a glass of water, and watched as I took the pills.

"I'm going back topside," she told me. "I hope you can take the bouncing, because I'm hitting full throttle for the Caymans."

For the remainder of the day, I was in and out of it, sleeping the wild and indefinable sleep of drugs and infection, dreaming dreams of unimaginable repugnance or pleasure. Then, as well, there were several periods of absolute lucidity, some even lengthy minutes of clear thinking and valid reasoning. When I wasn't sweating and hallucinating in my bunk, I was able to move about a bit despite my injured leg.

Minnie only came down once during the day to find me sitting at the salon table. "Do you know what you're doing?" she asked peevishly.

"Writing a letter," I told her, surprised that she couldn't see.

"Who are you writing to?"

I couldn't quite think of whom.

"Kev, you don't have any paper," she said, reaching over and taking the pen away.

I stared down at the table and I could see a few marks where I'd been sure there had been stationary.

"Back to bed," she commanded, pointing to the companionway.

Reluctantly, I obeyed, shuffling after her to my stateroom, dreading the nightmares that I'd find there. "I'd really rather sit up," I told her as we entered and I plopped down on my bunk.

"Stay there!" she said in that demanding voice. "And don't get out of it 'til I tell you!"

I did what I was told and vaguely remembered her leaving. Then, it was back to that bizarre slumberland, where fantasy came without rhyme or reason, episodes without storylines, a phantasma of nightmares and eroticism.

■ ■ ■

Then, she was shaking me, wakening me to the darkness in the cabin. "We're here. It's night, and we're getting off. Think you can make it to the dinghy?"

"The dinghy?" I repeated, not really able to focus on what was happening.

"An inflatable. We're anchored off Grand Cayman, and we'll use it to go ashore."

"Okay," I agreed. I took a step on my bad leg, and would have collapsed if Minnie hadn't supported me. "You're one strong lady." I told her, my words as slurred as if at the peak of a non-stop drinking spree.

"Come with me," she coaxed. "Just take a few steps."

Vaguely, I thought of my money. "Are we coming back?"

"No," she answered, guiding me out onto the aft deck. "We're done with this."

"Don't they have a dock or something?" I said, looking at the fuzzy sparkles of light on the shore some distance away.

"They do, but I don't want to bring the yacht in too close. Someone sees all the bullet holes and shattered glass, they'll start asking questions."

Even in my fever-intoxication, I knew I should be mightily concerned about the money I'd hidden away, but I wasn't really thinking clearly at all. I was allowing Minnie to walk me along, and all I could concentrate on was that I was close to land and civilization. Somewhere here, there'd be somebody to make me feel better.

Even so, I persisted: "Are you bringing the money?"

"Already in the dinghy," she told me. "All there."

All there?

Somehow, in my foggy state, I knew something about the money should've troubled me more than it did at the moment. Whatever was happening to me, nothing was making sense as she guided me along the deck to the stern ladder.

"Here we are," she said. "We need to get you into the dinghy."

I sank down to the deck, wondering if I would be able to swing myself over and down into the small inflatable. "I'll do what I can, but you'd better hang on," I told her. "Are you that strong?"

"Let's give it a try," she responded, scrambling around me and down into the dinghy. "Come on."

I rolled over, my feet on the ladder rungs, and tried to let myself down, feeling Minnie's strong arms helping to ease me into the dinghy. Either the inflatable was bobbing excessively or it was me wobbling, but for an instant, I thought I was going to pitch right into the sea. I sank down - more like a fall - and settled gratefully on the rubber bottom. A few seconds later, I heard Minnie's coaxing murmurs as she pulled the cord on the outboard. I heard it catch, and felt the surge of motion as we started putt-putting toward a small marina dock.

The cool wind seemed to revive me a little as we cut through the water and, although I couldn't quite sit up, I did manage to raise myself a bit, suddenly remembering to ask another question: "What about my . . . backpack . . . my clothes?"

"You won't need them," she answered. "You can buy new stuff in town."

My mind, not yet sharp, seemed to be recovering. "What about the weapons?" I asked, sure that I would need at least something in my further travels.

"All deep-sixed," she said cheerfully. "We're far out of danger now."

"Not with your crowd," I muttered under my breath.

She didn't hear me over the outboard motor. "I know of a doctor," she said to me. "He's a chiropractor, but he's good as an MD. He'll fix your leg."

"Out of the goodness of his heart?"

"If you pay him enough," she answered. "Which shouldn't be a problem." She paused, then added, "I wouldn't say anything about us having a large amount of money. Just let me do the talking."

"Whatever," I responded, feeling myself beginning to sink; a drowsiness descending into insensibility once again.

I roused as the dingy bumped against a pier, and Minnie cut the motor. She heaved the money bag onto the jetty and vaulted up onto the pier, then tied the dinghy to the dock. She helped me out of it and, with one hand hauling the money bag and the other hauling me, we made it up to a shanty of sorts where she located a telephone.

"You going to be okay?" she asked anxiously.

With an effort, I nodded. The night air was rather crisp for the tropics, and seemed to help me to stay alert. While she was dialing, I looked around the small marina. There were no more than twenty boats, sail and power. On a couple, there were lights showing, but I could see no one on their decks. Hopefully, no one had noticed our arrival. I heard Minnie talking in a low voice, a mixture of Spanish and English. The conversation was short and, after she hung up, she turned to me with a bright smile. "He'll take care of you."

"The doc?"

She nodded. "He's sending a cab."

We stood for a while, me leaning against the shanty. It was good to be back on land even if the one leg wasn't really up to standing. I looked around for a place to sit down, but the only place would've been on the wooden walkway and, once down, I'd have a hell of a time getting back up.

Finally, the taxi arrived and Minnie hustled me and the money bag inside, then sat beside me and gave directions to the driver. We drove through the middle of the island's shopping area; Georgetown's swank diamond and fine china shops, intermingled with touristy tee-shirt and baseball cap emporiums. We turned a few times on side roads, finally arriving at a rather large and well-kept two-story house. Minnie paid the driver and, dragging our baggage, we lurched up to the door where she knocked, waited, and then knocked again.

"How'd you know this guy?" I asked.

"Never met him," she replied. "Bruno told me about him."

The door opened and a gray-haired Hispanic man, slightly stooped and thick-bodied, gave us a gracious welcoming nod. He peered at me in a professional mien, looked down at my bandaged leg, and then ushered us inside. The hallway had a bit of a musty smell, but not necessarily an unpleasant one. It seemed to speak of a home lived in for many years, furnished with old and familiar things. The doctor moved ahead of us to open a side door and, once again, gestured for us to go before him.

Inside, there was a well-equipped examining room; everything appeared very neat, very clean. The doctor waved me toward an exam table, and nodded Minnie into a nearby chair.

"You have the money?" he asked, looking from one of us to the other, surprising me with his good English speech.

"I do," she said, taking a sheaf of bills from the pocket of her shorts. "Five thousand?"

The doctor nodded, accepted the money, made a quick count of it, and then put it in his pants pocket. He turned to Minnie. "I'm going to be some time with him. You can wait across the hall in my living room if you'd like."

"Won't I disturb your family?" she asked.

"No family," he told her. "Not any more."

"You live by yourself?"

He nodded. "For several years now."

She went out, closing the door behind her.

He instructed me to get up on the examining table, a task that I was barely able to accomplish. He took off the bandage and frowned at what he saw. "That's a pretty nasty looking leg," he said. "Much longer, you'd have been in trouble."

I didn't want to say bullet. "She said it went clear through."

He nodded.

He went to a cabinet, took down a brown bottle and cotton swabs, then returned preparing to clean around the wound. The strong smell of alcohol preceded the cold shock of the liquid that turned into sharp and lasting sting. I gave a small gasp, and he gave me a sympathetic smile. He coated the wound with an orange antiseptic, then said: "I'm going to give you an antibiotic shot . . . are you in great pain?"

"We had some pain pills," I told him. "Percoset."

"I'll give you something better," he said as he moved back to his cabinet where he prepared two syringes from different vials. He laid both aside on a nearby table, swabbed my arm with alcohol, and injected the fluid from the first hypodermic. "That'll help with the pain," he told me. He laid aside the first syringe and reached for the other. "This should take care of the infection."

After he finished the second injection, he did a thorough inspection, nodding his satisfaction. Next, he began to bandage my leg by placing a sterile pad over the wound. "Are you a violent man, sir?" he asked in a conversational tone.

The question surprised me.

"I . . . don't really think so," I stammered. "Although after the last couple of days, perhaps I am."

He nodded. "I appreciate your candor." He wrapped gauze around my leg, over the pad. "Dealing with questionable men, such as you, will likely get me killed some day."

"How so?"

"Because some day," he said in his soft voice, "I'll treat a man who'll repay my efforts with a shot from a gun or knife across my throat." He finished the bandage and stepped back. "You'll be very sleepy in a few minutes. The pain killer will have some effect on you."

"I don't know where—"

"You don't have to go anywhere else," he cut in. "The five thousand will provide you with a place for the night for you and Miss Cady. It's a big house with enough rooms." He cocked his head toward the door. "I've had a few dealings with her father, not the young lady. Is he with you?"

For a moment, I wondered if I shouldn't let Minnie tell him.

"You won't be dealing with him again," I told him.

He gave a nod to my injured leg. "Something to do with this?"

"Not by him, but he was involved," I answered.

"Well," he said, more to himself. "None of my business."

"I appreciate you offering your home," I began, "but I'm going to have to get going . . ." Suddenly, I felt woozy, a sort of heavy languor settling down upon me.

"I'll get you up to bed," he said, moving to assist me down from the table. "You can stay until you're feeling better, you and Miss Cady." He paused. "She's assured me that no one knows that you're here."

"I need to leave now—"

"No, nowhere but to bed," he said, guiding me to the door, opening it, and leading me out into the hall. Minnie came from another door to join us. "Help me get him up to bed, would you please?"

With Minnie on one side and the doctor on the other, they helped me up the stairs, then through an open door into a large room with a double bed.

"This was our guest room," the doctor informed us as he turned back the covers. "There's a beautiful view of the ocean in the morning."

"I've seen enough ocean," I said, instantly regretting my cynicism. "I'm sorry," I apologized. "I'm dopey enough to talk dopey."

The doctor nodded. "You'll feel better in the morning."

Then, I was in the bed, and I had a fleeting impression of them leaving the room, not even hearing the door close. The room wheeled and I swirled, down and down, into a senseless void; a gentle and painless oblivion.

31

The sun was well up in the sky when I awoke, feeling much better if not altogether well. I was surprised to find I was totally naked, and I wondered who had removed my clothes. The doctor or Minnie? Vaguely, I remembered a long night, at least a part of it, tossing and moaning. This morning, I was surprised at my quick recovery. I looked down at my leg and felt a gratifying sense of relief that it looked well bandaged, and not particularly swollen or ulcerated. I stood on my good leg and tried my weight on the bad one. It was sore and stiff, but usable. I limped over to the window to gaze out upon the sight that the doctor had so praised. Indeed, it was a beautiful view of land meeting sea. I stood for some time, enjoying what I believed to be, if not the dawning of a new life, perhaps the mid-morning of one.

My clothes were nowhere in sight, but a terrycloth robe had been placed on a chair and I put it on. I wondered if my only dirty and ripped clothes would be fit to be worn, or whether the good doctor might have something to wear instead.

I hobbled to the door and went out into the upper hallway, then limped down past a couple of closed doors to one at the very end. I opened it cautiously, and found it to be the bathroom I'd expected. I freshened up as best I could, washing my face and body, then rewrapped myself in the robe. The noise

I'd made in my ablutions seemed extraordinarily loud. I wondered if I was the only one up and about at this time of the day, and I wondered if my noise had disturbed the others. I moved quietly along the hallway, limping steadily and painfully down the stairway to the lower part of the house.

I found the doctor, still in his pajamas, at a kitchen table, drinking coffee.

"Good morning," he greeted me. "Coffee?"

"Please, make it black," I responded, awkward in sitting down across from him.

"Feeling better?" he inquired as he rose. He walked to a nearby cabinet where he took a cup from a shelf, then moved to a coffee machine and filled it.

"Much better, thank you," I responded. "Surprising what a night's sleep and the right medicine will do for you."

"Two nights," he said casually. He returned to the table and placed the coffee cup in front of me.

"Two? Two nights? I don't remember—"

"Oh, you were up a number of times the first night, trying to make conversation," he cut in with a gentle smile. "Sometimes, we were there . . . sometimes, we were not." He paused. "Last night, your fever went down, and you began to sleep normally."

I gave him a chagrined smile in return. "To me, I got here last night."

He leaned over to look at my leg. "Much better," he said in his professional manner. "I think you'll do just fine. You'll have some scarring, but it should heal without problems."

"I have you to thank for that and . . ." I looked around, listening for sounds in the house. "Minnie's not up?"

He didn't answer immediately, then said, "Long gone."

"Gone?" I asked, greatly surprised. "When?"

"Yesterday afternoon." He pushed a brown paper package across to me. "She left this."

With a sense of dismay, I opened it, and found several packets of money and a folded notepad page. I opened the page and read:

Sorry, Kev.

I know you deserve more, but I'm a greedy bitch and I wanted it all. I paid the doc, and I'm giving you back your original $4000. Good luck. Hope you make it!

There was no signature.

"The lady is a disappointment?" the doctor said in solemn sympathy.

"A disappointment indeed," I sighed. "I need a cab."

He shook his head. "You're in no condition to go out, and you'll never catch—"

"I won't try," I cut in. "I do need to take care of some unfinished business."

"You should spend a couple of days here," he protested. "You're mending, but you need to have some rest—"

"I'll be back, but there's something I have to do," I interrupted urgently.

He regarded me for a few silent moments, then shrugged with an appearance of aggravation. "It's your risk, your health." He paused. "I don't know what kind of business you feel you must take care of, that's your affair. Just don't bring trouble to my house."

"Of course I won't," I assured him. "You've been more than kind, but I do need that cab."

He sat quietly for several seconds, then rose and walked out of the kitchen and down the hall. I drank my coffee and thought bad thoughts about Minnie Cady.

A few minutes later, the doctor returned and gave me a single nod of his head. "A taxi will be here in a few minutes."

"Do you have anything I could wear?" I asked.

He looked at me, sizing me up. "I have some walking shorts and a shirt. From years ago, they might fit."

"That'll do."

He left the kitchen again and came back with a clean pair of shorts and a faded Key West tee-shirt. I put them on, pulling the shirt over my head just as the taxi horn sounded outside the house. I suddenly realized that I had only high denomination bills.

"Could you change this for something smaller?" I asked, holding up one of the hundred-dollar bills.

He gave me an amused look, got up, and left the kitchen once again. He returned as the taxi horn sounded once more by an impatient driver. "Here," he said, handing me five ten-dollar bills. "Keep your money."

"Thank you," I said. "I appreciate what you've done."

"I've been well paid," he responded. "Take care of your leg."

I signaled my agreement, and walked out the door to the cab.

"Take me down along the docks," I told the cab driver. "I'll tell you where I want to go when I see it."

■ ■ ■

We drove back through the business district, and cruised along a waterfront street that I vaguely remembered. We passed several boat landings, and I had a few anxious minutes with the thought that I wouldn't be able to find the one I sought. Then, I saw the marina and I thrilled at the sight of the *Bonnie Sue*. She was right where we left her, floating at some distance from the shore. I noted with satisfaction that the inflatable dinghy was still tied at the end of the pier.

"Let me out here," I told the driver.

He stopped the cab, and I handed him a ten. "Any chance you could wait for me?"

He shook his head. "How long will you be?"

I glanced at the distant yacht. "Fifteen, twenty minutes at the most."

"I can come back for you if you'd like," he told me. "Thirty minutes? Give or take?"

"Good enough," I said. "Here's another twenty, and there's more if you really do come back."

He gave a head bob of agreement, and then drove away.

I limped down to the dock, somewhat concerned at the activity of the morning. There were casual sailors getting their crafts ready for pleasure cruises, and mid-morning fishermen motoring their small watercrafts out to sea. Still others were apparently living on their boats, up and around on their decks, some sitting and enjoying the sights of the bay.

I ignored the curious stares of those in the marina, those likely wondering who I might be. I hobbled straight to the dinghy, untied the line, and clumsily eased myself off the dock and onto it. I fumbled with the outboard, pulling several times, trying to get the damned thing to catch. It seemed like every eye in the vicinity was on me as I labored, swearing under my breath, wondering if I would have to paddle my way out to the yacht. The engine finally caught, and I nursed the throttle, bringing a satisfying, steady whir of sound. I managed the turnabout from the jetty with a landlubber's lack of skill, and then headed for the *Bonnie Sue*.

It took about five minutes to reach it and, by then, I was handling the dinghy with somewhat greater proficiency. I brought it to the rear of the cruiser and killed the engine. Line in hand, I pulled myself up the stern ladder, rolled aboard, and tied the dinghy to a cleat. I looked around, now thankful that Minnie had anchored so far away from the dock, so far from scrutiny. I crossed the deck, went down the steps, and moved as quickly as I could through the salon, and into the forward cabin.

I went to the drawer where I'd stashed my money belt and, summoning strength, I ripped it completely out of the teak cabinet. I tossed the broken drawer aside and reached into the cavity, elated as my hand touched what I was seeking.

I brought out the money belt and laid it to one side.

Then, I broke out two adjacent drawers, and began to pull out the rest of the money.

The rest of money?

Indeed! The cash was right where I'd hidden it; in the drawers on either side of the one with my money belt.

Minnie hadn't discovered her loss, and why would she? Hadn't the two of us counted out the millions, and placed it all in the big soft-side bag?

On my intermittently hallucinatory day, in one of my lucid periods between deliriums, I had a larcenous epiphany. While she was on the flybridge, I had imagined the thoughts that might be racing through her mind. She was aiming the yacht to an exciting new life, a life to be bought with lots and lots of money.

Why would she share any of it with me?

On our celebratory night, I believe I'd read her mind. I had seen the sparkle that all that money had brought to her eyes, as well as her smiles of delight as we counted it. Perhaps she had missed similar avaricious signs of my own. I knew, that night, that her promise of a generous split was an empty one.

So, groggy as I was, while Minnie was speeding us over the waves toward the Caymans, I had counted out a million dollars of real money for myself from Cady's soft-side bag. I'd pulled out other drawers and, as I'd hidden my money belt, I had stuffed the bill packets in the spaces at their bottoms. I'd been barely able to close the drawers when I finished, but I had thought she wouldn't notice.

Then, finally finding a reason for having carried them all this time, I replaced the real million with a like number of those counterfeit bills. I shoved them into the soft-side bag, burying them deep inside the surrounding genuine currency which I'd left for Minnie.

Now, I stuffed my backpack with my own considerable fortune, the packets placed in and around the few articles of clothing I still possessed. I sat for a couple of minutes, thinking about Minnie:

So much for honor between loving thieves.

Wherever she was - and I was sure she was no longer on Grand Cayman - had she discovered her loss? I didn't feel particularly bad about my deceit or of the avarice that prompted it. After all, I'd taken only a third and left her a full two million; there were now windfalls enough for the both of us.

I strapped my money belt under my shirt, and carried my backpack out onto the deck. I unfastened the line from the cleat, scooted over the stern, and carefully lowered myself and my precious load into the dinghy. I pushed away from the *Bonnie Sue*, gave the dinghy's outboard a couple of strong pulls, and I was on my way back to shore.

When I got there, I hoisted my precious backpack onto the dock, and was struggling to pull myself up when a hand reached down to assist.

I looked up at the cabbie.

"You look like you could use a little help, mister," he said. "I got back a little early."

"Thank you!" I said, taking his hand, grateful for the assistance as I swung up onto the dock.

He reached down and picked up the backpack. "Let me carry this for you."

For a moment, I started to protest, but changed my mind. "Thank you once again," I told him.

We walked to, the cab, and he started to place the pack in the trunk.

"Just put it in with me," I told him.

He nodded, placed it on the rear seat, and then held the door open for me. He got in behind the wheel and started the engine. He turned around to me. "Where to, sir?"

I leaned back, content for the first time in years.

"South America."

Epilogue

The million or so paved my way to a different life. On Grand Cayman, with the help and knowledge of the chiropractic doctor and with a number of high denomination bills, I found an expert craftsman who provided a beautifully forged passport and other valuable false documents. I had now acquired what I needed to give me a new name and relatively safe passage to many other parts of the world.

I arranged for a flight to the island of Antigua - in an airplane with all its doors. Shortly after arrival, I deposited my newfound fortune in one of the numbered-account banks. To let my leg further heal, I stayed for a while in a rented seaside cottage, enjoying the warmth of the sun and the cool breezes from the Caribbean.

At the beginning of the third week, I booked still another flight to Buenos Aires. There, after some discreet inquiries, I made contact with a skilled and avaricious plastic surgeon. With money enough to buy his confidential services, I now have a new face that I've learned to accept, and I've almost forgotten the one I had before. It's too bad in a way because I liked that old face. As I remember, it had a sort of innocence that my new one seems to lack. This one has sort of a devil-may-care expression, perhaps better fitting the man I've become. Over time, I've often wondered:

Was it really the surgery that caused such a change? Or was it the cumulative effect of arrest, trial, prison, and the terrors compiled during my escape?_

After Buenos Aires, I became a man without a country, no longer able to live in my homeland. However, I did find refuge and pleasure in many other nations. I discovered that it was possible, with a new appearance and a new identity, to travel the world pretty much as I pleased. I did take certain precautions that have become standard with me: I keep a low profile, never doing any particular thing that would draw perilous attention.

These days, I dress carefully and casually, appearing neither too rich nor too poor. I make it a rule to never buy property or to stay too long in any one locale. For example, I would lease a pleasant house in the quiet countryside of Ireland for a few months, and then move on. I'd rent a comfortable flat in Paris or stay in a row house on a stately avenue in London. I've spent time in various cities of the Orient - Hong Kong, Singapore, Tokyo. I stayed for several months in Brazil, many more in New Zealand, still other days and weeks in Sydney and Brisbane.

In the course of such wandering, alone for too much of my time, I met a woman whom others considered pretty, and I considered beautiful. Near my own age, we found common interests and, eventually, adoration for one another. After she'd learned to know and love me well, I shared my story with her, one she believed without doubt. We live together and, understanding my circumstances, she travels with me and willingly shares this nomadic life. In return for her support and sacrifice, I see to it that we live well and graciously, if not ostentatiously.

Even so, you might ask, how could my mere million afford such a style of living?

Concerned that I should make the most of that considerable yet limited sum, I became an avid student of investments, determined to make my fortune grow. I studied stocks and bonds, and discovered that I had a real ability when it came to evaluating companies and their potentials. I was a quick study of the business of acquiring growth stocks, and how to reap rewards from opportune purchases and timely sales. With sufficient capital to master this newfound vocation, it became an exciting and satisfying occupation. Through the convenience of the computer and internet opportunities, my million multiplied and, in a very short time, I added considerably more. Today, my wealth continues to grow, and my business is to invest wisely and, sometimes, boldly.

For all my success, for all my comforts in the wide world in which I now reside, I am saddened to realize that I will never again be a citizen of the United States. For all my talk of contentment, it still bothers me to be a fugitive from my native land. Still, as much as I might dream of it, I know that I can never return. However, I remain curious as to what new events have occurred and what has happened to the people in my earlier life. One of my indulgences has been to satisfy my curiosity. Through a labyrinth of precautions, I have hired investigators to find out what I wanted to know:

■ ■ ■

My parents?

In his late fifties, my father developed Parkinson's disease, the disability coming on swiftly and mercilessly, and his surgery came to an end. He still tries to practice, in some sort of an advisory capacity, although a surgeon without skillful hands is of limited value to either the medical profession or to patients. His gruff, disdainful manner of the past works against him, and whatever former respect he demanded has been greatly diminished. He now lives alone, retired for all practical purposes although financially secure for the remainder of his life.

My mother filed for divorce, not long after my father's onset of affliction. It was, to me, a matter of conjecture whether she left him because of the disease, or to rid herself of the surname of shame that my conviction had brought upon her. She resumed her maiden name, and has returned to her native state where she is currently playing the social butterfly in her circle of affluence. Still a mature beauty, she hopes for a new and advantageous marriage. I wait with amusement to see who might become my stepfather.

■ ■ ■

My ex-wife, Gloria, remarried. She apparently found her hopes and dreams fulfilled in the personage of a used car dealer who appears in appalling 30-second television ads wearing ridiculous costumes. Despite the clownish behavior of her mate, she's found happiness, giving birth to two children, a boy and a girl. To her credit, on a national television show regarding our marriage, she recanted her accusations against me, and expressed hope that I was still alive somewhere and happy.

■ ■ ■

Howard Warnell gave up the practice of criminal law not long after representing me. He has devoted himself to handling personal injury lawsuits, where he has found success in defeating legal representatives of insurance companies. I understand he's quite successful, even without resorting to television advertising. Asked repeatedly by the press and various media sensationalists about my innocence or guilt, he has consistently replied, "No comment."

■ ■ ■

Christopher Munoz, my cheerful cellmate, was released from prison a couple of years after my escape. He's found an occupation in the landscape business. He married soon after, and he and his wife have a couple of small children. He has apparently become a law-abiding citizen and no longer has interest in dealing or doing drugs. I've thought of sending him enough money to help him with his landscaping enterprise, but I'm holding off. My informant has assured me that he seems to be making it on his own, and I think that's far more satisfying than through the receipt of a gift. Nonetheless, I'll keep an eye on him and back him if there's a need.

■ ■ ■

Through a representative, I sent a sum of $50,000 to an exclusive bank account we set up for Kim Palmer, the Oriental lady who deserved far better in her life than Mr. Palmer. The bank is located in Denver, and she was carefully notified that the money was to belong to her alone, to do with whatever she pleased. We also discreetly provided the name of a very good divorce attorney. From what I've learned recently, she left Palmer in the doughnut shop, got the divorce, took out her citizenship papers, and is now living happily in San Francisco with a new and caring husband.

◼ ◼ ◼

A year after Minnie Cady and I parted company, she was arrested, jailed in Mexico, and charged with trafficking in illegal drugs. She is currently serving a three-year sentence in a Mexican prison. My information did not disclose whether or not she still had the two million dollars she'd taken on the Grand Cayman.

◼ ◼ ◼

I have been content to live my new life, certain that I have taken every precaution to rid myself of every vestige of the past, secure in my belief that I've successfully become a new person with the promise of a prosperous and useful future.

One morning, a doorbell sounded in my rented villa in Spain. My companion and our maid were at the market, and I was alone in the house. When I opened the front door, two big men stepped in, brushing past me.

"Kevin Mathias?" one man said, not really a question.

"I'm sorry—"

"Don't bother to deny it," the other man said. "We know who you are."

I didn't know what to make of them. They were muscular men, early forties, dressed in casual clothing, making their entry in a forceful, assured manner. They could've been cops.

"We ain't cops," the first man said, reading my mind.

"Then, who are you?"

"We have some questions," the first man spoke again. "You answer 'em okay, and we go away."

"Who am I talking to?"

"I'll ask the questions," the first man responded, his manner brusque. He was a dark-haired man, heavy featured with sort of a coarse complexion. His partner was of similar size, but slimmer, handsome in a mature way, gray hair at the temples.

They walked past me into the living room, and stood looking out of the floor-to-ceiling windows that gave a breathtaking view of the coastal scenery. I followed them, wondering if I was in danger. If so, I was really in trouble. I hadn't kept a gun since my adventures in the Gulf of Mexico.

The blunt-featured man turned suddenly to confront me. "What happened to Vince Gianntana?"

Now, I was afraid.

"He's . . . dead," I stammered.

"How?"

I took a deep breath and told them the story. They listened without interruption, intently, nothing showing in their faces to indicate that they believed or disbelieved. When I finished, they sat quietly for several seconds before exchanging a look between them.

"That's it?" the first man asked.

I nodded. "Every bit of it the truth."

"You left him there in the garbage dump?"

I dreaded my answer, afraid of what they'd do. Undoubtedly, they'd resent what I'd done - or rather, what I hadn't done - for their respected underboss. "I had to leave him," I said apologetically. "I had no choice."

Again, there were a few moments of silence.

"That's good," the slim man said unexpectedly, showing a bright smile with perfect dentures. "Serves the sonofabitch right."

His companion nodded, showing an ugly smile of his own. "That's where Vince belongs . . . a grave in the garbage."

"You're happy about this?" I asked, trying not to show my relief.

"Absolutely," the heavy man said. "May he rot there for all eternity."

They started toward the door, the slim man turning to me. "Were you a friend of his? You and him, escaping together and all?"

"No, not at all," I replied. "Barely knew him as a matter of fact."

"About the money," the other man began.

I blanched, thinking about the original two million.

"People tell me that Vince was carrying several thou on him," the heavy man continued. "What happened to that?"

I hesitated.

"I took it," I admitted.

Both men looked at me.

"Well, keep it," the heavy man said. "You probably earned it."

Then, they were gone.

■ ■ ■

Finally, even though I had decried the possibility of being cleared of the murder charges, I was amazed to learn that an enterprising detective, in the Denver police department, had finally checked the ownership of the gun used to kill Turley and Wanda Dale. It belonged to a young Eurasian man who, under questioning, admitted the killings. He later retracted the confession, even saying that he'd sold the gun to me. Thanks to a better lawyer than mine, he'd been able to obfuscate the charge, and the prosecution of the case has been dragging on for more than two years. It would be nice if I'm eventually exonerated, but other charges are still outstanding such as escaping from prison, and a suspicion of drug dealing. I hold no hope of going back to the United States as a free man, but I take some comfort in that efforts to find me have lessened.

There is a possibility that you will believe none of this to be true. It may occur to you that I'm guilty of those first two murders, and a willing participant in drug trafficking and other nefarious deeds.

It doesn't matter.

I'm free!

The End